ISHTAR'S BLADE

LISA:BLACKWOOD

Edited by
Laura Kingsley

Cover Art Designed by
Ravven

Interior Design by Write Dream Repeat Book Design LLC
www.WDRBookDesign.com

ISBN-13: 978-1530609567
ISBN-10: 1530609569

other books by

LISA BLACKWOOD

The Avatars

Beginnings
Stone's Kiss
Stone's Song
Stone's Divide
Stone's War (Forthcoming Spring 2016)

In Deception's Shadow

Betrayal's Price
Herd Mistress
Death's Queen (Forthcoming)
City of Burning Water (Forthcoming Fall 2016)

Warships of the Spire

Vengeance (Forthcoming March 2016)

CHAPTER
one

AWN'S LIGHT CARESSED the mountain peaks of Nineveh and shimmered upon the reef-strewn waters surrounding New Sumer's greatest city-state. The ocean, still restless from the previous night's storm, tossed white capped waves toward the vast island's rocky cliffs and rocked the small skiff Iltani rode in.

The snap of the sail, the sound of the waves slapping the small boat's sides, and the stomach-dropping dips and rises of the bow all added to the excitement churning in her blood.

Iltani hardly dared to believe.

She was returning home for the first time after four long years of brutal, continuous training.

In truth, she'd dedicated her entire life to her training, but four years ago, she'd taken the final steps down that path, when Burrukan, the Leader of the King's Shadows had taken her on as his apprentice.

Now, almost four years to the day, Burrukan was returning her to her childhood home, Nineveh, the ruling seat of the Gryphon King. She'd left her island home a girl of seventeen and was returning a woman of twenty-one summers. While she couldn't guess if she could be considered wiser, she was greatly changed.

Four years was a long time. She sincerely hoped King Ditanu would be pleased with her progress and be happy to have her back at his side.

If he isn't? The small doubtful voice of her consciousness questioned.

Her mind shied away from that thought.

She supposed she'd find out later this day.

Not wanting to think more on the dark possibility of an indifferent king or worse, she turned from the sight of her childhood home and glanced back at her mentor where he worked the boat's rudder, guiding them safely past a reef. The wind shifted and two of the ropes tangled. With a grumble about needing to replace the fraying rope, Burrukan tied the rudder to maintain course. That done, he stepped over the bench Iltani sat on and started to work on the sail's tangled rigging.

She knew better than to offer her help. No one touched Burrukan's boat. He'd designed and built the swift little boat during the first year of her training, saying he wanted to shave time off the twice daily trips between the training island and Nineveh.

When she'd asked why he didn't just shift into gryphon form and fly, he'd rolled his eyes and said if he did that day after day, he'd be in no condition to beat her into shape and make a proper warrior out of her. Then he'd told her one of a Shadow's greatest strengths was their ability to remain silent, saying people with loose lips gave far too much away to their enemies. She'd frowned and he'd given her a fatherly pat on one shoulder and told her to go run a circuit around the island. She'd quickly learned not to question him about unimportant things.

It was probably for the best she didn't possess a set of wings. If she had, she'd have been tempted to fly back to Nineveh in the early days of her training when her yearning to hear the sound of Ditanu's voice, catch a whiff of his sandalwood and spice scent, or see the hint of a smile hovering on his lips grew too much to bear.

Sighing, she pushed away her internal musings and watched Burrukan work. That the ropes were in less than perfect condition could only mean the king had kept him busier than usual of late.

Iltani worried at her bottom lip as she stared at Burrukan's back. Today, the questions circling her mind were far from unimportant or frivolous. Dare she ask him what to expect? All she knew was that her mentor planned to present her to King Ditanu this day so he could perform the blooding ceremony, thereby honoring the ancient pact between gryphons and humans.

To most citizens of New Sumer, Iltani was just a human woman training to become one of the King's Shadows—a group of elite gryphon and human warriors who served and protected the king from all danger. She would have been content with that lot in life, but the goddess Ishtar had chosen Iltani for another role, that of her avenging blade. Only a select few people knew Iltani was Ishtar's Blade, the embodiment of the eight-thousand-year-old pact between the Queen of the Night and the line of the gryphon kings.

Iltani had spent the last four years preparing to become a living weapon forged by the Goddess Ishtar herself. One of flesh and blood and magic, but a weapon none the less.

At least, that's what Burrukan and High Priestess Kammani had drilled into Iltani from a young age.

Years upon frustrating years, Iltani had waited for Ishtar to rouse her magic. Even with Burrukan's reassuring words, she would have given up hope long ago had it not been for the deep indigo and gold birthmark marching down her spine, growing each year, and declaring that she was Ishtar's chosen weapon.

Her apathetic magic had finally roused for the first time this morning. Long before dawn, she'd jerked awake from a dream to find the mark throbbing with heat. After a good deal of twisting and turning, she'd gotten a look at it in her small handheld mirror. The mark had glittered with a soft gold and indigo power.

She'd bolted from her bed, pulled on yesterday's clothing, and ran to the dock where she normally met Burrukan each morning. Her mentor had already been waiting with the skiff, his expression as calm and devoid of worry as always.

It hadn't come as a surprise. Burrukan, like any good gryphon parent, missed nothing, always knowing what his brood was thinking, feeling, and doing. Unfortunately, Iltani was the only 'cub' in his brood and as such, she had all his attention. There had been a time or two in her youth when she'd very much wanted less of his eagle-eyed attention, but this morning she'd been more than happy for her adopted father's all-knowingness.

Otherwise, she would have paced a hole in the dock if she'd had to wait the two hours for his usual arrival.

If she was truthful with herself, it wasn't becoming Ishtar's Blade which scared her, it was meeting Ditanu again. Her four years on the training island had changed her. How much had those same four years changed the young king? He'd been new to his throne when she'd left. Would there be anything left of their unorthodox friendship?

Oh, great goddess Ishtar, I know it is impossible, but please let there still be room in his heart for me.

The thought had barely formed before making Iltani scowl at her own feeble willed yearning.

Oh, damn. Just stop thinking about him like that, she scolded herself.

It was easy enough to say, but, really, how could she stop thinking about the person who owned her heart?

Once, she and Ditanu had been the closest of companions, running wild as children. One never to be found without the other until that fateful morning after Ditanu's coronation, when she was sent from his side for the first time in seventeen years to finish her training.

The agony of the separation still burned deep in her soul, but she'd grown used to the ache over time until she could almost tolerate it.

Until now, with Nineveh within her line of sight again. The old ache had awoken fully born and Iltani couldn't pretend she'd mastered her unruly emotions during the four years of her training. Her sense of duty hadn't diminished, only grown—as had the strong emotional need which linked them. It never weakened or wavered in the intervening years since she'd last laid eyes on him. Even when that horrible letter arrived, telling her he'd taken a mate, her stubborn heart wouldn't relinquish its devotion to him.

It went beyond all common sense, logic, or reason. More than once, Iltani had wondered if she had been created solely to love Ditanu. If so, Iltani wanted to rail against her goddess's decision. Yes, it might be sacrilegious, but she still wanted to know just what Ishtar, the great Queen of the Night, Goddess of love, fertility, and battle had been thinking when she created her Blade to love the gryphon king so devotedly and then let him take another to mate.

Well, curse it! It wasn't like she hadn't had this particular internal debate a hundred times before, each one as ugly and painful as the first time. She sighed out the breath she'd been holding and stared down at her pack, her mind going back to the only thing that comforted her during these moments of melancholy.

Surely something of the bond they shared still remained buried in the king who now sat the throne? It was too powerful to simply be gone. Iltani and Ditanu had been together for seventeen years. His consort had known him less than three.

That hope gave her the strength she needed to face what was coming. Besides, her mentor had trained her well, even if the worst came to pass and every part of Ditanu's heart belonged solely to his consort—which it probably did since gryphons mated for life—Iltani could endure as long as he still valued their friendship. It wouldn't be easy, not with her heart desperately craving more, but her soul could live on whatever crumbs Ditanu might toss her.

After a good wallow in self-pity, Iltani finally looked up from her pack in time to catch Burrukan glancing over his shoulder at her. He held her gaze a moment, and then with a clear evasion, his eyes slid away again.

There was something in that look, a hint of guilt. Iltani's gaze narrowed, her mind sharpened, shaking off the internal musings like drops of sea spray. All her senses focused on her mentor as she realized something.

He'd been unduly silent on the short voyage, not speaking more than ten words since they'd left the training island of New Assur while the sky was still dark.

She might have thought his silence was brought about by the need to concentrate on navigating the dangerous waters, had he not sailed to New Assur each morning to continue her training and returned to Nineveh each evening to dine with the king and give his report. Burrukan had already mapped and memorized these waters so well, he could probably write his report while sailing the skiff at the same time.

No, it was as he'd always said. Talk betrayed things to one's enemies. While she wasn't an enemy, Burrukan's silence spoke volumes. There was something he didn't want her to know. The absolute silence was Burrukan's version of nervousness.

As if sensing her regard, his fingers twitched on the ropes, the sail shivering in his grip. His shoulders rose, betraying a slight tension in his body.

Someone less familiar with her mentor would likely have missed those small involuntary tells.

Iltani continued her silent study. She could wait. Patience wasn't a natural talent she'd been born with, but a skill she'd been forced to learn and master along with everything else.

Pushing her pack containing all her worldly goods aside, she stretched her legs out in front of her, shifting her position just enough to ease the stiff muscles of her lower back.

Burrukan remained with his legs braced for balance, attention fixed firmly forward. His right hand reached up and rubbed the stubble on his shaved head. He'd always said a King's Shadow didn't have time to fuss with all the tiny braids and hair ornamentation the rest of the court favored. Secretly, she knew it had more to do with Burrukan's receding hairline than lack of patience. Not that she would ever mention that.

His hand reached out and rubbed at the stubble a second time.

Burrukan was very nervous about something. Iltani smiled. She'd get him to tell her what was on his mind eventually.

With that knowledge a certainty, she allowed her attention to momentarily drift from her mentor back to Nineveh, which had grown in size to swallow the horizon.

After a final unneeded tweak of the sail, Burrukan returned to the rear and took up the rudder again and smoothly guided the small boat around the last dangerous patches of water.

The imposing wall of cliffs gave way to a vast harbor. Its calmer waters looking dark and mysterious in the shadow of the stone magnificence of Ishtar's Gate. Burrukan had told her this one was far grander than the one built long ago in their ancestral desert home of Sumer. Just how Burrukan knew that was up for question since he was nowhere near old enough to have witnessed that first gate's splendor.

Befitting the Queen of the Night, this newer version of Ishtar's Gate glittered blue in the early dawn light, its gold inlay bulls and dragons catching the light and winking it back.

Closer now, Iltani could pick out the artistic details she'd loved to study as a child, those intricately engraved dragon scales and the proudly curving horns of the bulls.

Iltani dragged in a deep, shaking breath, surprised at the tightness in her throat.

High overhead, the blue and gold design continued all the way up to the peaks of the towering turrets. Ishtar's Gate was the most imposing of the eight gates leading into the interior of the largest of the island city-states.

She had missed the beauty of Nineveh.

As the small boat sailed under the high, graceful arch of the gate and continued to sail the smoother waters of the harbor, Iltani knew this journey home was as much spiritual as physical.

Burrukan held his silence but guided the boat toward a small wooden dock just inside the gate. Rugged stairs carved from the stone of the island led up from the water line to a gatehouse where three of the King's Shadows waited for Burrukan to disembark from his boat.

Iltani watched her mentor tie off the boat to the moorings. She would have offered her aid if Burrukan was less of a stubborn old goat. Instead, she held her silence but allowed her gaze to narrow upon him.

The boat secured, Burrukan came to stand at the bow, his back still to her as he stared at the stone stairs, unmoving.

Iltani remained seated, her pack resting between her knees.

Burrukan dragged in a deep breath and then let it out on a chuckle. "There is something I promised to give you. I must do it now before we set foot back upon Nineveh or I will be guilty of treason. Wouldn't *that* give Ditanu's enemies on the council something to gorge upon?"

Iltani's breath stilled in her lungs.

Treason?

"King Ditanu gave me some items," Burrukan explained, "items I was supposed to deliver to you."

Iltani dragged in a breath and released it just as quickly.

What an interesting turn of events.

Yet she did not doubt Burrukan's loyalty to his king. Not for a moment. A King's Shadow never betrayed their king. They could not. The magic binding king and guard together prevented such. A Shadow saw to the king's safety first. That sacred vow even took precedence over some of the king's orders and most certainly his wishes. Besides, Burrukan had practically raised both her and Ditanu.

If Burrukan had defied Ditanu's wishes, it was for the king's own protection.

He turned to her with his own pack in one hand and started rooting around inside.

After a moment, Burrukan's searching hand stopped fumbling in the pack's deep recesses. He closed his eyes and tilted his face to the sky. She caught a few soft snippets of a prayer.

What could be so bad he prayed for the gods' protection and forgiveness?

Iltani folded her hands in her lap and fought for greater patience. She even smoothed her frown into a more peaceful expression, fearing Burrukan would change his mind.

At last, he pulled his hand from his pack. He held two small bundles of letters.

Iltani's eyebrows shot up. Those looked like...but no. It was impossible. She'd packed those letters in her own satchel just before she left the training island.

She suppressed the urge to tear open her pack just to see if Burrukan had somehow removed them from hers without her knowing.

He held out the letters. "What I did, I did for the good of our king."

Mystified, Iltani took the first bundle he offered. It was only then she realized these ones were pristine, not her much read and tattered, but still beloved, letters. Those were still in her pack, apparently.

The royal seal and the handwriting, Ditanu's elegant scrawl, were the same, though. She glanced down at them and shuffled through the bundle with growing unease and the first spark of anger.

The oldest of the letters dated back four years, with the majority of them from the first year of Ditanu's reign. There were far fewer from the second year of his rule. The newest letters being written almost a year ago by the date.

Every last one had been addressed to her.

Burrukan had been censoring the king's correspondence. She'd half expected that some of her own letters might have gone astray.

But the king's?

The facts were clear before her. Burrukan had withheld the king's letters. That would be considered treasonous by some.

"I merely promised that I would deliver our king's letters to you. I did not specify when."

Iltani snapped her mouth closed. So these letters were the 'treason' he spoke of. She wasn't sure if it wasn't treason after all. For what harm could have come to the king had Burrukan delivered them as he was supposed to? She didn't see how this fell into the gray area that allowed a Shadow to do whatever he must to oversee the king's protection.

"Don't give me that look," Burrukan scolded her. "I live to protect the king. Even from his own foolishness."

Frowning, she glanced between her mentor and the letters in her hand. "If whatever is written in these letters offers a threat to my king, why give them to me? Why not burn them?"

"Because," Burrukan said with conviction, "You need to find, acknowledge, and destroy anything that is a threat to our king. Even if it is something within yourself, an essential part of your very soul. If it is a danger to the line of the gryphon kings, you must grind it beneath your boot. If it goes against the king's wishes, then so be it. One day, you'll learn the delicate balance between protecting the king and serving him. Until then, follow my teachings and my lead. Surely between the Head Shadow and Ishtar's Blade, we can keep Ditanu safe."

Iltani's grip tightened on the letters. "I understand." And she did, but that didn't mean she was happy about it. Keeping something from Ditanu just didn't sit well with Iltani.

For seventeen years before their separation, they'd been constant companions. She couldn't remember one time—not even one event where she had done something that would constitute going against Ditanu's wishes. How strange that was. Stranger still, she had never noticed that oddity. Yet it wasn't that Ditanu intentionally dictated what they did as children. It was more like they simply thought with one mind.

"Take these ones too," Burrukan said and handed her another smaller bundle of letters. "You can give them to the king at some point should you wish—there is nothing in them that can harm the king now that you are finished your training."

She eyed the new letters—they were a selection she'd written to Ditanu over the years. "What, by the great goddess Ishtar, could I possibly have written that was dangerous for my king to read?"

Burrukan started to laugh. "Ditanu has always been protective of you, and he missed you terribly in those early years. All he needed was one hint of your unhappiness and he'd make an idiot of himself. The crown has mellowed him a bit and he is growing into a wise and capable king, but in the first years, he would have acted before the first rational thought had a chance to catch up."

"But, Burrukan, how...why now?" When there was no time to read through all the letters before she was to meet with the king.

"You will not read them this day. As you have probably guessed, there is no time. Later you will read them. Only then will you understand and uphold the reason for the deception."

Iltani wasn't so sure. The betrayal was a bitter taste in her mouth. How could she lie to her king, even if duty demanded it?

That's what she sensed Burrukan wanted her to do.

Just what did Ditanu write in those letters that could endanger his life? Why did he write it? Why to her?

Iltani frowned down at the letters in her hand.

Ditanu was wise enough to know that anything he wrote in a letter could find its way into the wrong hands. He would know better than to reveal things that could be used against him…unless something had slipped in that should not have, something that he could not help but share with her.

In the past, Ditanu had written many personal things to her before he enlightened others.

It was in one of those letters she'd learned he'd taken a consort.

That day, a year and a half into her training, Iltani had been waiting on the dock to greet Burrukan when she'd spotted the letter in his hand. She'd snatched it from him before he'd even disembarked from his skiff. Had she known then what she did now, she never would have opened that letter.

But she had, and Ditanu's flowing script told how he had taken a consort. Ahassunu was her name, a noble lady of ancient gryphon bloodlines.

The news shouldn't have come as a surprise. Even on the distant training island, she'd heard the rumors that the council was leaning hard for the king to take a mate. And well they should, the logical side of her mind knew, for Ditanu was the last of his line. Were he to die without an heir, much of the gryphon kingdom's magic would perish with him.

While her training demanded she remain on the island in seclusion, Ditanu had written to her on a fairly regular base in those first few months of his rule, sharing some of his day to day trials. She, in turn, shared hers as well, but not once had he hinted he was caving to his councilors' wishes.

That lack had felt like deepest betrayal but she'd come to see and understand the price of duty. There was also another unhappy explanation, she supposed. Ditanu had always been passionate about everything, never doing anything by half. It was possible his fiery gryphon nature had found his perfect match in Ahassunu and they'd fallen in love with a swift, all-consuming passion.

Iltani fidgeted at her sword harness's buckle as she eyed the unopened letters. Or perhaps he had hinted at it and she'd just never gotten the letter, until now. It hardly mattered how it had come about. Nothing could have softened that blow.

At the time, she'd tried to reason with herself, thinking that as his friend, she should be happy for him and his consort.

Iltani snorted with bitter humor. Logic never had had any effect on her obstinate heart's desires.

A few months after Ditanu had taken Ahassunu as his consort, another monumental letter had arrived. In it, he'd shared the news that his consort was carrying the first brood of royal cubs. The letter had gone on to say that he needed to share his great joy with his oldest friend, his Little Shadow, the only being to love him without reservation.

Even though she didn't exactly know what to make of that last admission on his part—for gryphons only took mates out of mutual love, respect, and a lengthy courtship, and there was no question his consort also loved him without reservation—his letter and the news it carried became Iltani's turning point.

While her new understanding still held a bittersweet tang to it, she also realized it didn't matter what her king's ambiguous phrase might mean, nor did it matter if Ditanu didn't love her in return. As Ishtar's Blade, she could remain at his side, and her love would protect both him and his heirs always.

She would serve and it would be enough.

A smile touched her lips at the memory. In the months following that letter, Iltani's youthful zealous ardor had mellowed from raging wildfire into more sustainable embers. It didn't mean she loved him any less. None, not even a consort, was as close to the king as his Shadows or his Blade. Iltani planned to become the Shadow that was ever at her king's back.

Glancing down at the pile of letters Burrukan had handed her, something occurred to her.

Perhaps it wasn't so strange that Burrukan had held back some of the king's letters.

When they were young, almost up until the moment of their separation, they had shared everything, every joy, fear, doubt, and guilty confession. Neither of them had living parents. The same group of assassins who had killed Ditanu's mother had cut down Iltani's parents when she was less than a year old.

Ditanu's two other siblings, a brother and sister of the same litter, were also killed that night. Later, the story was told that Ditanu, a cub not even two years old, had somehow managed to kill the single assassin sent to the nursery to kill him.

The truth was somewhat different by the story Burrukan told her. When the surviving King's Shadows made their way to the nursery, they found it blood drenched. Crimson covered the walls and floor and even dripped in sticky drops from the ceiling.

There had been many assassins—not just one.

It was whispered among the Shadows that the great goddess Ishtar, the Queen of the Night, danced in that room, and loosed her rage upon those who would dare harm a child of her blood.

It was in that room where a much younger Burrukan found the cub Ditanu covered in blood, but none of it his own. Under the curve of one wing, an equally blood-drenched baby snuggled against the cub's side. The baby slept peacefully as if unaware of all the violence and heartache visited upon Nineveh that night.

Burrukan told Iltani that when he reached for her to check her for injuries, he came close to losing a few fingers to Ditanu that day. He'd managed to separate baby and cub long enough to see the birthmark denoting Ishtar's Blade, glowing with power at the nape of the baby's neck.

That event had forged a special bond between her young self and the child-king.

The adult Ditanu may have felt compelled, even unwisely, to share things with her that were safer not expressed. If that was the case, and those things were, in turn, a danger to the king's welfare, then Iltani understood why Burrukan might have withheld the letters.

She didn't like it, but she thought she understood his underlying reasoning.

"Iltani?" Burrukan's voice brought her back from the past.

Mentioning her thoughts aloud could also be dangerous to Ditanu if his enemies overheard what she and Burrukan discussed, so she told a half truth.

"I was remembering back to when Ditanu and I were little. We were always so close until he sent me away. Do you still remember the story you told me about how you found Ditanu and I after the assassination?" It was common knowledge that she and Ditanu had been together in the nursery that night. Iltani's parents had been two of the Shadows killed in the battle, so the strange bond between her and the king brought about by their shared tragedy was not unknown, but no one knew she was also marked by the goddess Ishtar to become Her Blade.

With a bark of laughter, Burrukan flexed his fingers as he made a show of counting them. "He was such a fierce little cub, so protective of you. The years have not changed that." He sobered and then continued. "It's a miracle I was able to pry you from his clasp long enough to finish your training."

"It was you? I always thought Ditanu sent me away." She'd blamed herself, though. The night of the king's coronation, she'd gotten drunk out of her mind and been...an idiot.

As she'd grown, so too had her feelings for Ditanu. She'd craved more than just friendship between them. Blessedly, she didn't remember much of that night, but Ditanu had sent her away the next day so it couldn't have gone as she'd planned. Old embarrassment heated her cheeks.

Burrukan grunted, and then said barely above a whisper, "Ditanu needed to learn to be a king, and you, my young warrior, needed to become Ishtar's Blade. That was best done in secret, far from the watchful eyes of our enemies. Besides Ditanu, myself, and High Priestess Kammani, only one other knows your secret."

Iltani's eyes widened slightly at that confession. She'd always assumed the council and many of the other Shadows knew her secret, yet it seemed Burrukan or Ditanu were keeping that knowledge close. "Who?"

Burrukan laughed at her directness. "Consort Ahassunu."

So Ditanu's consort knew that she would become Ishtar's Blade. That wasn't surprising, newly mated gryphons never kept secrets from each other. "Just the four of you, then?"

"Yes," Burrukan said, "Ditanu didn't want to share that information with Ahassunu at first."

Iltani's eyebrows threatened to climb into her hairline. "Why ever not?"

"Ditanu is even more paranoid and overprotective of you than I am?" Burrukan grinned and shrugged. "You'll have to ask him yourself."

Was that need to protect her why Ditanu allowed Burrukan to send her away, to protect her secret until she was fully grown, her magic matured enough she wouldn't be vulnerable to the political and physical attacks that might target anyone who could help secure Ditanu's legacy?

After shoving the king's letters into her pack, Iltani took a steadying breath, and then slipped passed Burrukan and made her way up the steps. Once there, she turned and glanced back. When their eyes were level, she whispered, "I promise to do nothing rash. You have taught me well. I know my duty."

Relief flickered in his dark gaze and Burrukan gave her a sharp nod. Her mentor waved her aside while he had a private word with the three Shadows waiting at the gate house.

CHAPTER
two

As Iltani followed Burrukan, she trailed her fingers along the glazed brick of the wall to her right, touching the familiar decadence. Her eyes followed the Processional Way as it wound its way up through the many levels of the terraced city. Other roads intersected the city's main artery, diverging off in other directions, each marked by archways and walls decorated by their own glazed brick motifs or figures carved directly out of the stone of Nineveh's rocky bones.

Burrukan turned down a side road, leaving the bull and dragon motifs behind. This passageway was decorated with carved figures of tribute-bearers carrying offerings for the gods. Ahead, a mid-sized ziggurat rose up above the other city buildings. Lovingly tended gardens graced each level of the step pyramid and water cascaded down either side of the main stairway.

Stone genies, with their dual layered wings, braided hair and beards, and long flowing robes, stood guard at each corner of the ziggurat as human and gryphon worshipers made their way up the cut stone stairs and into the temple's heart for morning worship.

The stone genies, like the sphinx and the lamassu that guarded the royal palace, were far more than decoration and would wake to defend the city if they sensed danger coming to Nineveh's shores. A worrisome thought occurred to Iltani. "How long since the statues were last anointed with royal blood?"

"Too long," came Burrukan's solemn reply. "King Ditanu and Priestess Kammani do what they can, but ten island city-states are far too many for just the two of them to properly maintain. Ditanu's distant cousins have not the strength of magic needed to maintain, let alone wake the spirits sleeping within."

Iltani glanced up at one of the genies with its wide, blank eyes. The stone of its body was smooth, unmarked by cracks or salt damage.

"Burrukan," Iltani asked once they outpaced another group heading for the temple. "What of my blood? I'm not royal, but my blood is thick with magic. I've read every ancient text I could get my hands on, and while I never encountered a passage about other Blades performing these rituals, there are references of them creating many of the ancient defenses."

"Quick minded as always. Yes, I am confident that will become one of your roles. Fear not, you will have more tasks to complete than you will have time to accomplish."

They walked along the base of the pyramid temple, its first terrace reaching three body lengths above her head. Images depicting the history of the gods were skillfully carved into the stone and lovingly painted in vivid colors. The first series showed Ishtar's descent into the netherworld when she'd gone to challenge her sister Ereshkigal, the Queen of the Underworld. Ishtar had gone with the intention of lengthening the earth's growing seasons, demanding her sister forfeit the dying time when the earth rested and no crops would grow.

To reach her sister's realm, Ishtar had had to shed a portion of her power at each of the gates leading into the underworld. By the time Ishtar had completed her descent, naked and powerless, she'd confronted the Queen of the Underworld. Ereshkigal, affronted at her sister's audacity, ordered her dead on the spot.

Legend had it that all across the earth, lovers drifted apart, wombs turned barren and life stalled, for Ishtar was more than a battle goddess, she was also the source of fertility and desire. Seeing this, the other gods intervened. Tammuz, the god of the harvest, Ishtar's own husband, offered himself in her place. Had Ereshkigal not accepted Tammuz's offer, all life would have ended.

Iltani always wondered why Ereshkigal had accepted Tammuz's offer—it couldn't have been out of concern for the living, the Queen of the Underworld had none.

To cause Ishtar greater pain?

Perhaps.

Iltani wasn't likely to ever learn the answer to that question. She did pity Ishtar, though. Not being with the man she loved was a high cost for Ishtar to pay for her rashness.

Speaking of the cost of impulsive behavior, Iltani wondered if the last four years of her own life might have been different if she hadn't gotten drunk the night of Ditanu's coronation and foolishly tried to seduce him. He might not have agreed with Burrukan that she needed to be kept at arm's length until her magic matured.

Ishtar might have called upon them to perform the Sacred Marriage, and Iltani might have become Ditanu's mate instead of Ahassunu.

That was a great heaping pile of what ifs and might haves.

Iltani huffed unhappily, casting a glare at the next series of images that showed an ancient gryphon king performing the ritual marriage with his human Blade. The image seemed to silently mock her.

Burrukan cleared his throat.

She jumped and yanked her gaze away from the images. Without a word, they continued on past the temple and turned down another roadway.

Here lions and waterlilies were the motifs of choice.

They walked the narrow road at a slower pace, forced to weave their way around the thickening traffic of the day. Chariots made their way through the crowds, bearing officials and nobles. Iltani wondered why Burrukan hadn't ordered a chariot for himself, but discarded the thought a moment later.

He was obviously taking her through the less travelled part of the city for a reason.

The Processional Way was long and somewhat winding but was the most direct route to the palace from Ishtar's Gate. If Burrukan was taking her this slightly longer way, it was likely because it also conveniently led around behind the palace where only servants and other Shadows were likely to see them.

They continued to walk as the sun climbed higher into the sky and the city came fully awake.

The day promised to be warm and humid, but the ocean breeze offered welcome relief.

The royal palace, relatively close to the harbor and the Ishtar Gate when compared to the rest of the sprawling city, finally came into view.

Soon, she reassured herself. *Soon I will see my king again, and then I will set aside all this mental and emotional wool gathering and focus solely on my duty.*

Halfway up the stairs leading to the palace, Iltani watched for the strange behavior she'd seen when they passed the first two sets of guards. As she and Burrukan drew abreast, the guards snapped to attention and brought their right fist up to their left shoulder, which was Burrukan's due as leader of the Shadows. However, it was Iltani's name they murmured.

"By Ishtar," Iltani said, not bothering to keep the demanding note from her voice, "What is that all about? I thought no one knew my little secret."

"They don't. I may have let slip that I was grooming you as my heir."

They passed the last set of guards and crossed under the archway and on into the palace itself.

"Well, that's one way to divert attention, I suppose."

Iltani was secretly pleased. Burrukan was the closest thing she had to a father—a stern, hard to please father who was always drilling her to be faster, better, stronger, and smarter.

"Enough talk." Burrukan's gruff voice softened a touch, "Besides, I'm famished and if we hurry, we should make it to the throne room in time to eat with King Ditanu and Consort Ahassunu before the morning's court descends on our rulers like jackals on a kill.

Jackals? Iltani smiled at the thought of the island jackals even knowing how to hunt. Beg? Most certainly. Hunt? Never.

Some four thousand years ago, when Ditanu's ancient ancestor realized that the primitive humans were a threat to the powerful Gryphon Empire, she prayed to the gods.

They answered, showing that the best way to solve the dilemma was not a genocidal war to wipe out the human race, but instead to relocate far out into the ocean to a vast island chain created by the gods for that purpose.

The gryphons, ever mindful of the will of the gods, abandoned their old city-states for their new home. Being protective and territorial, the gryphons took those few humans still loyal to them and then preceded to uproot every other plant and animal in their domain.

Somehow, the jackals had taken advantage of the move and gone from self-sufficient wild animals to fat, loving household pets.

Iltani wondered if those ancient gryphons had viewed the humans living in their territory as 'pets' as well.

Then wondered if the gryphons today might still view the humans living among them in the same light. Having descended from mostly human bloodlines herself, she knew if the goddess Ishtar ever stripped away her gifts, and Iltani was no longer Ishtar's Blade, then she would be as human as many of the island's other residents.

Her lips turned down with that unhappy thought.

I'm more than a well-trained pet, she mused.

Burrukan grabbed Iltani by the shoulder and pulled her off balance as he started down another corridor. "Stop your wool gathering and pay attention."

Iltani felt heat climb her face and neck. She tucked her chin and scowled at his back as she doggedly followed in his wake.

She kept her lips firmly sealed and her mind focused on the coming meeting. She would not give either King Ditanu or Burrukan any excuse to send her back to New Asurr for more training.

They passed through the outer courtyard and finally reached the great bronze throne room doors, which were thrown wide as if in invitation or welcome.

Only the two colossal stone lamassu statues standing silent guard on either side of the door suggested something other than welcome. From within their mighty shells with their winged bulls bodies and human heads, their spirits thick with ancient knowing and magic looked out at her, taking her measure, judging her.

After a moment of scrutiny, both guards seemed satisfied with what they found and returned to their slumber.

Ah. The small circle of those who knew she was Ishtar's chosen just grew a little bigger. However, her secret was still safe. The city's stone guardians communicated only with their king.

And possibly Ishtar's Blade, Iltani realized. Not yet back half a day and she was already finding gaps in her training. Possibly, some knowledge had been lost to time. It had been over five hundred years since one of Ishtar's Blades had last walked the earth.

Were the gaps intentional or accidental through honest ignorance?

"Burrukan, welcome." The voice was familiar and emerged from the shadows to the right of the throne room doors. "And you've brought our Little Shadow home at last. The king will be pleased."

Etum, a King's Shadow only a few years older than Ditanu, stepped from his place by the door and clasped a hand to Burrukan's shoulder in welcome before turning to Iltani and giving her a hug.

Growing up, Ditanu didn't have many companions, but both Etum and his twin, Eluti, were Shadows, and only ten years older than Ditanu. The king viewed them as friends while Iltani viewed the twins more like older brothers.

"Etum!" she returned his embrace. "It gladdens my heart to see you. Your brother, he is here, too?"

"Never far," Eluti answered as he tossed back the hood of his gray cloak, appearing as if out of nowhere. The cloak's magic hummed along her senses a moment more before its spells went dormant. He shoved his brother aside for a hug of his own. "We were just on our way to start our shift when we heard of your arrival and guessed Burrukan would soon bring you here." He glanced over his shoulder and through the open throne room doors.

Iltani followed his gaze. Both guards wore human forms which meant King Ditanu was currently in human form as well. The guards always echoed their ruler's current form or risked not being able to follow him into the air. She would have preferred Ditanu in his gryphon form for this first meeting. At least, it might act as a visual reminder to her of how impossible her love for him was.

The twins might have said more if Burrukan hadn't grabbed one by each shoulder and steered them through the bronze throne room doors. Once inside, he gave each a shove in the opposite direction and continued on into the throne room.

As Iltani followed, taking in the forgotten grandeur of the vast room, her own appearance seemed twice as shoddy in comparison. Her brown hair was wild and windblown, not even in proper braids, merely tied at the nape of her neck. Salt spray from the ocean voyage had left a whitish discoloration on her otherwise dark training vest and leather pants—both comfortable and well worn, not something one would wear before their king. And, oh yes. Yesterday's shirt. Most definitely not something one wore before their king.

Why hadn't she thought of that before now?

Oh, right. She'd bolted from her bed and ran for the dock in a fit of excitement even a six-week old jackal pup would be hard pressed to match.

Why hadn't Burrukan allowed her to settle in before she was presented to the king?

Oh, Great Goddess, there was only one reason for the hurry. Burrukan hadn't yet informed King Ditanu that she was returned from New Asurr, and he wanted to inform the king in person before he could hear about it from other sources.

She tugged at her vest and smoothed a hand down her pants and slid a despairing glance at the twins' attire.

They were both dressed in graceful flowing robes with weapons belts strapped around their hips and each had a bow slung around one shoulder and a quiver full of arrows at their back. Sensible sandals encased their feet and laced up over their calves. They each saluted her with their spears as if acknowledging her dilemma, but also with silent amusement.

Ah, she was home indeed—and soon to be the butt of the twins' jokes."

What would palace life be like without the twins finding brotherly amusement at her sake?

She didn't have time to dwell on the problem because Burrukan had stopped his headlong flight across the vast floor to scowl over his shoulder at her. His one long-suffering look saying 'why are you still over there?'

Iltani rushed to catch up. She managed to match pace with him just as he was approaching a smaller alcove, shrouded in potted plants.

A table laden with food and comfortable benches took up a good portion of the area.

She stumbled to a halt as Burrukan executed an elegant bow. The benches were occupied she realized belatedly. A woman sitting on the other side of the table looked up and offered Burrukan a smile and then graced Iltani with a surprisingly honest grin. On the near side of the table, mere feet from where Iltani stood, a broad-shouldered man sat with his back to them. Due to the sultry heat of the day, he was bare-chested.

Her eyes roved over his back, taking in the familiar old training scars. Three of which she'd accidentally given him when they were younger. They'd been mock fighting in the forest during a bout of hand to hand combat. It had been an impromptu fight started by Ditanu and they hadn't checked the area first. She'd managed to flip him on his back, and he'd landed just off the path, where he'd skidded down a small slope. The rocky terrain had proven far less forgiving than the sands of the practice ring. Healers had spent half a morning picking bits of gravel, twigs, and other debris from Ditanu's back while Iltani had gripped his hand and offered apologies. He'd only laughed and said it was his fault for starting the fight.

The scars were familiar, but in contrast, the rest of him had changed. He'd filled out...nicely. She watched with purely female interest as his muscles bunched and flexed under his skin as he turned to glance over his shoulder. As the familiar angles of his face came into profile, Iltani belatedly dipped, half falling into a deep bow even as her cheeks burned with embarrassment at almost being caught staring.

"Burrukan, welcome," the woman said. "I see you have returned my husband's Little Shadow."

Iltani was slowly straightening from her bow, seriously thinking of hanging back while Burrukan made introductions, when her gaze landed on a pair of sandal-clad feet directly in front of her. Slowly, she followed the ankles on up to powerful calves and then up a bit more to the hem of a richly embroidered robe. Her eyes tracked to the side. The bench where the king had sat seconds ago was empty. Heart pounding in her chest, she studied the fine quality linen. She followed the stylish cut higher up to where it hugged powerful thighs and a trim waist. She got as far as a thick belt made out of hammered gold links. It reminded her of fish scales the size of her thumbnail.

"Iltani?" Ditanu said, "Great Gods look how you've filled out."

At the sound of his voice, she jerked her gaze up to look in his face. The youth she'd known was gone. In his place, a stranger with far sterner features looked back at her. The hard line of his clean-shaven jaw, high, well-defined cheekbones and strong brow that hooded his eyes all added to the harder look of a king. Only the slight softening of firm lips and a bounty of dark lashes ringing his hawk-like gaze softened the king standing before her enough that she could still see hints of the boy she'd grown up with.

She couldn't get her mind to formulate a thought or her mouth to string together words. Instead, she just stood there and stared at her king like a dolt.

With a second, hoarser 'Iltani', she was swept up in powerful arms and pressed into that hard chest. It was Ditanu's voice, alternately whispering her name and laughing in almost tearful emotion.

The feel of his warm body, the sound of his heart, the scent of his skin, it was all too much for Iltani's starved senses. Snaking her arms around his waist, she clung to him. Then she merely stood, absorbing everything about him in detail, more than happy to stand there for half an eternity if he would allow it.

His arms tightened around her, pulling her closer. Just when she thought he was going to smother her, he loosened his hold and held her out at arm's length to study her.

"Gods." Ditanu's rich voice had steadied a touch. It no longer shook with emotion, but his face was still full of wonder at seeing her again. "My Little Shadow, you can't imagine how much I've missed you."

That voice. She just wanted to close her eyes and listen to its familiar cadence. It *was* a touch deeper in tone but still sounded like the Ditanu she remembered.

Requiring a bit more willpower than she wished to admit, she snapped her mouth closed and schooled her expression into what she hoped was polite attentiveness as she fought for something intelligent to say.

When her mind stayed stubbornly blank for ten whole beats of her heart, she dodged the awkwardness by retreating into another deep bow.

Coward, her internal voice scolded and she couldn't debate the issue. She'd taken the coward's way out after Ditanu's strong showing of affection.

"My king," she said, hoping a formal turn of phrase would cover her earlier social blunder. "I come before you as your loyal servant. Please take my humble gifts into your house and use them as you may."

"Humble gifts?" King Ditanu chuckled, "I doubt there is anything humble about your gifts, but even if you had no magic at all, you would still be welcome into my house for the rest of your days." A long fingered hand settled on her shoulder, its weight and warmth the only things that seemed real at that moment.

She fought the urge to rub her cheek against the back of his hand. Instead, she forced her gaze up to his deep brown eyes with their golden flecks and found all the warmth, humor, and love she remembered reflected back at her. Ditanu slung an arm around Iltani's shoulders and dragged her toward the table laden with fruits, cheeses and nuts where Burrukan already sat, deep in conversation with Consort Ahassunu. King Ditanu guided her over to the bench and then pushed her down when she would have balked. Before she could shift over, he settled next to her. Close enough their thighs brushed when he reached for various items on the table.

She felt half intoxicated by Ditanu's scent—that mellow sandalwood fragrance which was purely his own blended with the sweet spiciness all gryphons carried even when they were in human form.

Her heart very much wanted to convince her nothing had changed in the years she'd been away, that she was still the only one in Ditanu's heart. Alas, no matter what her foolish heart wanted her to believe, her mind knew better.

In all their species' long history, never once had Iltani read or heard a ballad mentioning a mated gryphon taking a lover. Even Ishtar respected that bond, for the most part. Only once had the Queen of the Night interfered. That time, a gryphon queen had lost her consort before they had sired any young, so to save the royal line, Ishtar had that queen and her male blade perform the Sacred Marriage. That had been nearly three thousand years ago now, and the scroll she'd read hadn't given much detail. At first, Iltani had imagined it was only possible because of Tammuz and Ishtar's passionate love, but then she'd got thinking. There must have already been a very strong and loving bond between that queen and her blade, for she hadn't descended into grief madness at the loss of her consort. She wouldn't have felt lust for her blade, but she must have loved him enough to live for him, and Ishtar must have assured they had a fertile union.

But she'd often wondered about that poor man. Had he been in love with his queen, desperately looking forward to each future Sacred Marriage? Or had he just seen it as his duty? For his sake, she hoped it was only a duty and he had not been in love with his queen, for outside of the Sacred Marriage, those two could not have shared an intimate relationship. Iltani wouldn't wish her own misery on another living being.

"Eat," Ditanu said, shoving food before her and drawing her out of her glum thoughts. "If I know Burrukan at all—which I do—I'm sure he hasn't given you time to eat yet." He pressed a finger to her lips. "Don't argue. Burrukan trained me. Well do I remember his demanding ways." Ditanu rotated one shoulder as if trying to ease a phantom pain while giving her one of his boyish smiles she remembered so well. The same one which often haunted her dreams.

Iltani felt her own lips curving in response. As she had done in her youth, she leaned closer to whisper in his ear that he was a terrible liar, but glanced across the table and found both Burrukan and Consort Ahassunu watching them. Betraying heat raced over her cheeks and she glanced down at the food on the table. Spotting a tall glass of some drink, she picked it up and sipped at it. Lemon mixed with something a touch sweeter, but her mind was too preoccupied with Ditanu's nearness to reason out what that other fruit might be.

Ditanu suddenly reached around behind her to snatch the stoneware cup on her other side. While he was pouring himself a new drink—faster, she noted, than a servant could come forward to do it for him—Iltani's befuddled mind remembered Ditanu was dominant on his left side. The cup she just took a drink from had been his.

She'd just stolen the king's drinking vessel.

Great goddess Ishtar, please don't let your humble servant embarrass herself further in the coming hours.

King Ditanu topped hers up.

Frozen in horror, Iltani stammered out an apology. Ditanu brushed it off and then turned to one of the other Shadows standing guard along one wall. "Have Uselli bring the cubs. They should be awake now."

Iltani's stomach plummeted. Knowing Ditanu was mated to another was one thing. Seeing the living evidence of Ditanu's love for Ahassunu was something else altogether. She barely maintained her composure as it was. How was she supposed to handle this? How could she possibly think she would be able to do any of this?

A warm hand landed on her thigh as Ditanu patted her in reassurance. "My cubs will love my Little Shadow. You'll see."

Ah, I see Ditanu can still read me as easily as always, Iltani thought with growing despair. While Iltani was fighting her churning mess of emotions, Ditanu returned to his meal with a hardy appetite.

Iltani, feeling more nauseated than hungry, forced herself to eat so as not to draw any more attention. Blessedly, Burrukan and Consort Ahassunu were still deep in conversation and had already forgotten Iltani's painful moment.

CHAPTER
three

A LOUD QUESTIONING squawk had Iltani jerking her gaze up from the food she was pushing around on her plate. She tracked the sound to the open throne room doors. Well, actually the sound was traveling from somewhere beyond that point.

A second more excited shriek echoed down the hall. A fluffy gryphon cub, its tiny wings flapping and its sharp talons clicking against the tiled floors as it scrambled for traction came hurtling through the door. Two more identical balls of fur and downy feathers rushed in after, chased by three flustered looking servants and eight silent Shadows.

Iltani found the sight of the three servants trying to herd the cubs and losing, somewhat entertaining. It was clear they'd been trying to catch the cubs before they made the throne room. King Ditanu merely chuckled good-naturedly at their difficulties. For their part, the Shadows merely kept a watchful eye on the cubs and kept pace with them, but didn't attempt to restrain them in any way.

"You should see them at bath time," Consort Ahassunu added in a dry tone. "You'd think you were trying to force a full grown mountain cat into an ice cold lake."

The cub in the lead charged toward the consort, his beak gaping and head in the air as he ran. Tracking a scent he liked? That was doubtful. He was too young to be hunting his own food yet. He would still be drinking his mother's milk.

His wings only had the beginnings of flight feathers sprouting out among the soft fur and downy feathers covering his lion-cub like body. The one in the lead squawked again, skidding to a halt. His head waved around to better catch whatever scent he was tracking and then his small legs began scrambling to gain traction as he headed for Ditanu.

The cub leapt onto his father's lap, but his momentum was too great and he overshot. Iltani's lap was suddenly filled with a wiggling bundle of feathers and fur. Before she uttered an exclamation, two more of the soft, squirming bodies were in her lap, which wasn't big enough to hold three gryphon cubs. When the first to land on her was pushed off by the two newer arrivals, she scooped him up and held him safe in the crook of her arm while she shoved the other two more firmly into her lap before they tumbled to the floor. The one in the crook of her arm climbed up to her shoulders where he proceeded to shove his beak in her hair and began to purr. His claws, still dull in infancy, left marks but didn't break the skin.

Gritting her teeth, she reached up and stabilized the cub so he wouldn't fall. While she was distracted, the other two took advantage and escaped her lap, trying to get to her head or shoulders.

Great goddess Ishtar. No wonder the servants look frazzled.

Ditanu plucked one of the cub's up from her lap. "Easy, easy. She's not going to disappear."

That's when Iltani realized she was being sniffed over and scent marked by the cubs. *Whatever were they doing that for?*

One of the two still in her lap nuzzled its beak against her breasts as if hoping for breakfast. "I'm sorry little one. I think you're confusing me with someone else." Iltani glanced up across the bench to see the consort looking on with a curious expression on her face. Iltani was glad it wasn't a hostile look. Many gryphon mothers were territorial and overly protective of their cubs.

"Your mother is over there." She scooped the tiny female cub from her lap and set her on the table. She knew the lone female cub was called Humusi, so that was easy enough to figure out.

Iltani gently pushed her on the rump to get her walking toward her mother. The cub looked over her shoulder at Iltani, gave a little questioning squawk and then shook herself. It was too early to decide which parent the cub would take her coloring from; she was still just fluffy and brown like her brothers. Though Iltani hoped a couple of them would look like their father. She was fond of Ditanu's gryphon form with his rich golds and lustrous browns.

Now that her lap was empty, she reached up with both hands and gently pried off the male clinging to her shoulders and deposited him in her lap again.

Looking down, she watched as the cub nuzzled her clothing and licked sea salt residue from them. After a couple moments of that, he decided he'd had enough and settled down to chew her sword's harness. She reached to pick him up, intending to put him on the table and encourage him to go to his mother. He hunched down and pressed its head into her lap, making a pitying sound, part cry and part thrill.

Iltani froze, uncertain what to do, half expecting Ditanu to snatch his cub away from her since male gryphons were just as protective of their young as the females.

Ditanu chuckled, looking astonishingly relaxed considering the sound his cub was producing. "He likes to be petted. He won't stop until he gets what he wants."

Hearing his father's voice, the cub paused in his crying, but it was to Iltani that his dark soulful eyes looked. His tufted ears twitched uncertainly like he was thinking about renewing his crying, so she reached out and attentively caressed the soft downy feathers between his ears. He began to purr. She felt her heart melt toward the little one. If he really wanted to sit in her lap that badly, he could.

Ditanu cleared his throat. "Like this."

He reached out and rubbed the cub along the back of the neck, ruffling both fur and feathers into disarray. She glanced to the side to see him watching her, not his cub. His expression didn't show even a hint of disgruntled, overly protective gryphon parent as she'd half expected. Strangely, he looked somewhat sheepish. Iltani was missing something here. She looked toward the other side of the table where Burrukan and the consort were still talking. The cub Iltani had encouraged to return to her mother was now climbing Burrukan like he was her favorite tree. Again, to Iltani's surprise, Ahassunu seemed fine with Burrukan parenting her cub.

"I must beg pardon on their behalf," King Ditanu said. Again that flash of sheepishness crossed his expression. "The little ones don't understand that they shouldn't run roughshod over guests. Perhaps I may have spoiled them more than a good parent should."

"Nonsense," Iltani said as she grinned down at the cub in her lap. The lone female was easy to put a name to, but she didn't have a clue about the males. "Is this Ilanum or Kuwari?"

"Kuwari," Ditanu said with a grin in his voice when the cub rolled onto his back for a belly rub.

Just like that, the cubs were no longer just a painful reminder that Ditanu wasn't and never could be hers. They were a part of him, and they were beautiful in her eyes.

Her magic rose up within her, dancing along her skin for a moment before vanishing. The reaction wasn't strong enough to be visible to others, but it was enough she knew Ishtar acknowledged the cubs as under her protection.

Even without a goddess's blessing, Iltani would still have protected these cubs, because they were a part of Ditanu.

"Or maybe I just spoil Kuwari the worst since he's the runt of the litter." He said it fondly as he gazed upon the cub in her lap, so she knew he wasn't passing judgment on the smallest of the three cubs.

She wrapped one arm securely around Kuwari so he wouldn't roll off her lap and then with a touch more gusto, she started on the food set out before her. While they ate, Burrukan told Ahassunu embarrassing stories about when Iltani and Ditanu were children.

If her mentor's purpose was to put Iltani at ease, it worked. For she was soon telling the consort about her training on New Assur, and much to Iltani's surprise, Ahassunu seemed to honestly want to know more about her. Together, the four of them laughed and joked of days past as the cubs chewed on whatever item of clothing they could get their beaks on while the adults pretended not to notice. The laughter transformed Ahassunu's somewhat plain features into something truly beautiful.

Could Iltani ever forgive Ahassunu for catching the king's eye and his heart? No, she admitted as even that reminder caused pain deep in her soul, but Iltani couldn't hate Ahassunu. One of the earliest gifts Ishtar had gifted to her was the ability to see what was in a person's heart. Ahassunu was a good person.

Iltani almost wished Ditanu had instead mated a haughty, beautiful shrew.

She sighed.

King Ditanu was far too wise to pick beauty over brains. Iltani was certain his consort was every bit as intelligent and politically cunning as the king.

They were a perfectly matched pair. All of New Sumer was fortunate to have them to rule over and guide the ten city-states.

Ishtar had chosen wisely.

Iltani accepted that truth. At least in her mind.

Her heart?

That would take a little longer.

CHAPTER *four*

AFTER THE MEAL was finished, servants came and moved the table, screens and plants to other parts of the throne room while King Ditanu and Consort Ahassunu relocated to the two imposing thrones on the raised dais at the north end of the vast hall. Lesser priests and priestesses drifted into the room from one of the side entrances and took up their customary stations halfway up the wide stairs.

From her position behind and to the right of the king's throne, Iltani watched as other nobles, both gryphons and humans, trickled in next and executed elegant bows.

Ignoring the nobles, she rolled her gaze to her mentor, where he stood at the king's left shoulder, whispering something into the king's ear. Focusing on them, she caught the tail end of the conversation.

"I want the ceremony performed tomorrow night," Ditanu was saying as he took a sip from a goblet of wine. The heavy cup hid his lips from view as he spoke, effectively hiding what he and Burrukan said if anyone in the room was trying to read lips. "The moon is in its dark phase and Iltani is ready."

Burrukan looked unhappy as he bent down to whisper in the king's ear, but Iltani's heightened hearing still caught his words. "If it were up to me, I'd like to see her settle in first, familiarize herself with the court and all the politics that goes with it. As soon as others see what she is, she'll become a target."

"It doesn't matter what we want or think is best," Ditanu said, sounding a touch impatient with Burrukan. "Ishtar has given her blessing."

They could only be talking about her blooding ceremony. Iltani hadn't thought much beyond that she'd be returning home and seeing Ditanu for the first time in years. However, Ishtar had declared her ready, and the blooding ceremony was the first step to becoming Ishtar's Blade and renewing the pact between the Queen of the Night and the line of the Gryphon Kings.

Yes, it would likely cause a few ripples in the court as Blades were rare and Ishtar hadn't anointed a Blade in nearly five hundred years. Most of the nobles and council members wouldn't know how much power she would wield, or if she would challenge them for a seat on the council.

In the past, Ishtar's Blades had proven very diverse in their powers and roles. Some simply watched silently from the shadows, only acting to strike at dangers that came too close to the crown while others took on a much more active role. From the little she'd gleaned from ancient texts, those that engaged in politics and the day to day rule, did so because the king or queen at that time required that form of aid.

If she was given a choice, Iltani wanted nothing to do with the ruling of the ten city-states. She'd much prefer to be a Blade that waited in the shadows to strike out at threats as they came. Besides, she figured she had a good chance of having her wish granted. Both King Ditanu and Consort Ahassunu were competent rulers, in no way needing Iltani's input.

That notion was reinforced as Iltani watched how they handled the business of the day. During the morning hours, both Ditanu and Ahassunu listened to grievances and other petty squabbles, doling out their judgments in a fair manner.

Second meal came and went, and still Ditanu sat his throne and listened to more bickering. In the afternoon, more nobles and council members arrived from the outer city-states. By Ditanu's clipped replies, she assumed this was an old argument he and his councilors had been over several times. It revolved around the fact he and Ahassunu had not picked a regent to raise his cubs should there be another successful assassination attempt like the one which had killed his parents and siblings.

Iltani fought the urge to smack certain councilors alongside the head with the flat of her sword. What a terrible thing to remind the king of, repeatedly.

Ditanu merely frowned at the marble steps leading down from his throne while deep in thought. Long heartbeats crept by as his councilors waited in silence. Iltani fisted her sword's hilt and visualized what she'd like to be doing.

Then at last, when the sun was starting to sink toward the horizon, Ditanu stood and stretched. Iltani shifted her position to limber up stiff muscles and sluggish circulation, being careful not to draw attention from the king.

"I have taken your suggestions under advisement," Ditanu addressed his councilors. "Tomorrow we will travel to Ishtar's great temple where High Priestess Kammani will bless and formally anoint my oldest cub as heir. After the ceremony, I will announce my choice of regent for my cubs."

CHAPTER *five*

ILTANI WAS A touch surprised at the king's sudden compliance to his councilors' wishes when it seemed this was an old, bitterly disputed argument. Until she figured out King Ditanu was probably using this as an excuse to hide the blooding ceremony required to seal the pact between the gryphon kings and the Queen of the Night.

Shrewd.

Though now he really would have to pick a regent for his cubs. Many councilors would like to have that prestigious position, but few would willingly relinquish their power later. Should something happen to either Ditanu or his mate, there was always the possibility the surviving mate might succumb to grief madness, and with Ditanu being an only child, it would leave only his aunt to raise his cubs. High Priestess Kammani raised him, and she'd been a wise and loving influence on both Iltani and Ditanu when they were children, but Kammani had more responsibilities now that she was High Priestess. It didn't rule her out as a regent, but the other councilors would use her responsibilities to Ishtar as an excuse to undermine her as a possible regent.

Ditanu rounded his throne so quickly, the hem of his robe brushed Iltani's salt-stained leathers. Consort Ahassunu came around her throne just as quickly, but Burrukan was ready and didn't have to scramble to catch up like Iltani did. She closed in on Ditanu's retreating form just as his other Shadows closed ranks around him.

Iltani might have found herself part of the rearguard had King Ditanu not shortened his stride as he turned a corner and reached back with one hand to grip Iltani by the arm and pull her up even with him.

"My consort needs to nurse the cubs, but she will join us later to talk in private about tomorrow night," he said. "You will accompany me for the time being. I hate eating alone, and Burrukan will need to stay with Ahassunu and the cubs while she nurses them."

Iltani's eyes sought Burrukan. She desperately didn't want to be alone with Ditanu without her mentor present. "Surely you both have things you need to discuss. I can keep Consort Ahassunu and the cubs company while you and he go over plans…"

Ditanu jerked his head in her direction, pinning her with an intense look. "If I am not with my cubs, then Burrukan is. That is our rule."

It made sense to assure that his cubs were guarded by the best when Ditanu couldn't be with them, Iltani acknowledged with growing dread. Unfortunately, it also meant Ditanu likely intended for Iltani to entertain him over his evening meal. It wasn't like she had daily reports to share with him yet. How did one entertain a king?

This wasn't the Ditanu she'd grown up with. Oh, there were still hints of the boy she'd known buried deep within the ruler. This morning, when he'd hugged her and called her his Little Shadow, she had thought this transition might not be so hard, but after seeing the stoic king all throughout this day, it drove home how much he'd changed, or maybe how much the throne had changed him.

She wasn't some great lady able to hold an audience enraptured with her voice or ability to tell great ballads. The only songs and games Iltani knew were the coarse kind soldiers played.

What were they supposed to do, compare training scars?

Oh, great Ishtar, hear your humble servant and grant me even the tiniest drop of your grace so that I may survive the next few hours with my pride intact.

Iltani was sure her earlier prayer must have gone astray and never reached Ishtar's ears. As soon as King Ditanu reached his suite, his guards did a thorough search of the area, stationed pairs at each of the doors and windows, and then the last four inquired if the king required anything. Ditanu shook his head and dismissed them. They gave him swift bows and then took up positions outside in the hall which left Iltani standing ten feet across the room from Ditanu, casting fugitive glances around the area looking for a nice wall to stand guard against.

She'd just picked out a spot when he cleared his throat and tilted his chin toward another room branching off the one they were in.

"Come, the servants have already set out food." Ditanu parted a gauzy curtain and proceeded out of the chamber. When Iltani didn't immediately follow, he reached back and held the curtain aside to peer at her.

Making a pretense of adjusting her pack, she mumbled a hasty apology and hurried across the room.

"You guard that almost as carefully as you guard me," Ditanu said with a chuckle, arching one brow. Humor glinted in his dark eyes. "Should I be jealous?"

Iltani straightened her spine at his question but told the truth. "Your letters. I wanted to keep them near."

"Ah." He rubbed a palm across his face, but she still caught the crooked smile he tried to hide. "You value my words so much?"

"Yes." *Why lie to him about something so innocent?* "They kept me company and provided a distraction when I was exhausted from training and every muscle burned. Your words kept me from missing home so much."

"I'm glad I was able to keep you company in that way." He hesitated, and then glanced away, breaking eye contact.

It was an old habit, a telltale sign he was feeling a touch insecure about something. Her?

"Each of your letters brought me moments of joy," she said as she eased by him in the doorway. The gauzy curtain tickled her bare arms. While she was studying the pattern of the weave, she whispered, "Even the painful ones."

"I still have every letter you sent to me, too." A matching note of pain echoed in his voice.

Was that...? His tone...it sounded like he...what? Had he once wanted more than friendship between them?

She glanced up and her stomach did that foolishly-hopeful, excited little flip it did whenever she looked him in the eyes. With them both half in the threshold, she found him uncomfortably close, but the pain in his voice wasn't imagined on her part, there was a secondary instance of it reflected in his eyes.

"I would not have sent you away if I'd had a choice." He eased on into the room and allowed the curtain to settle back in place. Without glancing back at her, he said, "There were many things that did not turn out how I might have wished, but you are here now. The past is what it is. Tonight I am hungry and would simply like to sit, eat with my childhood friend and forget for a time that I am a king."

Oh, Great Goddess, the pain in his words and the echo they caused in her own heart nearly brought her to her knees. It was such an impossible mess they found themselves in. She wanted him and would likely yearn for him the rest of her life, but at this moment, the pain in his tone eclipsed her own needs and she simply wanted to comfort him.

"I would enjoy that, too," she paused and then added with a smile. "Ditanu."

At the break in protocol, Ditanu turned back to her with a broad grin. "Good, I think that is the first time you addressed me by my name instead of my title. In the future, when we are alone, you will always call me by my name, not my title. I hear it enough times in a day. I don't need it from you too."

"I understand, my k…Ditanu."

His grin grew broader, his entire face transforming into something living and breathtakingly handsome. With a laugh, he removed his crown. Then a piece at a time, he started plucking out all the other bits of gold hair ornaments. When there was a substantial pile laid out on a table, he started to remove the tight braids from his hair. Unlike many of the nobles, Ditanu's bountiful hair was not a wig. "The servants usually do this," he admitted as he felt around for more gold beads in his hair, "Did I miss any?"

She reached out and plucked a couple more gold pins from his hair and then laid them on the table. "That's all."

"Tradition," he grumped. "I should make sweeping changes and declare such excesses an affront to the gods."

She cleared her throat to cover a cough. "Ishtar might be the one to take affront. She likes her people to glitter in the sun or like stars in the night sky, or so the texts say." Those same texts said the Queen of the Night also liked her lovers. Somehow, Iltani imagined Ishtar would still find Ditanu pleasing to look upon even without all the gold and luxurious robes. Iltani certainly wasn't immune to his broad shoulders or defined abdomen. It was always a fight to keep her eyes from travelling down to where that trim waist disappeared under his low-slung belt.

"Our food grows cold," he said and gestured her over to where the servants had set out food next to the hearthstones of the fire. Pillows and blankets were artfully arranged, allowing the diners to sit or recline, which-ever they preferred. Iltani swallowed hard as she took in the intimacy of the meal. This must have been intended for his mate.

He didn't seem bothered by that fact, so maybe he normally had meals like this. Perhaps even with Burrukan? A grin tugged at her lips at the image that conjured. No, not likely.

Ditanu knelt and poured two goblets of heated, spiced wine and then selected a few choice bits of meat, cheese and fruits. He then held the plate out toward her. Iltani just stood and looked at the offering. He sighed and gave it a little wiggle without looking at her.

Court etiquette aside—as a king just did not serve others—Iltani found everything about the situation awkward. Was it some kind of test?

"Iltani," Ditanu sighed out her name. "Just take the plate. I have another rule you probably are not aware of. When I am in my personal chambers, I am not a king. I am just myself and can do whatever I want. You'll get used to it."

She took the plate. "Yes, my king."

"Ditanu." He drew the name out slowly as if he suspected she may have forgotten it.

"Yes, Ditanu." Formal tones still edged her words.

He shook his head and then took a sip of his wine. He braced one arm behind him and tilted back his upper body in an exaggerated way to look up at her. "Fine. Don't dispense with the formalities. But Iltani, if you don't sit down, you're going to give your king a terrible kink in his neck."

She dropped to her knees so quickly, she bumped one of the plates of fruit. At least, she hadn't sent it flying. With exaggerated care, she edged the dish a bit closer to the fire. Ditanu was sipping from his wine again, but she could still see the corners of his mouth turn up in a smile.

Well, she supposed, she *was* entertaining the king after a fashion.

Flustered and a touch desperate for a distraction, she looked around, anywhere but at him. Her eyes settled upon a wall panel of carved and painted stone. Much of the city was decorated in a similar fashion, but this piece was far more intricate and detailed. It showed the beginnings of the gryphon kingdom and the birth of the eight-thousand-year-old pact between them and the Queen of the Night.

The first part of the wall carving depicted Ishtar as she returned from the underworld. She had been struck by both grief and rage at Tammuz's loss, and from the heady mix, she brought forth a new creature to walk the desert sands and stride into battle at her side. A fierce beast, part lion and part eagle—but all cunning hunter.

She'd called them gryphons.

They were unfailingly loyal to her but bloodthirsty and wild. Fearing nothing and hunting all.

The next section of the carving showed those early gryphons hunting Ishtar's human worshipers. Iltani frowned at the evidence proving Ishtar wasn't infallible.

However, not wanting to witness the wanton slaughter of her human worshippers, Ishtar changed her gryphons, introducing human blood into them alongside the lion and eagle parts. The new breed still possessed their hunting prowess, but their temperament had been moderated by the addition of human compassion and other gentler characteristics.

Over time the new breed of gryphons interbred with the old, taming them and giving rise to the first of the shapeshifters. To create a lasting bond between her two peoples, Ishtar took the strongest, fiercest, but also the most compassionate of the new gryphon shapeshifters, and upon him she bestowed the right to rule, elevating him to king. Then Ishtar took a human female with the same characteristics and infused her with a substantial power equal to the gryphons, making her the first of Ishtar's Blades.

Iltani was very familiar with the story and already knew what the next scene would show, but hadn't seen this artist's version, so looked anyway. Besides, it gave her something to look at other than Ditanu's naked chest and muscular thighs. She scanned the images.

It showed Ishtar and her Blade summoning Tammuz from the underworld. With the newly made gryphon king acting as the harvest god's host, the four beings came together in two bodies and performed the first Sacred Marriage, thus ensuring the harvest and the continuation of all future life. Each spring after that Ishtar and Tammuz were honored by a ritualized Sacred Marriage performed by their respective high priest and priestess. But the true rite happened every few hundred years when the pact would be renewed between a gryphon monarch and one of Ishtar's human Blades.

The last scene in the carving showed a gryphon queen and her male Blade honoring the gods in rather explicit detail. Iltani felt a betraying blush race up her cheeks and down her neck.

"You should see the one in my bedchamber," Ditanu said with a healthy dose of humor. "My aunt had one of her artisan priests create it. Took him two years to finish. It's very beautiful and skillfully worked, but it depicts a gryphon king and his female Blade in a very…ah…inspiring fashion."

Iltani felt her stomach tighten unhappily. In times past, Ishtar would create a new Blade to protect the line of the gryphon kings when there was some strife threatening the kingdom. That was a Blade's primary role. Yet, like the scene the artist had created, many Blades had also been participants in Sacred Marriages, reuniting Tammuz and Ishtar. In such cases, the Blade and their gryphon ruler became mates.

Iltani thought she could be forgiven for her youthful naivety in believing she and Ditanu were fated to be one of the mated pairs. But that wasn't how it happened, and it was a bitter reminder that not every Blade was mated to their monarch. Only about a quarter ever were, but it hadn't stopped a young Iltani from dreaming.

"You should come see it sometime in the daylight," Ditanu continued, unaware of the pain his words caused. "It is striking when the afternoon sun illuminates it."

Iltani reached for her wine goblet and drained it in moments.

CHAPTER
six

S IPPING AT HER third goblet of wine, Iltani eyed the king as he talked. During their meal, he'd told her stories about his first days of rule, things he hadn't included in his letters, at least not the letters she'd read. He also talked about Burrukan's training, his aunt's over protectiveness and the petty bickering among the nobles and even his council of advisors. Most of all, he talked about his cubs. His delight in them was obvious and Iltani had to admit the littlest fur ball was well on his way to having his claws firmly entwined in her heartstrings.

Strangely, Ditanu didn't talk much about his consort, and Iltani had a suspicion that he was censoring his conversation so as not to raise painful feelings within her.

Am I so easy to read?

Even with that question flirting around in her mind, she couldn't help but relax and actually enjoy dinner. She'd missed hearing his voice, the animation in his tones as he told his stories. Though his voice held an almost hypnotic quality that was presently threatening to put her to sleep. A yawn escaped before she could stop it.

She stammered an apology, but Ditanu only chuckled.

"I will assume it is the long day and not my storytelling skills that are putting you to sleep. Ah, you should go find your bed soon and I should discuss a few more things with my consort and Burrukan about your blooding ceremony tomorrow night." He started to gather up their plates and Iltani hastily jumped up to help. He shooed her away. "While Burrukan is with me, you'll stay with my cubs in the suite across from this one. I've had a bed made up for you there. I'll find you a more permanent place tomorrow."

"Of course," she paused, not wanting to question him but curious too. "If I may ask, what's wrong with my old room?" Her old room was actually the old nursery where she and Ditanu had both lived as children. Apparently after he'd taken up the kingship, he'd moved into the royal suite as was fitting, but she wondered what was wrong with her old room that she couldn't sleep there.

He didn't look up at her question but she saw him stiffen. "It is too far away."

His harsh tone surprised her and she wondered at its cause. The wine was making her muzzy headed, but it hadn't dulled her senses enough to overlook her king's emotional disquiet.

"Ditanu?" she asked softly.

When he finally looked her way, she saw the pain in his eyes and tension in his jaw. "I have been having bad dreams again. The same ones I had as a cub, before…"

He didn't have to finish his sentence. She knew. The dreams he'd had before his parents and siblings were murdered. Her hand fisted around her sword hilt. "I will do all in my power to protect the line of the gryphon kings."

"Knowing either you or Burrukan are with my cubs at all times gives me peace."

She drew her blade and brought its hilt to thump softly against her breast. "Ishtar's Blade is yours to command."

"I know." He came to his feet, and towered over her by a good head, but that wasn't what she found disconcerting. It was the warm caress of his fingers as he brushed a few loose locks of hair from her cheek.

"My fierce Little Shadow has always done my bidding." Again, he surprised her as he leaned down and placed a kiss on her forehead. His brotherly kiss did things to her heart and body that no brotherly kiss should do.

He inhaled sharply and Iltani stepped back.

"Your hair smells of the ocean," he said simply as he grinned.

"My skin and clothing, too, probably," she said in a disgruntled tone as she wiped at the salt stain on her leather vest.

"Burrukan was in a hurry this morning, wasn't he?"

"When isn't Burrukan in a hurry?"

"True," Ditanu agreed and then surprised her again by dragging her into his arms for another fierce hug. "But I'm glad he brought you home."

He released her before Iltani thought to return his hug, but he didn't seem upset and with a laugh, shoved her in the direction of his bathing chamber. "Go, the servants have already drawn a bath for me, but I think you will appreciate it more."

"I will not steal your bath. I'll survive until the servants round something up for me."

"Stop arguing with your king."

He said it with a lopsided grin, Iltani decided he rather liked the novelty of having someone argue with him.

"I thought here, in your chambers, you were simply Ditanu. You can't have it both ways."

"True. However, trust me. Once you're at the nursery, the cubs will not leave you alone long enough to bathe. They want nothing to do with their own baths, but if someone else is trying to get a bath without them, you will never believe the hew and cry those little ones can make."

"Perhaps they are too used to getting their way."

"Likely."

"A family trait perhaps?" She grinned when he arched an eyebrow at her audacity.

"I don't doubt." A lazy smile spread across his face. "Then they can't really be blamed for being irresistible either. Alas, another family trait I have no control over."

Iltani huffed at his boast but didn't deny it. Ditanu was irresistible. She still had wits enough to know she was as drawn to him as a night flier was to a torch. "Irresistible and dangerous."

Drat, she'd said that last out loud.

"Never dangerous to you." He reached for her again.

"I've had too much wine," she said in haste and turned away to evade another of his touches. She stalked away from him and made straight to the royal bathing chamber. After all, she did want to wash off the salt essence, and Ditanu always got his way. It was a forgone conclusion.

"A servant will bring you clean clothes." A hint of pain laced his words.

Iltani cast a glance over her shoulder at the tone, but Ditanu had already taken a seat at a large ornate table. It was piled high with paper, ink, and numerous unopened missives. He broke the seal on the first letter just as she brushed aside the veils providing a privacy screen between the two chambers. Hesitating a moment, she fought the urge to go back to him, to soothe whatever small hurt he might feel.

Her emotions hopelessly out of balance, she ducked into the bathing chamber.

Alcoves lined the walls of the room, housing towels, soaps, linens, fragrant oils and a whole host of other luxuries Iltani had never taken the time to use herself. Numerous candles, oil lamps, and a fire burning in the large hearth along the north wall provided more than enough light to make out details on the beautiful screens that flanked one side of the vast pool-like tub embedded in the floor.

The bathing pool took up a good third of the floor space, and steam still rose from the tranquil waters. This one was much the same as the ones in the public baths. They were built large enough for a full-sized gryphon to bathe in, which made them almost deep enough for swimming. To overcome this minor problem, ledges had been cut into the rock to act as seats. Like the public baths, the king's personal pool was fed by a fountain head, which at the push of a lever allowed water to run across the small streamed of enchanted heating rocks and on into the pool.

Iltani didn't care if she was breaking some archaic royal law by being here and headed for the decorative screens. There she stripped off her clothes and made a side trip to one of the alcoves to select some mildly scented soap, a sandalwood scent that reminded her of Ditanu, before crossing to the large pool and slipping into the water's warm embrace.

The warm water had soothed and settled Iltani's earlier turmoil far better than the wine had. Or maybe simply being away from Ditanu for a while allowed her to calm her chaotic thoughts. Whatever the case, as she exited the tub and wrapped a towel around her body and another around her hair, she felt in control again.

That was a first since she'd woken up this morning.

A slight noise, the brush of a sandal against the polished stone floor, had Iltani turning to the sound in time to see two young servant girls entering the room. Seeing her, one came over carrying a pile of clothing and the other went to the pool.

The one by the pool turned a lever and the bath began to empty into a drain. Iltani knew the water wouldn't be wasted, and was even now making its way through a purification system where it would eventually find its way into the irrigation lines for the farmers to use.

The girl with the clothes approached Iltani and bowed.

"I am not of noble blood," Iltani told her. "The bow is not necessary. In fact, I'd prefer if you treat me like any of the other servants. I am a Shadow."

The girl smiled. "I know who you are. You are our king's childhood friend and Shadow Burrukan's heir." The girl's smile grew into a grin. "Consort Ahassunu sent me and said to treat you as I would her."

Well, even though that was a touch unsettling, it made sense. Ahassunu was one of the few who knew that Iltani was Ishtar's Blade. That elevated Iltani's status enough to warrant the occasional bow. She supposed she might as well get used to it because come tomorrow night, everyone within the ten city-states would know as well.

"I will do your hair for you and then we'll help you dress for bed."

Iltani was going to say she could dress and do her own hair, but she was tired, and she hated working the tiny little braids back in. She'd been going to wait until morning, but it was better if they were put in while her hair was still wet. If someone else wanted to do it for her? All the better.

The girl picked up another basket and skirted the bench Iltani sat on. The basket contained combs, pins, an assortment of gold beads, and several delicate ribbons to weave in her hair. Iltani pulled another towel up around her shoulders for warmth and just sat, allowing her mind to wander as the girl worked on her hair.

Iltani was half asleep by the time the servant had finished.

"You have beautiful hair," the servant said. "I love the color. It reminds me of the royal cubs."

Fighting back a laugh, Iltani only nodded. Her hair did have something in common with the cubs. They both had thick brown pelts that bordered on wild and wiry. She allowed the girl to take the damp towels and then dress her in a long sleeping gown. Ribbons tied at the shoulders held it on and intricate needlework along the bodice and waist provided the only touch of modesty as the fabric was so soft and sheer that it hid almost nothing. A matching robe of the same material was laid out on the bench beside her. Iltani supposed the two layers together would almost provide enough fabric for warmth and modesty.

A slight sound of surprise escaped the girl. Iltani glanced over her shoulder and saw the girl's gaze was riveted on her back.

Ah. Ishtar's mark. The sheer robe probably allowed the mark to show through.

Iltani normally bathed by herself so no one had the opportunity to lay eyes on it.

The girl dropped into a deep bow. This, of course, alerted the other servant that something was amiss and she too approached with caution. Iltani knew the exact moment the second girl spotted the mark and registered what it was. She dropped to her knees and bowed her head to the floor.

When it became apparent neither one planned to get back up, Iltani cleared her throat. "Get up, please. This isn't necessary. I am a servant as much as you." Which was true. For as Ishtar's Blade, she was a servant to both a goddess and a king.

Still the servant girls didn't move.

Iltani was still coaxing the servants to stand when Ditanu brushed aside the veils and entered the bathing chamber. He took one look at Iltani's expression and laughed.

"Off with you," he ordered the servants. "Ahassunu will need your help getting the cubs to bed."

As if his words had broken invisible chains securing them to the floor, both girls rose, bowed to their king, and hurried from the room.

"I'm sorry. I didn't mean for them to see Ishtar's mark, but they spotted it through the nightdress." Iltani glanced down at her bare feet. "Close to twenty-one years I've managed to keep it hidden. One day back and now the servants know."

Ditanu brushed aside her words. "They were handpicked by Ahassunu because she knows their families and knows they will be discrete. You have nothing to fear. Besides, in less than a day the blooding ceremony will have unlocked the first tier of Ishtar's power. Your enemies will find you a fierce opponent."

His hand landed on her bare shoulder and at his insistent tug, she turned. Neither of them said anything as he traced the mark through the fabric of her nightdress and robe. He grunted something and pushed her toward the bench.

Ditanu strolled from the room. He wasn't gone long. When he returned he held a large dagger, its blade bare. If it were anyone else, the sight would have had her snatching the nearest item to use as a weapon, but this was Ditanu. She trusted him with her life, so she just sat and watched him as he came.

He halted and frowned down at her. "This may be a bit premature and likely to anger my aunt. But I don't care. We're going to perform the first of the blooding ceremonies tonight. Ishtar has sent me her nightmares and awakened your magic this day for a reason."

She understood his reasoning and the fear which prodded him into action. "Aren't there rituals and prayers and blessings and a whole assortment of priestly things that go along with it all?"

"Those are trappings only. Three things are all that's required. Ishtar's blessing, her Blade and her gryphon monarch. We already have her blessing." He then gestured first to himself and then at her. "What more do you think we need?"

Iltani admitted he had a point. "Then we just need..."

"For me to shed blood for Ishtar, yes."

She saw no reason to postpone the first ritual, certainly not if it would allow Ditanu to sleep peacefully this night.

She shrugged off the robe and then reached for the ribbon ties at her shoulders. She tugged them loose. The delicate material fluttered down to pool at the flare of her hips. While she was debating if she should shed it completely to save it getting ruined, Ditanu took the decision from her and straddled the bench next to her. Mimicking him, she swung her leg over the seat and faced away from him, exposing her back and the mark that ran along her spine from the base of her neck all the way down to her tail bone.

Turning her upper body slightly, she watched him over her shoulder. He was already bare-chested and dragged the tip of the dagger across his right pectoral as she watched. A slight grunt at the first cut was all the sound he made.

Afterward, he made a second, matching cut on the opposite side. The cuts sloped down at a slight angle, funneling most of the blood toward the center of his chest. He reached around her to place the dagger on the bench in front of them. Iltani braced her hands against the stone just behind where the dagger lay. Tension made all her muscles ridged, but commanding herself to relax simply didn't work.

Overly aware, she tracked his every move. At last, he shifted closer and pulled her against him until his bleeding chest was pressed against her back. "Ishtar, this night we come together to renew the pact between the gryphon kings and you, oh great Queen of the Night. Your Blade has been anointed with king's blood as the ancient rites demand, bless her now with your power so that we may serve you to our fullest potential and never fail you."

Even before he'd finished his plead to the goddess, Iltani felt her magic stir awake with greater strength. Ditanu's blood trickled down her spine and Ishtar's mark flared to life, absorbing it.

An unfathomable sensation spread outward from her spine as her body and Ishtar's power reacted to the blood of a gryphon king. It began as numbness, slowly changing to a tingle and then morphing into a burning sensation. Before she could tense farther, the burning receded, replaced by a pleasant warmth that left her body feeling heavy.

He spread his hand flat against her stomach and shifted closer to better hold her in place. "I'm sorry. I know this part must make you feel vulnerable."

Iltani twisted just enough to look back at him and grinned. "I have been away too long if you think you can make me feel vulnerable."

An answering smile crossed his lips, breaking what could have become a very awkward moment. "Yes, there's no denying you've been away too long."

Her muscles all threatened to turn to putty and Iltani had to lock her elbows to keep upright as more of Ishtar's power raced across her senses. When she, at last, allowed her eyes to drift closed, she sensed another presence. It probably should have come as a shock realizing Ishtar was manifesting in the room with them, seemed actually to be caressing them with her power, but Iltani was too far gone to worry.

Ditanu's fingers kneaded her skin where they rested against her belly. The power rising in her blood made her aware how it felt with him blanketing her. Her breath came faster and magic danced along her skin. A wave built, rising within her, answering a goddess's call and resonating with something of equal potency sleeping in Ditanu's blood.

Needing to touch something, to hold on in some way, she wrapped one hand around his left forearm. At her touch, the muscles flexed under her fingers, but he made no other protest, so she changed her grip, sliding her fingers down his wrist and then covering his hand.

The wave of power that had been threatening, rose up, and then came crashing down upon her, their magic a bright swirl of color to her vision, engulfing their bodies and the room.

Ditanu sat back on his haunches, dragging Iltani with him, never breaking the contact between them. Behind her, a shiver wracked his body and both arms wrapped around her middle almost convulsively. He uttered words too slurred and guttural to understand.

"Ditanu?" The power slowly began to ebb, receding back to where it had come from.

"I'm sorry. Just give me a moment." His head dropped to rest on her shoulder as he fought to catch his breath. "Our goddess has a wicked sense of humor."

Thinking was hard with him still pressed close, his warmth sinking into her bones. "You felt her, too. I didn't imagine it?"

"You most certainly didn't, and you can stress the 'felt' part." His voice still held a hoarse edge and mild disgruntlement. After another long moment, he pushed away from her and sat heavily on the bench behind. "This isn't quite how I imagined this moment. It's far rawer than I expected."

Already missing his heat and warm sandalwood scent, Iltani sat up and flexed her stiff joints. Several more times, she and Ditanu would have to do this over the next six moon cycles.

Great Ishtar, Iltani questioned, *is it wrong to look forward to the next ceremonies simply because it forces Ditanu and I closer together?* Reaching around behind her, she touched her mark but felt no blood.

"It's gone without a drop to show I ever spilled blood." The fingers of Ditanu's right hand brushed down her spine, a slow caress that measured every little bump along her spine and made her breath hitch. "Though it glows, and I can feel the power within you nearly twice as strong as it was before."

She tugged up her robe and Ditanu helped her tie the ribbons.

"My king, are you truly all right? At the end, it seemed...painful for you."

Pausing in his task, the ribbon spilling from his fingers, he glanced into her eyes. "You're still within my chambers. It's Ditanu, here. And no, that wasn't it."

Iltani tilted her head in question and wouldn't be dissuaded from her hunt. "What did you mean?"

"Some of the ancient texts you studied must have eluded to Ishtar's... appetites."

Iltani's eyebrows shot up nearly into her hairline. "Ishtar showed you her favor?"

So that's what had him so disconcerted. Ditanu must feel he'd somehow been unfaithful to his mate. Iltani rolled her eyes at the ceiling. She should tell him something to soothe his worries.

"You in no way dishonored your mate by catching a goddess's interest." Iltani laughed at his expression. "She could have demanded far more than a stolen caress."

A slight red hue shaded Ditanu's cheeks.

"Hmmm, it was just a caress, wasn't it?" Iltani might have been jealous of her goddess, but she wasn't. In a tiny wicked part of her mind, it felt more like she and Ishtar were working together to seduce their king.

"Ha! There's the Iltani I've always known." He grinned back at her and then pushed off the bench and started toward the steaming pool. "I might tell you about it one day."

For the first time all evening, Iltani allowed her eyes to devour Ditanu's form. With his back to her and his attention on the pool, she deemed it safe enough.

Ishtar wasn't the only female whose interest he'd managed to snare whether he wanted to or not. When he halted at the pool's edge and began working loose his belt, Iltani decided it was better not to torture herself. She looked away. Her eyes landed on her own sword and harness. She retrieved them and belted the harness on simply to give her fingers something to do.

"You said you needed to speak with Burrukan and Ahassunu?"

"Yes," he sighed. "With my earlier announcement about my cubs' regent, there is sure to be an overabundance of hurt feelings and new ambition among the nobles. Don't be surprised if they approach you wanting to forge alliances and discuss mutual benefits and the usual politics. The rumor that you are Burrukan's chosen heir is sure to have already spread far. They know Burrukan has my ear, and you have his. Once they figure out you have unhindered access to me, they'll grant you no peace either." Ditanu paused, and while she couldn't see his grin, the tone was there in his voice. "You'll be wishing for your quiet life of training back on New Assur within a quarter moon cycle. If they become too persistent, just do as Burrukan does and find some stairs to stretch your legs on. He says the soft nobles soon leave him alone."

Iltani found herself nodding at his words even though she wasn't facing him and didn't know if he was even looking in her direction. The soft rustle of clothing sliding to the floor told her he was still undressing. "I'll follow Burrukan's wise council."

"Good." There was a small splashing sound as he stepped down into the pool. "And, Iltani?"

"Yes, my king?" Her gaze instinctively slid back toward him.

He was half in the pool, the steaming water lapping at his hips. Continuing down the last two steps, he reached the bottom and waded over to the side of the pool where soap and cloths were laid out for him.

But the image of him half in the pool would likely return later to haunt her dreams.

"Watch yourself." At his words, her eyes jerked from where his strong hands were working soap into a cloth to guiltily meet his gaze. She was sure her own face must be revealing her embarrassment again, but his expression was serious, a king's blank mask. "Report anything you see that disturbs your peace, anything at all. Our enemies are still out there, and if unable to strike at me directly, they will gladly harm my loved ones."

"Yes, my king."

"You will be a target as much as any other member of my family."

Her stomach did its silly little flip. He'd just called her one of his loved ones in a roundabout way. "I don't see why they'd…"

He cut her off. "Just listen to your king for once."

"Yes, my king."

"Be safe, my Little Shadow."

Dismissed, Iltani bowed to him and then turned and left the room all without letting her gaze fall upon him again.

He'd lumped her in with his family. Her foolish heart had thrilled at his words, but her mind knew they could never be lovers. Even if he'd wanted too—and she might be misreading the situation—he couldn't. After the first mating, a male gryphon only grew aroused at the scent of his mate.

Once outside the bathing chamber, she drew a relieved breath and continued through the suite heading for the main hall. She wasn't running away, she told herself, she was doing her king's bidding.

It wasn't cowardice at all.

Nope.

But his bewildering words caused such a chaotic mess of her emotions, she exited the king's suite and turned down the hall heading in the wrong direction. Burrukan, Ahassunu, and the cubs were all in the opposite direction.

Curse it.

Worse, the guards in the hall all watched her as she passed. She probably did look an entertaining sight with her sword and harness strapped over her delicate nightdress and robe. She didn't care if her garb gave them something to chuckle over later, she wasn't going unarmed. Ever. She kept to her brisk walk and didn't slow until she reached a set of large double doors which marked the southern entrance to the royal wing. There were guards spaced every twenty paces along the hall, and a half dozen stationed at each doorway. Out of the entire number, she counted only ten in their gryphon forms, and none at all among those other guards walking patrols along the intersecting corridors where visiting nobles were housed.

There were a suspicious number of nobles and servants still 'going about their business' this late at night. Iltani's eyes narrowed.

"Report," she barked out the order and was pleased to see the guards snap to attention.

A bulky Shadow bristling with weapons brought his fist to his heart in a show of respect before he stepped away from the alcove he'd been standing sentry within.

With that formality over, he grinned widely, which contrasted his white teeth against the blackness of his beard. "Hah! The king's littlest Shadow has grown up, indeed. My nephews boasted of seeing you. Etum claims you like him better since you hugged him first. Everything is a competition with them."

An answering grin stretched her lips. "Kurumtum," she greeted the twins' uncle. "How have you been?"

"Well enough. I see Burrukan's training hasn't killed you yet, so you're doing well. You as good as he says?"

Iltani flashed another grin. "How should I know? He never tells me anything."

"Damned tight-lipped, isn't he?" Kurumtum chuckled again. "We'll have to test you in the ring later after all this ruckus has died down." He lowered his voice a notch until it was just loud instead of booming. "Now that rumor has openly declared you Burrukan's heir, you'll be too busy fending off overly enthusiastic nobles for the next few days to get any good practice time in. Already turned away four since I came on duty."

Iltani saw through his outward humor to see the truth behind his words. He was more concerned that his guards would be so busy fending off nobles that they might get distracted and miss a true threat. Acknowledging his concern, she gave him a sharp nod.

With a grunt, he thumped one of the guards nearest him on the shoulder. "Iltani asked for a report."

The guard, a girl a good five years younger than Iltani herself, looked shocked at the sudden attention turned her way.

Kurumtum didn't give her time to think. "Huh. What's this? Swallowed your tongue?"

"Sir," the girl managed.

"Report to Iltani, not me."

The girl wasn't dim-witted and launched into an account of everything that had happened since the king returned to his suite. Which in actual fact wasn't much. Iltani didn't comment, not wanting to get the girl into more trouble. It wasn't until the girl fell silent that she recognized her and turned to Kurumtum. "Is this little Takurtum?"

She couldn't believe how much his daughter had grown in four years.

He nodded. "She can't shift to gryphon yet, but she's done well in her training. She'll make a fine Shadow one day. She beat out all the other trainees and won the right to stand at guard."

Iltani tuned out the proud father as an arctic chill fingered along her soul and crept across her consciousness. Her heart raced with sudden adrenaline and all her senses sharpened, demanding her attention elsewhere.

"Excuse me," she said.

Eyes scanning the hall, she stepped away from Kurumtum to face the east corridor where a figure was making her hip-swaying way towards them.

After a moment, she recognized the newcomer. Her name was Beletum, a recently appointed councilor according to one of Ditanu's letters. Iltani didn't remember much about her, but she seemed calm and confident with her power. It didn't really come as a surprise. Her father, Ziyatum, was also a councilor and governor of the island Kalhu. Beletum had likely overseen much of her father's duties during the day to day running of the smaller city-state.

The newly made councilor was a few years older than Ditanu, but had not spent much time on Nineveh until recently, so Iltani hadn't had any opportunity to interact with Beletum before her training started on New Assur.

Even if they had known each other as youths and been friends, Iltani doubted it would have survived into adulthood. Ambition, greed, and a relentless hunger for power radiated off the councilwoman. If Iltani wasn't misreading Ishtar's warning, something greater here constituted a threat to either Ditanu or his kingdom.

"I have urgent business to discuss with Consort Ahassunu," Beletum said as she made to sweep past the guards.

Iltani stepped out to block her. "The Consort is bedding down the cubs and does not want to be disturbed."

She didn't know if that was the truth but there was no way she was letting the councilwoman anywhere near Ditanu's cubs.

"Then I must speak with the king."

Iltani kept her face neutral. "King Ditanu is not taking visitors. If your message is urgent, tell it to me and I will pass it along."

She didn't miss the flicker of annoyance as it crossed the other woman's face. But she had to give her credit for a well-preformed bow.

"Then I will return in the morning. Good evening to you."

Ha! Good evening indeed. Iltani doubted that one wished anything good toward her and evening was already a fading memory. If she were to guess, she'd say it was closer to midnight. Once the councilwoman was out of earshot, Iltani turned back to Kurumtum. "Make sure she isn't ever left alone with Ditanu, the consort, or the cubs."

Kurumtum didn't even blink at her command, merely nodding his agreement and glowered in the direction Beletum had gone.

CHAPTER
seven

KING DITANU WOULD be wondering why Burrukan and Ahassunu hadn't come to him yet. Iltani had allowed herself to get postponed too long already. She had an errand to complete. Turning away from where the councilwoman had vanished, Iltani started down the length of the hall where Ahassunu's quarters and the nursery were housed.

It wasn't a long walk and she arrived at another door guarded by four Shadows. They saluted her. She brushed past them and on into the room without announcing herself. The last thing Consort Ahassunu would appreciate was for Iltani to wake the cubs if they'd finally fallen to sleep.

There was no sign of Burrukan. Maybe he'd already returned to Ditanu?

The nursery was laid out similarly to the king's chambers though these rooms were a third again bigger to house the nursery. Using that design as a guide, she headed for what she assumed was the consort's receiving room and paused outside another door. There was a guard standing at attention and he opened the door for her.

Within, Iltani didn't find Burrukan or the consort either. Though she did find the sleeping cubs safe in their nest.

Iltani scouted around the nursery and found an alcove the servants had prepared for her. It was larger than she'd expected, the walls softened with tapestries and colorful veils. The floor was covered in plush carpeting. The bed on its raised platform was decked out in piles of woven blankets and pillows that matched the room's rich burgundy color scheme.

Ditanu must have remembered her favorite color and had been thoughtful enough to instruct his servants to find something fitting in those tones. Iltani was touched by the gesture.

Hoisting her pack off her shoulder, she stowed it under the bed for now. Later, she'd unpack her few personal items and store them in the beautifully carved wardrobe. The letters twanged at her conscious for a moment, but she wasn't going to be gone long, just long enough to alert Burrukan and Ahassunu that Ditanu required them.

Which reminded her. Just where was Burrukan? He was supposed to be with the cubs. It was possible the Consort Ahassunu might have sent him on an errand, but then where was she? A gryphon mother didn't normally leave her cubs alone for long.

Brushing aside the heavy veil that doubled as a door, she exited her room and wandered over to check on the cubs. They slept in a raised platform nest, with waist high padded walls that offered a sense of security to the young cubs. Inside, large down filled pillows softened the nest and kept the cubs warm and snug. It was large enough that an adult gryphon could climb in as well.

At the moment, it only held three fat round cubs. At the sight, Iltani felt herself relax. Here she would be free from political intrigue and inappropriate desires for her king for a few hours.

There was something soothing to the soul about the cubs' milk scent and their sleepy coos of inquiry. She leaned over the side, stretching to caress each of their fuzzy heads. Kuwari, the one she'd held in her lap during breakfast, blinked sleepily at her. Then his dark orbs sharpened in recognition and he rolled away from the others to scramble over to the nest's side where he attempted to scale the wall. When that failed, he begged to be picked up. His tiny voice growing louder until Iltani scooped him up in her arms.

"Easy, little Kuwari," she crooned softly to the cub. "No need to wake up the world."

He made a couple more huffing cries and then settled in her arms, nuzzling against her breasts.

Voices from the adjacent chamber reached Iltani's ears. The deeper tones were Burrukan's, so he was still here.

She made her way over to the door to find it open a crack. The chamber beyond was dark and deserted. The only light came from the glowing embers in the hearth. Directly across from the door where she stood was another doorway, this one rigged with hanging veils like Iltani's own sleeping chamber.

The room beyond the curtains was better lit and Iltani saw movement.

"I'll go check on the cubs." Burrukan's voice came clearly through the veils.

"You might want to get dressed first." The second voice was female and familiar but Iltani's mind refused to make the connection. It was not possible. Or...or she was coming to conclusions while lacking all facts.

"I heard the servants leave a while ago. Why bother? Unless you simply enjoy stripping a man." Burrukan's voice again. "I'll be but a moment. I'm sure one of the cubs is only dreaming."

Iltani started back the way she'd come, all the while being certain not to make as much as a whisper of noise. She was easing back toward the nursery when Burrukan pushed aside the curtain. Luckily, he was looking behind him, back into the consort's bedchamber so he did not see Iltani.

She eased behind the door and into deeper shadows. Calmly. Moving with stealth, her training rescued her even as her mind spun with confusion, shock, and disbelief.

An equally naked consort joined Burrukan at the curtain. She held out his pants. "Ditanu will likely send Iltani to seek her bed soon. She's to bed down in the nursery if you've forgotten."

Burrukan took the offered pants with a sigh. "If I know Ditanu, he will keep her up late into the night reminiscing. I'll be surprised if we see her before dawn, and I'll be doubly surprised if she's still sober."

"Don't tempt fate. Get dressed."

Burrukan grumbled something under his breath, but dropped the curtain and went to dress.

Treason. Burrukan and Consort Ahassunu had been committing treason against King Ditanu.

How was it even possible?

Gryphon mating bonds created an unbreakable link, their hearts, minds, and bodies synchronizing until mates only craved each other and resulted in one unified fertility cycle. Unlike the human citizens of the city-states, gryphons did not—could not—seek out other lovers.

She didn't have time to solve how the treason was even possible at the moment. For now, the greatest priority was not letting either Burrukan or the consort know they'd been found out. Iltani couldn't risk them doing something desperate in retaliation. She had to think, plan and then figure who to tell.

But first, she had to make it look like she'd only arrived.

Switching the cub to one arm, she raced back to her sleeping area and snatched her pack from where she'd shoved it under the sleeping platform. Barely pausing, she hoisted it over one shoulder and made her way back to the nest in the main room. She placed her pack next to her feet and stood with one hip cocked and began to rock the cub in her arms.

Humming softly, she sang a lullaby she remembered Burrukan singing to her when she was young. She was halfway through the third verse when the door between the two chambers opened.

"Iltani, I didn't hear you come in." Burrukan's voice held a note of surprise but no guilt.

She held her finger up to her lips and indicated the cub in the crook of her arm. She answered in a whisper. "I only just arrived. I heard this one fussing so came over to investigate."

Burrukan wasn't the only accomplished liar. She'd been lying since shortly after she'd first learned to talk. In the court of the Gryphon King, one learned the fine art of deception early if they wished to survive. Although she'd never lied out of maliciousness, only to hide Ishtar's mark and to protect Ditanu. In point of fact, Ditanu was the one person she always told the truth.

Omitting to mention that she was in love with him wasn't a lie, and if he ever asked her plainly, she'd answer him truthfully.

If he never asked, that was one bit of awkwardness which need never see the light, but this newest treason was something that must be handled with utmost care. She couldn't lie to him about this, but she couldn't just blurt it out to him either. It would crush him, and that pain would make him vulnerable.

With the cub still in her arms, she leaned back against the nest's high walls. "I'm sorry. I think the cubs may have heard me talking with the guards outside, just before I entered. Ditanu wanted to discuss plans with you and Ahassunu before retiring for the night and ordered me to watch the little ones."

She smiled at Kuwari and rubbed his belly. "Watching over the cubs is no hardship."

"You'll change your tune come bath time." A fully clothed Consort Ahassunu swept into the room and smiled at Iltani.

It seemed a genuine smile, full of warmth and welcome, but that smile was as false as Ahassunu had been to Ditanu.

With the cub still in her arms, Iltani executed a court bow. She straightened a moment later with the sleeping cub none the wiser. "The king wished your council and he asked that I stay with the cubs tonight."

"Of course," Ahassunu said and came over to ruffle the downy feathers and fur on Kuwari's head. "My cubs are in good hands. If they are any trouble at all, bring them to me. The youngest can be a touch fussy."

Ahassunu turned to Burrukan and inclined her head. "Come, the night isn't getting any younger and Ditanu likely has much he wants to discuss before morning."

With that, the two traitors to the crown turned and exited the room.

Iltani watched them go, wishing she had a valid reason to keep them away from the king. Unfortunately, there was nothing she could do that wouldn't look suspicious.

She needed a plan.

Only the knowledge that they weren't likely to do Ditanu harm in the next few moments kept her from rushing back across the hall with her sword drawn.

Iltani started to pace while she mulled over this new distressing news.

All three of the cubs were most certainly Ditanu's. Their blood called to her mark, confirming the cubs were his. At least, his heirs were truly his. Her line of reasoning turned down another road.

Gryphons mated out of love, but what if ambition overruled that emotion? Could Burrukan and Ahassunu have mated in secret even before Ditanu had laid eyes on his consort? Did they plan this all along?

Had Ahassunu actively seduced the younger Ditanu as a way to gain the power and prestige of the crown? That seemed likely. But to what end?

How was this even possible? Iltani massaged the back of her neck, but it did nothing to alleviate the tension.

She had to report this mess, or at least, share it with someone.

Who would believe her? She was having difficulty accepting what her own eyes had seen.

If she hadn't witnessed it, Iltani would have sworn Burrukan was loyal to his king.

Perhaps if she took some proof before Ditanu's aunt, Priestess Kammani? Ishtar's high priestess would, at least, listen to Ishtar's Blade.

Iltani pinched the bridge of her nose and attempted to massage away the beginnings of a headache.

How could Burrukan have done this?

That was the hardest part to swallow.

Burrukan was the only father she knew.

For now, her own feeling of betrayal and confusion would have to wait. Ditanu's safety came first.

Yet, how was she supposed to keep him safe when she was here instead of there?

The cub in her arms, perhaps sensing her distress, stirred awake and made a mewling cry in question. She rocked him and sang softly. The cub soon settled. Iltani glanced down at him, studying him in a new light, and the beginnings of a plan grew as she glanced between him and his siblings who were also waking to see what the youngest had been fussing about.

Iltani grinned. "Did you have a nightmare, little Kuwari?" she crooned to him and kissed him on the head. "Of course, you want your father's reassurance. It's entirely natural."

Then she gently deposited him on the floor next to her pack and scooped up the other two cubs. They wiggled in her arms and tried to burrow deeper, not particularly distressed or wanting to visit their father, but Iltani insisted.

Soon, the youngest was doing some very loud insisting of his own. He clawed at her boot and cried piteously to be picked up again.

Once she'd deemed he'd made enough noise that the guards outside couldn't possibly have missed it, she picked the cub up again. The door creaked open just as she was trying to figure out how to juggle three upset cubs.

"Do you require assistance?" the guard asked.

Iltani grinned. "Sorry. I think they miss their mother. Ahassunu said to bring them to her if they started to fuss." Having finally managed to get a good grip on all three cubs, she marched out into the hallway and on toward Ditanu's suite before the guard could make other helpful suggestions.

The Shadows outside the king's suite took one look at Iltani and tapped softly on the door before opening it and ushering her forward. One of them had the audacity to grin as she marched past. She didn't dignify his grin with a response.

Let them think what they would. Iltani had other concerns.

Once she entered the outer receiving rooms, she soon picked up the soft mumble of conversation and followed it to its source. For the second time, she found herself in the king's study.

The king in question was sitting cross-legged by the fire. Ahassunu was kneeling behind him, working his wet hair back into intricate little braids. Burrukan sat cross-legged beside the king, holding out a bowl of beads for Ahassunu to pick from as she required them. All three fell silent and looked up at Iltani's sudden entrance.

After executing a hasty bow, which earned three delighted squeals from the cubs, Iltani sought out Ditanu's gaze. "I am sorry to interrupt, but Consort Ahassunu said to bring the cubs over if they started to fuss. I think they worried when they awoke to find only me."

Ditanu brushed away Ahassunu's hand where she was tying a gold bead into one of his braids. He unfolded himself and came to his feet. "The little ones will have you well trained within the week," he said, a smile softening what might otherwise have been a rebuke.

Iltani would have replied had her mouth not just turned dry as a desert and her tongue cleaved to the roof of her mouth. Ditanu approached her with a masculine grace that she couldn't help but appreciate, but it was his attire or mostly lack thereof which made her speechless. His only adornments were the beads in his hair and a white and gold knee-length loincloth that left much of his golden skin bare.

Forcing her eyes away from her king, she looked down at his cubs instead. Three sleepy faces looked back at her, destroying her ploy about them being fussy. "I swear they were whimpering just a few moments ago."

Ditanu leaned forward, using the pretense of scooping two of his cubs from her arms to whisper in her ear. "You shouldn't lie to your king."

"We need to talk," she answered truthfully, already deciding to tell Ditanu of Ishtar's warning about Beletum. One threat at a time. She'd figure out what to do with Burrukan and Ahassunu later. "In the hall earlier, I ran into Beletum and my magic flared a warning. You said to come to you if anything disturbed my peace." She paused. "My peace is disturbed."

Her words caught Burrukan's interest and he drifted over from where he'd been leaning against the mantle. "I'll increase the guard." He swung his gaze from Ditanu and speared Iltani with a dark look. "Why didn't you mention this sooner?"

Maybe because I caught you and the consort together? Aloud she said, "The cubs distracted me. Besides, I didn't take Ishtar's warning to mean an immediate threat, only one that needed watching."

Burrukan held her gaze and then grunted unhappily. His look slid sideways to where the consort was taking one of the cubs from Ditanu.

She could see him wondering if she'd been distracted by something else she might have seen. Iltani kept her expression neutral, not willing to give anything away that might, in turn, endanger Ditanu.

Thankfully, he didn't challenge her or show any outward signs of nervousness.

Still Iltani was a little surprised when she heard herself saying. "Ditanu and the cubs stay together tonight. I can't keep them both safe if they are on opposite sides of the damn hall."

"Agreed," Burrukan barked and then marched out toward the corridor.

Iltani heard the door open, and then Burrukan's sober voice issuing orders. The guards said something in exchange and then her mentor returned. "I've doubled the night watch. Three of the guards will stay in your quarters at all times."

"Does your king get a say in this?" Ditanu asked with humor glinting in his eyes.

"No," Iltani and Burrukan echoed each other.

Ditanu sighed. "You know I hate having an audience while I sleep."

"Yet, I sleep better knowing you'll wake in the morning." Burrukan snipped back.

Iltani's fists tightened. Did Burrukan really mean that, or was he such an accomplished liar, that everything she'd grown up believing was actually false?

"One guard." Ditanu's gaze slid toward Iltani and she didn't know what to make of the look he gave her.

Burrukan snorted. "Two. And, yes, you can keep Iltani with you."

The king's boyish grin reminded Iltani of the youth he'd been. She was glad to know her childhood friend still lived within the man, even if his charms had her emotionally off balance every moment she was with him.

Her eyes tracked toward Ahassunu where she was grooming her oldest cub, Humusi, in a loving manner, all without looking even slightly nonplussed by Ditanu's clear joy at keeping Iltani with him. Shouldn't Ahassunu, at least, pretend to be upset or disturbed by her husband's focus on another woman?

Just what, by Ishtar, was going on here?

CHAPTER
eight

N O ONE ANSWERED Iltani's unasked question, of course, so she simply shrugged it off as another intriguing mystery she'd unravel in the coming days. Tonight, she was too tired and flummoxed to attempt it.

Ditanu motioned for her to join him by the fire. She did, transferring her cub from her arms to her lap. The king did the same and then glanced over at his consort. To Iltani's surprise, Ahassunu was stripping off her robe. Eyes widening in alarm, she snapped her gaze back to Ditanu.

She wasn't...Ditanu wasn't...they weren't. Because there was no way Iltani was staying for that. She could guard her king from the hall.

"If I only had a mirror," Ditanu drawled, "so you could behold your expression. Ahassunu is going to shapeshift so she can nurse the cubs before they go back to sleep."

Iltani felt a fiery wave of embarrassment course down from the top of her head all the way to the tips of her toes. "I knew that."

"Liar."

When Iltani chanced a glance over at Ahassunu a few moments later, it was to behold a tawny colored gryphon flicking her wings to settle the long primary feathers in place. Her lion's tail flicked gently as she gathered her powerful haunches under her and paced over to where Ditanu and Iltani held the two male cubs.

Iltani held perfectly still. Even the mildest mannered of gryphons could become predatory, territorial and reactive while in full gryphon form. Add to that a mother's natural tendency to be territorial and volatile, and Iltani was suddenly feeling on edge.

"Relax," Ditanu said, not looking alarmed by the massive presence of the gryphon towering over them while they sat on the floor. "Ahassunu is as familiar with your scent as the cubs are."

This time, it was Ditanu's turn to look embarrassed about something.

"What?"

"You never noticed some of your clothing going astray?"

Iltani arched an eyebrow. "It was common on the training island to misplace items of clothing since it all went to the central laundry area for the servants to clean."

Ditanu cleared his throat. "Your worn clothing always made another stop first." He groomed the cub in his arms gently as he spoke. "It was important to me that my cubs know your scent, so I instructed Burrukan to always bring an item of yours when he returned each night."

Again, Iltani was stunned by Ditanu's actions and touched by them as well.

He didn't elaborate more, and Iltani didn't question him.

"Not one of my prouder moments—stealing woman's underthings," Burrukan groused from where he was gathering up Ahassunu's discarded garments. "At least when the new litter is born, you will be here for it."

"New litter?" Iltani blurted it out before she could stop herself. Ahassunu was carrying another litter? She eyed the consort's sleek and trim gryphon form. Nothing showed yet. The consort couldn't have been far along since Iltani hadn't noticed any telltale bulge when she'd been in human form.

Were they even Ditanu's?

"The healers say I am only a month along, but the little ones are strong," Ahassunu said in hissing gryphon speech. "I just told Ditanu the news yesterday after the healers confirmed it."

Ditanu grinned at Iltani. "I was going to write you, but then you came in person and I got sidetracked. You'll be here for this litter's birth, and all my cubs will know the love of my Blade."

Iltani just hoped Ditanu was the father.

When Ahassunu issued a soft cry, the cubs jerked awake from where they were dosing and bolted toward their mother. The oldest two got there first just as Ahassunu laid down, curling on her side to allow the cubs to nurse. Kuwari showed interest in the offered meal, but simply sat and looked up at Iltani expectantly.

"What?" she asked the cub, wanting something to think about other than another litter where Ditanu may or may not have been the father. Iltani acknowledged Kuwari's intense, hopeful gaze. "Aren't you hungry?"

The cub yawned and then nipped at Iltani's fingers with his still soft beak, making purring noises in the back of his throat. He butted his head against her breasts when his first attempt didn't elicit the response he'd hoped for.

"As well as being the fussiest of the three, he doesn't understand that not all breasts produce milk on demand," Ditanu said, humor glinting in his gaze. He sobered a moment later. "I think he's also inherited my gift for true dreaming and may see glimpses of the future, but he doesn't yet have a way to communicate his worries. Your scent has always calmed him—he knows Ishtar's Blade will protect him."

If he'd inherited his father's ability, which Iltani thought of more as a curse than a gift, then poor little Kuwari had a good reason for being clingy.

With tears pooling in the corners of her eyes, she picked up the cub and planted a kiss on his head before carrying him over to his mother where he burrowed around until he found a teat. The sound of the suckling cubs was relaxing but it still didn't dull the sorrow she felt. Her eyes slid to

Ahassunu and Burrukan and the sorrow turned to anger. She still hadn't forgotten or forgiven their betrayal, but she didn't have the first idea what to do about it either.

Nor did Ishtar's warning flare when Iltani was near them. Could it be that while Ahassunu and Burrukan *were* committing treason, they *weren't* actually a threat to Ditanu's welfare?

Iltani fought off a yawn as she listened to Ditanu and Burrukan discuss plans for the trip to the island of Uruk, home of High Priestess Kammani. Perhaps after the blooding ceremony, Iltani would find time for a private moment with Kammani to ask her advice about what to do about Burrukan and Ahassunu.

Ditanu's aunt was wise and kind, as well as being quick to forgive, but equally quick to react should she deem something a danger to her nephew. There was not much that happened in the ten city-states that Kammani was not either privy to or lacked the means to find out.

That dilemma postponed until tomorrow, Iltani let her mind go blank and allowed her eyes to wander for a few moments.

Ahassunu was curled up with Humusi sleeping on her flank while Ilanum was snuggled in Ditanu's lap and Mite, as she had taken to calling Kuwari in her mind, was asleep in her arms where she stood against the wall, keeping watch.

Though she admitted, it was hard to look like a properly fierce King's Shadow with a cub purring softly in her arms.

"We've talked this topic to death. I'm in danger of losing my voice." Ditanu stood and stretched, the cub still asleep in his arms. "Off with you."

It took her a moment to realize he was talking to Burrukan. She'd only just begun to relax when Ditanu swung his attention back to her.

"Come, help me put these ones to bed." He gestured at the cubs.

She couldn't really say no, so she followed him as he headed toward his bed chamber. Burrukan scooped the cub off Ahassunu's flank and then handed his tiny burden over to Ditanu.

With that, Burrukan uttered good night and left.

Iltani paused at the threshold and held the door for the consort to follow.

Ahassunu stretched and started in the direction that Burrukan had gone.

"Consort?" Iltani called, not really wanting her to come but curious what she would do.

Looking over her shoulder, Ahassunu laughed. "Ditanu snores. Enjoy."

Well, wasn't that blatant?

Iltani just shook her head and promised to get to the bottom of whatever deception was going on under the king's very nose as soon as possible. Another thought occurred to her. Ditanu was equally as sharp as his aunt.

Could he be aware of what was going on—and, what? Didn't care?

She scowled. It made no sense. At least not yet, but perhaps Ditanu had mentioned some of his suspicions in one of his letters and that was why Burrukan said they were dangerous if they fell into enemy hands. Sighing, she rubbed her temples with her free hand and looked down at Kuwari.

"I guess I'll worry about tomorrow's troubles tomorrow, eh little Mite?"

After Ahassunu had left, Iltani checked on the guards posted at each location. Content that the area was as secure as it could be, she made her way back to the king's bedchamber. Before a case of nerves could overcome her, she marched into the room. Another guard was already stationed in one corner, pretending he was invisible. Iltani spied the opposite corner and mentally claimed it as her own. From there, she could watch both the bedchamber door and the door leading out to the balcony.

She'd almost reached the location when her eyes adjusted to the darker bedchamber and she began to pick out details of the wall. It was another of those wall carvings. Her eyes narrowed and then one brow arched.

Well, my...wasn't that...something to make Ishtar proud, Iltani decided after she ran her eyes over the life-sized image of a female blade astride her gryphon king.

Iltani cleared her throat and spun on her heels.

She made her way over to the balcony and surveyed it and the three Shadows standing guard directly outside. She knew there would be others stationed throughout the gardens. Her magic already told her Ditanu's location. Even without that, she could hear him reading softly.

Drawing a deep breath she marched over to the large raised bed, stomped up the four stairs and peered around the heavy drapes that were only partially drawn. Ditanu sat with his back propped against a stack of pillows, a book in his hand and Humusi and Ilanum play fighting on his lap. A heavy coverlet offered protection from tiny claws.

He stopped reading long enough to glance in her direction. "If I keep reading they will eventually fall asleep. It doesn't seem to matter what I read them. Guess my tone must bore them to sleep."

Patting the coverlet to the right of his hip, he gestured her to bring Kuwari to him. Iltani eyed the distance and winced. There was no way she could reach. She'd have to crawl. That *just* had to be in violation of some court edict somewhere.

"Your bed is so large it borders on obscene," she groused as she hoisted herself up onto it and crawled one-armed toward him, the cub tucked against her side. "And this is completely destroying my fierce Shadow warrior persona I've worked so hard to maintain."

Ditanu laughed, the rich tones sounding far too intimate trapped within the bed's drapes.

Her long night dress didn't help at all. She kept getting tangled up in it as she tried to crawl. Kuwari awoke and gave a questioning cry, which had the other two cubs bolting toward Iltani. "Oh, for the love of Ishtar!" she cried as they piled into her.

She rolled to her side so she wouldn't crush any of them, but it left her vulnerable to their assault. They clambered over her, grabbing any bit of lace and cloth they could find, or pouncing and pawing at it. Kuwari, having decided to get into the game as well, pounced on her sword belt, chewing and biting the leather. When that didn't gain him anything, he started on her scabbard, trying to pry off the jewels embedded in the leather.

"Gah! Stop. Don't eat those." She pushed his head away and only succeeded in having him attack her fingers instead. It didn't hurt, his beak still too soft and rubbery to really cause damage, but it felt peculiar and ticklish at the same time.

Humusi had moved to the hem of her nightdress and started yanking and growling playfully. She heard the sound of tearing fabric. Kuwari abandoned her scabbard and was now pawing at her hair. "Hey, the servants just fixed that!"

She twisted and lunged at Kuwari, rolling him onto his back and tickling his belly.

As children, she and Ditanu play-fought for hours, and while she'd been outmatched physically when he was in his gryphon form, she was cunning and had found all his ticklish spots.

A few exploratory wiggles of her fingers and she found Kuwari shared a lot of his father's ticklish spots. The cub squealed in delight and batted at her hands with his paws. He kept his claws sheathed, thankfully. Ditanu hadn't always bothered when they'd used to play fight as younglings. The other two cubs charged back toward her though she found they were after Kuwari as much as her.

Iltani turned her attention toward the other two. Laughing and lunging at them, her guard completely down, she didn't see the attack coming. A full grown gryphon slammed into her side, his massive paws flipping her as easily as she had his cub. She rolled across the bed twice before coming to rest on her stomach. As she lay there with the breath knocked out of her, she realized her fatal mistake. Ditanu was a full blooded gryphon, possessing the heightened protective instincts all gryphon parents shared.

She still had the wherewithal to go limp as she waited for Ditanu to make the next move.

The killing blow she half expected didn't fall. She cautiously raised her head a few inches only to have one of the cubs leap at her. It was Kuwari. The sweet little fellow didn't know the game was no longer a game.

She expected Ditanu to nudge the cub out of immediate danger, but he didn't, confusing Iltani no end. She knew gryphons. She should have been dead.

A heavy paw landed on her butt, holding her down as a rather large and wickedly sharp beak started nuzzling her. His purr echoed around the room.

That wasn't an aggression sound.

Slowly, Iltani's adrenaline filled mind cleared enough to think. She wasn't going to die. He had simply wanted to join the play fight with her and his cubs. Well, she didn't want to disappoint him. A grin of challenge spread across her face.

Thoughts of how to retaliate were floating through her mind when the tufted tip of his tail found its way into a tear in the side of her nightdress. Giggles burst forth from deep inside her, but she didn't admit defeat so easily.

A skillfully placed heel jammed into a tender place had the large gryphon grunting and leaping away before she could land another blow. While Ditanu was stalking her from the left, two cubs were circling from the right. Kuwari, at least, sided with her and together they attacked the other two cubs. Ditanu launched himself at them all. They scattered out of the way with only moments to spare, then in lightning fast agreement, Iltani and the three cubs changed tactics, coming together to face a greater foe.

Before they could formulate a plan, the big gryphon charged them all, opening his forelegs wide and scooping them all up. Instinctively, Iltani snatched all three cubs into her arms as Ditanu's momentum carried them off the large bed. A pile of arms, legs, and wings, they rolled across the floor. Iltani and the cubs weren't hurt. Ditanu had curled around them, taking the brunt of the impact. While he was still getting his feet under him, Iltani leapt backward, flipped clear of his limbs and landed with her legs planted on either side of his head.

She dropped down and hooked her legs around his thick neck and wrapped her arms around his head and then hauled back with all her might. "Get him," she yelled.

The cubs leapt upon their father with squeals of glee and Iltani's laughter echoed theirs. They ran their beaks along his tidy feathers, tickling and biting and pulling until a few feathers drifted to the ground. Ditanu mock growled at the sight, but those feathers were likely loose anyway, so she shouted encouragement to the cubs.

"That's it Humusi! Three points for the big feather."

Of course, she couldn't hold Ditanu for long. He hoisted himself back to all fours, his cubs rolling harmlessly out of the way. Meanwhile, Iltani found herself dangling across his back, trapped in place by his great wings while he chased each cub. He paced them at his leisure, eventually pinning them down one at a time and blowing hot breath into their baby down, making them squeal with delight.

After a time, Ditanu finished his play discipline. Then he ducked his head and heaved his great shoulders, sending Iltani rolling down his neck. Knowing what he planned, she hit the ground, rolled and then sprang back to her feet and bolted for the massive bed, using the obstacle to try and evade Ditanu's pursuit.

Every moment she remained free was a point in her favor. If she managed to complete a circuit around the room, she won the game. At least, that was how they played it as children.

Behind her, Ditanu bound over or around anything in his path, keeping an even pace, never hurrying. The cubs had switched allegiances again and were now targeting Iltani, too.

"Why you little traitors," she called between gales of laughter. Even as she continued her mad run around the room, she already knew the end of the pursuit was a forgone conclusion, and the longer she made Ditanu chase her, the longer her tickle session after was likely to last.

"I surrender!" She stopped running and Ditanu knocked her down. One large paw caught her and prevented her from slamming into the ground full force but it didn't deter the three cubs and they landed upon her, tiny balls of fur, hissing and growling mock fury. Ditanu sat with his paws planted on either side of her body as his cubs gloried in their win.

A long time later, when the cubs finally tired of the game, she backed out from under Ditanu's bulk and glanced up into his face. Both the earlier merry cant of his tufted ears and the glimmer of humor in his eyes were gone, replaced by a much more soulful expression.

"Promise me," Ditanu demanded in his deep, gravelly tone. "You'll never leave me again."

The breath froze in her lungs, her heart pounded and she swore her stomach had just plummeted to the ground.

Oh, my king, I never wanted to leave you in the first place.

His tone completely extinguished her playfulness and she returned his gaze with her own level look, all the while fighting the urge to tell him of her love. Coming to her feet, she stepped up to him until she was standing on his left side, then she wrapped her arms around his neck and buried her face in his feathers as she had as a child and hugged him fiercely.

"Even if my duties as Ishtar's Blade should require me to hunt down our enemies and leave you for a time, I will always return."

"I suppose that will have to do," he whispered back to her reluctantly and then fell silent. She thought he was done until she heard his deep purring voice wrap around her senses. "I will hold you to that, my Little Shadow."

Her heart overflowing with joy, Iltani squeezed harder. It was a fight to let him go.

While she was still futilely attempting to brush out the wrinkles and snags in her nightdress where the cubs had clawed and chewed it, she slid her gaze sideways to Ditanu and witnessed him take the hook of his beak to his forearm.

"While I have you here," he said, his deep gryphon voice vibrating along her breastbone. "I see no reason not to go ahead with the second blooding."

Iltani arched an eyebrow and glanced between his determined gaze and the new wound. This slice wasn't as neat and clean as the ones he'd made on his chest earlier, but his beak did a sufficient job.

"You're really out to annoy your aunt, aren't you?"

"In this instance, Ishtar's high priestess will forgive us if we forgo some of the trappings of the ceremony. The safety of my cubs comes first. Maybe if someone had listened to my childhood nightmare, we might each have had a chance to know our parents."

Iltani merely nodded and then turned her back to him and dragged the nightdress over her head. She knelt, bowed her head and dragged her braids off to one side. This time was less nerve wracking than the first time. While she was honest with herself, she admitted she found Ditanu as a gryphon surprisingly less intimidating than Ditanu as a man.

A brush of feathers along her side was the only warning before he pressed his bleeding forearm against her spine. Unlike the first time, there was no sense Ishtar was present. However, her body did react to Ditanu's blood, eagerly drawing it in and adapting her body to be more like him.

"I wonder," his voice rumbled loudly next to her ear, "what color of gryphon you'll make."

"You're so certain that I'll advance that far? Most of Ishtar's other Blades never did."

"The strongest did. You hold the potential to be one of Ishtar's greatest Blades."

"How very brash of you." It was easier to bait him than acknowledge how much she would one day like to be able to fly, wing to wing, as his equal.

"It's not speculation. Ishtar told my aunt, and she told me. If you don't believe me, go ask High Priestess Kammani yourself."

Iltani held her breath and fought not to grin like a fool. Even knowing it would one day be possible, she still had trouble imagining herself as anything other than human.

They were silent after that, but Iltani was still aware of the environment around them. The cubs sleeping curled nearby, the night breeze blowing in from the ocean. Even the silent regard of the Shadow standing at guard in one corner. That one now knew what she was, but he, like all his brethren, was not inclined to gossip.

Iltani hadn't forgotten him, but like the king was pretending he didn't exist.

Ditanu shifted at last, taking the weight of his forearm off her back and licking to close the wound. When his own wound was closed, he nudged Iltani in the side, urging her to stand up.

She would have obeyed at once, but at this second blood exchange, she now felt a deep sense of lethargy seeping through her body. She'd be content to sleep on the floor. The carpets covering the king's floors were plush enough.

Ditanu nudged her with his beak. "Up with you. Ishtar's Blade does not sleep on the floor."

"Not even just this once? I won't tell if you don't." She turned her head enough to see him pad softly toward his bed. With a heavy sigh, she scooped up her discarded nightdress and stood.

It wasn't until she poked her head out the top and wiggled the bunched fabric down her hips that she noticed Ditanu sitting on his haunches watching her. His tufted tail flicked softly and his dark bird-like eyes studied her in that unfathomable way shared by both gryphons and birds of prey.

He watched her a moment more, as if he wanted to tell her something, but then his gaze slid away from her to land on the other guard in the room.

At his soft call, the cubs stirred awake from where they were having a power nap, and then followed him back up onto his bed. There the big gryphon curled on his side and offered his warm flanks and belly fur for the cubs to nestle in. They did and soon Iltani heard their soft snores.

"Come here and sleep with the cubs. You need time to rest and allow your body to process my blood. Tomorrow will be a long day and I don't want Ishtar's Blade falling asleep at her own blooding ceremony."

Iltani snorted with humor but realized she was tired and her body did need rest.

"Do not worry," Ditanu offered. "I will stand watch over both you and my cubs this night."

She hesitated a moment more. Then with a shrug she went to the head of his bed, grabbed a pillow, gave it a couple savage fluffs and then flopped down next to the cubs, circling them protectively. Little Kuwari grumbled softly and then shifted closer to her and began to purr.

The whole time, she felt Ditanu watching, but she didn't look up at him. After a moment, a large wing curved over both her and the cubs. Iltani sighed, closed her eyes, and slept peacefully for the first time in four years.

CHAPTER
nine

AWN HAD BARELY painted the clouds with the first rays of light and already gryphons darkened the skies. Iltani stood at the edge of the cliff overlooking the ocean as she waited for the king's entourage to ready themselves for flight. King Ditanu and Ahassunu, as well as many of their Shadow guards, had already taken on gryphon form. As was customary, a third of those in gryphon form already wore harnesses and saddles so they could carry armed riders as a precaution.

Burrukan, still in human form, was holding a heavy bodied crossbow in one hand similar to the one Iltani carried. Although, hers was slightly lighter. Given what she'd learned the night before, seeing the crossbow in Burrukan's hand was more worrisome than reassuring. He adjusted the harness and saddle of the gryphon that would be his mount.

Other bits of armor and weapons were strapped to those gryphons not caring a rider. The king's cubs were also bundled onto three gryphons like so much baggage. When King Ditanu finally gave the order to mount up, Iltani thanked her gryphon mount and settled into the saddle and clipped herself into the harness. With a barely discernible signal, the king ushered the vanguard of his escort into the air. They were soon followed by Ahassunu, the three gryphons carrying the cubs, and then Burrukan. Iltani's own mount followed next, and then Ditanu took wing next to her. He darted forward, taking his place in the formation to the right of his cubs. The rest of the escort followed a few wing beats behind.

If Iltani hadn't been preoccupied with worry for her king and his cubs, she might have enjoyed the flight. However, she imagined she would like it better when she had her own wings. She rather hoped her king was right on that account. Though she honestly didn't know if Ishtar would bless her so greatly.

Personally, Iltani thought Ditanu might be wrong. She was no great war hero or wise advisor to her ruler. To be a Blade was blessing enough. She wanted no honor or glory, especially if it meant something might happen to Ditanu or his little ones.

Iltani cursed herself for woolgathering again. She was just reacting to Ditanu's talk of his and Kuwari's returning nightmares.

⋈✛⋈

By the time the island of Uruk came into view, the sun was well above the horizon. It promised to be a bright, clear day. The gryphons in the lead began their descent. Iltani's own mount followed suit. Soon, the entire entourage was landing, their wings kicking sand high up into the air as they touched down upon the beach.

The island home of High Priestess Kammani had some of the nicest beaches she'd seen. As children, she and Ditanu had come here to play many times. It didn't surprise her that Ishtar would demand a temple built here.

The Queen of the Night loved things of beauty and claimed them as her own. Be it a stretch of scenic beach, or the grace of gryphons on the wing—Ishtar appreciated them all.

Iltani jumped down from her mount and landed on the sun-warmed sands. Already several of the king's councilors, and what looked to be half the court had gathered on the beach between them and the stairs leading up to the cliff-side temple. Iltani would have preferred if the escorts could simply have flown straight to the temple, but one did not approach Ishtar's temple with anything other than humble bearing.

The first of the councilors had already cornered Ditanu while he was still in gryphon form. The escort circled the king, his consort, and his cubs protectively. Iltani pushed her way through the throng, not caring if it was a priest, a noble, or a councilor she shoved out of her way. Being a Shadow and having to answer only to the king and his safety was a benefit. When she finally reached the king's side, she stood so close to his flank she could feel the heat of his body. The tip of his flicking tail occasionally brushed her arms. Ditanu was not annoyed with her, his grumpy expression was for anyone else who ventured too close to his cubs. Ahassunu was giving her own growls of warning. Ah. Here was the gryphon parents she'd expected to see last night.

Taking her clue from them, she glowered at anyone who tried to get to close.

As the other Shadows started to clear a path to the temple stairs, Iltani manhandled more councilors and nobles. When they still didn't take the hint, she tossed back her cloak and rested one hand on the hilt of her sword.

They finally took the hint and backed off a few steps, enough the king and his entourage could move toward the stairs unhindered. At this rate, maybe they'd make it to the temple before sunset.

Iltani steeled her spine and prepared for a very long day.

While it hadn't taken half the day just to reach the temple, unfortunately, it was a long drawn out affair. Once they'd reached their destination, High Priestess Kammani and several of her priests and priestesses were already there waiting for them with refreshments and quiet places for the gryphons to shapeshift back to human form and dress.

The king chose to remain in gryphon form, saying it was to comfort the cubs. Iltani had interacted with the cubs for less than a day but already knew the cubs were familiar with their parents' ability to shape-shift and were not stressed by Ditanu in his human form in the least.

Ditanu must have another reason for wanting to retain his gryphon form. Iltani would bet it had something to do with his returning nightmares. While they waited for half the Shadows to take on human form in the side chambers, Iltani took the opportunity to join Ditanu as he stood by a window, looking out toward the ocean. In gryphon form, he stood a head taller than her but probably weighed five times as much.

"You're worried about something?"

His closest tufted ear flicked in her direction while he stared steadily out the window. "I am a king—there's always something to worry about."

"Yes, but unless you've changed more than I believe you have, this is something more."

Turning to her, he dipped his head, rubbing against her side in a showing of gryphon affection. Iltani returned his loving gesture by reaching up and grooming the feathers on his head. He leaned into her scratch, shifting every so often so she could reach the best spots. His eyes drifted closed in pleasure.

They stood like that for a few moments. Not king and Blade, but simply friends.

"My King?" Burrukan's voice prodded them out of their moment of shared affection. "We are ready. Whenever you wish us to leave, we can."

"Then we should go," Ditanu agreed. Giving himself a shake, he ruffled all his fur and then flicked his wings before slicking all his feathers back in place.

Once Ditanu's entourage emerged, Kammani dropped her persona of High Priestess for a short time and greeted her nephew with a warm welcome. To each of the cubs, she gave a kiss and a good head scratch before clasping Ahassunu's shoulders and kissing each of her cheeks.

The welcome done and over with, the business of prayer, politics, and court intrigue commenced.

For the majority of the ceremony, Priestess Kammani and Consort Ahassunu took the lead. Iltani decided the naming of an heir was a direly serious business, which even at half the length of time, would still have been deadly boring.

Throughout the ceremony, the king scanned everything around him, his dark eyes missing nothing. Iltani endeavored to outperform him. Though, in the end, she doubted it was possible. She wasn't a gryphon parent.

The afternoon waned and the sun sank lower in the sky while high up in the temple the priestess held the oldest cub aloft and declared her the crown princess, Ditanu's heir, and future guardian to all those of gryphon blood.

Iltani echoed the prayers and chants as required, thinking that should nothing untoward happen in the next hundred years, Humusi would be the next Gryphon Queen. Glancing at the tiny cub chewing on the priestess's belt, Iltani grinned, having a hard time visualizing this little one all grown up into a fierce ruler.

The rites droned on for some time afterward. Iltani stopped paying attention to the ceremony, but her attention to the world around her never waned, nor did Ditanu's. At last the ceremony was over, the nobles cheered, servants brought out platters of food, and wine began to flow.

The celebration would run long into the night, but Iltani wouldn't see it through to the end. She would be at her own ceremony. At last, Ditanu called his escort to him and announced he and his family would retire to the temple for private prayers to Ishtar. If some of his guests thought he wanted to give his cubs rest from the noise of the celebration, she imagined he was all right with their assumptions.

They left behind the noise and drunken bustle of the celebration and Iltani felt the peace of the temple wrap around her. Currents of Ishtar's power played against her skin and raised goose flesh. Once again, she felt Ishtar's attention upon them. Ditanu must have felt the same thing for the big gryphon shook out his wings and his tail twitched gently as he looked over his shoulder at her. Outwardly, he showed no other signs of his nervous apprehension or the eagerness she felt reverberating along their link.

Priests and priestesses came forward, bringing with them bowls of water for washing, goblets of wine, and more platters of food. The room Iltani found herself in was warm sandstone with beautiful carvings and paintings of Ishtar. Ringing the outside of the walls, were more of the large stone archways allowing in the ocean breeze.

From her east-facing vantage point, Iltani watched the first of the stars appear against the night sky. Soon the moon would rise and it would be time for the ceremony.

The servants came forward offering the king food and drink. He waved them away with a flick of his tail but instructed them to serve the rest of his entourage. Then with a glance over his shoulder at Iltani and a flick of his tail in invitation, he paced away from the rest of the escort, his large paws silent on the stone floor. Four equally silent Shadows followed.

Iltani started after him but was waylaid by Kuwari. He cried and clawed at her boots, begging to be picked up. She reached down and scooped him up. He was shivering as if afraid.

"Oh, little one, there is no danger here in the heart of Ishtar's temple. You are safe." When Iltani looked up from the cub in her arms, she found Burrukan was there to take him off her hands. "I will come back for you, little Mite. I won't be gone long. You have my word." She kissed the cub on the forehead and gave him to her mentor. Kuwari continued to fuss, but Burrukan walked him back to his mother.

Glancing where she'd last seen the king, she found he'd halted, waiting for her. High Priestess Kammani stood at his side now too. Not wanting to keep either the king or the high priestess waiting, she hurried over to them and ignored the soft cries of Kuwari.

Priestess Kammani hadn't changed much in the four years since Iltani had last seen her, the familiar warm glint was still in her eyes, so too was that smile which lurked at the corners of her lips. When Iltani reached them, the high priestess spread her arms and took her in a fierce embrace.

Perhaps it was breaking some formal protocol, but Iltani hugged her back, for Ditanu's aunt was the closest thing either of them had to a mother.

"Look at you," Kammani said with an approving tone. "You've grown even more beautiful, and it's nice to see Burrukan hasn't completely turned you into one of his stern-faced, disapproving Shadows. Unfortunately, as much as I'd love to reminisce, we have another ceremony to prepare for. I have instructed my acolytes to prepare baths for both of you. There you will also find your ceremonial garb."

Ditanu huffed softly in agreement and allowed himself to be led deeper into the temple. Iltani follow.

CHAPTER
ten

Iltani had thought the blooding ceremony would not begin until she was outside, under the stars and in the moonlight.

She was wrong.

The ceremony began the moment she and Ditanu were led away by the priestess. She and the king paced side by side as they entered the bathing chamber.

She supposed it represented unity and balance and being in accord, and other such drivel but she was secretly pleased for it allowed her to stay near the king. When they made it halfway across the room, priestesses, priests, and novices descended upon them.

They took her sword and daggers, and then her harness and bow and arrow. While one novice was removing Iltani's few hair ornaments, another was unlacing her sandals while a priestess was stripping away her robes.

A priest to Iltani's immediate right was droning on about going before Ishtar bare to reveal one's true beauty.

While the priest droned on in his monotone, the two acolytes flanking him continued to chant prayers to the gods and Ishtar in particular.

Rolling her eyes in the king's direction, Iltani swallowed a smile at seeing his tufted ears threatening to pin themselves to his skull. Upon first glance, it looked like the priests were grooming his feathers for him until the first feather was carefully selected and pulled free with considerable force.

Iltani knew this was the part of the ceremony where the gryphon king gave offerings for his Blade. The feathers would later be woven into her ceremonial garb. The number of feathers donated was always determined by the king. Curious, she watched wondering how many he would allow pulled for her.

Between the two priests, they pulled six of the king's secondary flight feathers, enough to leave unsightly gaps when he spread his wings, but not enough to ground him. That was far more generous than many a king had been in the past, and still Ditanu stood to allow them to take more.

One of the priests paused and glanced at the High Priestess. Kammani nodded. After a brief hesitation, the priest resumed, taking smaller feathers from Ditanu's body.

The king allowed them to continue plucking him until they had fifteen feathers by Iltani's count, at which point he suddenly growled, his tail switching. The priests dropped and prostrated themselves on the floor.

Had Ditanu been in his human form, Iltani was certain he would've worn a scowl.

Iltani was flattered by the number Ditanu had bestowed upon her.

They were ten paces away from the ceremonial pool when Ditanu halted. His sandalwood and spice scent intensified and Iltani felt the brush of his warm power against her overly sensitive skin. Goose flesh raced over her body.

The shift was too fast to see much of anything, just a shimmer of light and then Ditanu was standing beside her in human form. Forcing her eyes away from him, she turned her attention back to the bath.

Small wisps of steam rose from the ceremonial pool, promising that the communal bath was warm. The priests and priestesses aiding them began removing their own robes as they prepared to enter the water. A sideways glance showed a delectably naked, golden skinned king watching her back, his eyes hooded and his expression presently unreadable.

What did he see when he looked at her? Had there been a time in their youth when he looked upon her as a woman and not just his Shadow?

She shook off the webbings of old longings and stepped into the bathing pool. Perhaps this night would wash away that dull ache in her heart, and she could finally start anew, as Ishtar's Blade.

The ceremonial bath did not actually take that long. She and the king simply walked the expanse of the pool, as the priests and priestesses sang their chants and blessings upon them. When they reached the other side, more priests and priestesses were waiting with scented oils and towels. She continued her slow pace, allowing the priestesses to buff her with warm towels and then anoint her body with sacred oils. King Ditanu was undergoing the same ritual.

Directly ahead, two benches were burdened with their ceremonial garb. Iltani arched an eyebrow when she reached her bundle. She must have made some sound for Ditanu laughed. She glanced at him to see his attendants tying on his ornate loincloth. He tossed her own words back at her. "Ishtar demands her people embrace their own natural splendor."

Iltani grunted, her eyes sliding back to the clothing and then over to Ditanu. He was grinning at her. She flushed and grew more flustered at the glint of humor in his eyes. He might have spoken in jest, but Iltani could help but think Ishtar might not be the only one to enjoy the sight of a nearly naked, well-made body. Her eyes lingered upon Ditanu longer than they should. Ishtar wasn't the only one to enjoy the king's natural grace.

Turning back to her own attendants, Iltani held her arms out from her sides and allowed them to fasten her garments in place. A golden chain went around her waist, its many translucent veils, like streamers of light, fluttered in the breeze coming in through the archways. Iltani supposed she should be grateful for the clothing. The ancient texts said that the Queen of the Night was often depicted in her winged form nude save for the golden chains in her hair.

Next a young priestess wrapped a length of fabric around Iltani's breasts. She wasn't modest, which was good because the length of fabric barely met the needs of modesty. Of greater annoyance was the fact that the strip of fabric would be next to useless as a breast binding. Granted, it was highly unlikely that she would need to do battle in such an outfit.

When she glanced across to the king, he was grinning. She frowned at him darkly. His grin grew larger.

"When all this is over," he said, that damn smile still lurking at the edges of his expression, "I will have armor made, something suitable for Ishtar's new Blade."

High Priestess Kammani interrupted Iltani before she could make a response. Urging them both forward, she led them out onto the temple's roof. Torches circled the outer edge, marking the boundary of the roof and illuminating the area with an orange glow. In the center of the space, a small fire burned in a shallow depression carved from the stone of the roof. Next to the fire was a long bench-like altar. This one was far older and far more ornate than the simple one she and the king had used to perform the first blood ceremony. As she approached the altar, she could feel its age and power. This was the place where other kings had shed blood to anoint Ishtar's Blades throughout history.

Perhaps it was not such a long list Iltani's supposed, but she was still humbled by the ancient stone.

Priestess Kammani led them on a winding path to their destination. Some of the lesser priests and priestesses joined their voices together as they chanted blessings upon Ishtar's newest Blade.

When Iltani reached the altar, she calmly straddled the bench and sat with hands braced in front of her while she waited. Her tension increased. The fire's heat caused sweat to bead on her flesh. She would blame the heat. It certainly couldn't be nerves. They had already completed the blooding ceremony twice.

She swallowed. This time was different. Now they had an audience of priests and priestesses. There was also the growing suspicion that here, on top of Ishtar's own temple, the Queen of the Night would make her presence known far more intimately than the first two times.

A stolen glance in Ditanu's direction showed he had his blank mask in place. So, he was tense, too. Knowing he was as nervous, made her feel better in comparison.

While Iltani had been deep in her own thoughts, Priestess Kammani had handed the king an ancient blade. It had a smooth bone hilt and a blade of ancient hammered copper.

The king approached the bench and then hesitated. She sensed his unease and something else, another's presence on the roof with them. A banked, simmering magic.

Ishtar was upon the roof with them.

Iltani squared her shoulders and waited. The next part was up to the king.

After another long hesitation on his part, she finally sensed him moving and heard the soft scrape of cloth as he settled on the bench behind her. Her ears straining, she heard a slight intake of breath, likely at the first cut. Inhaling a deep breath, she caught the sharp coppery scent of his blood. He shifted closer until she could feel his body heat. One arm reached around her waist and dragged her back until the length of her spine was sealed to his chest. The warmth of his blood began to flow, trickling down her spine. In its wake, her birthmark began to tingle.

As before, he braced the arm not wrapped around her waist against the bench in front of her, leaning over her forcing her forward. Again, she was cocooned in his warmth, his scent, his strength—all of it so very addicting.

His power and essence flowed into her with his blood, drawn in along the length of her spine. From there it spread out to every corner of her body. It was glorious, painful, and powerful all at once. Her magic stirred and flared, her body beginning to glow from within. Ishtar's mark pulsed with heat, echoing the beat of her heart. It took her longer to realize it matched Ditanu's, but she could feel her king's powerful heart beating in tune to hers.

She felt his essence stamped into her soul. It had always been there, but now the link was greater. There would never be any doubt as to where he was. She could be in another land, many months distant from him and still she would know where on the planet he was. His cubs, too. She would sense their joy and pain and sorrow. She would always be able to find them. Keep them safe.

Perhaps Ishtar's greatest gift was a secret, unseen one. Iltani now owned a piece of Ditanu, it was rooted into her soul. Just as surely, she belonged to him. Happiness bubbled up inside. She wanted to throw her arms open wide and laugh joyously in thanks to Ishtar. It battled with the urged to turn and wrap her king in a fierce hug.

Ditanu moaned softly, the sound tumbled over her, caressing her skin. He made another guttural sound of protest.

What? Iltani shoved aside her internal musings and took note of what was going on around her for the first time in several moments.

Ishtar's presence had increased tenfold while Iltani's body had been adjusting to the new infusion of blood. The Queen of the Night was a goddess of many aspects. She could be a wager of war, a healer, or a bringer of life. During a normal blooding ceremony, it was an aspect of her battle magic that forged the ties between Blade and King, but the thickening magic swirling around them now wasn't the scorched scent of Ishtar's battle magic. No, this power was warmer, mellower, but shared a familiar tinge with that destructive power. Warm passion and rich fertility. A mix that was usually saved for fertility rites or the Sacred Marriage.

What was Ishtar planning? Ditanu wasn't a candidate for either rite.

No wonder the king sounded distressed.

"Ishtar's probably just being playful like she was during the first blooding ceremony in the bath," Iltani whispered. Wanting to give him some kind of reassurance, she reached out and patted his arm where it was wrapped around her waist. His muscles were so tense she might as well have been touching stone. Turning, she realized his forehead was pressed against her shoulder. A fierce swirling magic radiated off him. It was potent, a sultry heat pressing against her skin, raising the tiny hairs along her arms and the back of her neck. She gasped, but only dragged in more of Ditanu's scent and Ishtar's magic, each lungful adding to a growing desire and a heavy throbbing deep inside. Iltani wanted to touch Ditanu, feel his warm skin brush against every part of her. She could only imagine what it was doing to Ditanu.

Yet that was not what made her gasp in surprise.

All around them, the priests and priestesses, even High Priestess Kammani herself, lay prostrate upon the ground, foreheads pressed into the stone. Only one winged being still stood, glorious power radiating off her as she stood at the king's shoulder, her hand resting upon his back.

The Queen of the Night had come in person to lay claim to her King and her Blade.

CHAPTER
eleven

A HEADY MIX OF fear, anticipation and confusion spiked through Iltani's blood, setting her heart pounding. Ishtar had only ever appeared in person a handful of times during blooding ceremonies. Each of those times, she'd demanded the Sacred Marriage. It was a great blessing, but those participants had been unmated until the ritual forged mating bonds between them.

Ishtar touched Iltani and all higher thoughts fled her mind. Great need flooded her, radiating out from the spot on her shoulder where a goddess had laid her hand. Above her, the king shuddered almost convulsively, but he didn't try to pull away or struggle.

For a time, Iltani floated cocooned in power and heat and need. One sensation blended into another until there was a great fiery ache centered low in her belly. She pressed back against the male body above her.

Her hearing crackled with white noise and raw power, but slowly she sorted through the chaos and realized the king was speaking.

"I won't. I will not force her."

Iltani shook her head, trying to clear her muddled thoughts. A moment more and she schooled her mind enough to focus. When she did, his thoughts came to her. His panic was the most forefront of his emotions. She stroked his arm, wanting him to know it was all right, that she was willing.

"I will not take her, not even at your command. You cannot make me."

"Ditanu, it is all right."

"No!" he roared. "I do not want this, not like this."

Ditanu didn't want her?

Emotional pain lanced through Iltani's heart and mind, his words a swift kick to the gut, a sharp blow to the head. They were still piercing and excruciating and startling to hear even though they were a cold truth she'd known all along. Of course he did not want her, he could not want her. He already had a mate—it didn't matter that Ahassunu was unfaithful to him, he still loved her. He would not, could not, perform the Sacred Marriage with Iltani.

Her mind started to work again.

Even if Ishtar persuaded Ditanu, or worse, forced him, what then? Ishtar would return to her spiritual home, and they would be left to deal with the fallout come morning. There was no way Iltani would willingly harm her king, even emotionally. Worse, it would drive a wedge between them that at some later point could damage her ability to keep him safe.

Unfortunately, the Queen of the Night seemed disinclined to listen to pleas from her gryphon king and was simply overwhelming him with her power, for Iltani felt the unmistakable evidence of his desire.

A part of her knew it was simply a reaction to the Queen of the Night's power and had nothing to do with Iltani herself, but she was starting to think that did not matter. Ditanu wasn't going to be able to control himself. Ishtar wouldn't let him. Afterward, the guilt would set in. She knew Ditanu.

That's how it would happen and it would destroy a part of him. Iltani couldn't let that happen, but she didn't have the power to deny a goddess.

Hmmm, but what if she and Ditanu gave the Queen of the Night some of what she asked? Would it be enough to keep her from demanding everything?

Perhaps if she beseeched Ishtar directly?

Not that she knew if her thoughts and prayers would even touch the goddess in their presence, but it was worth a try. With nothing to lose, Iltani shrugged and prayed.

'Great Ishtar, long have you been revered for your strength, beauty, and passion,' Iltani began, hesitant, but growing stronger. *'Once called Inanna, by the humans of the outer world, but to the gryphons, you have always been our great Ishtar, Queen of the Night.'*

Your gryphon king is loyal to you, and he would gladly offer himself to you if he were free to do so. But he loves his mate, as his instincts dictate—instincts you infused all gryphons with at their creation. Oh, great Ishtar. Please do not punish my king because he is as you made him.'

'Punishment? This is not about punishment. It is about protecting New Sumer.' Ishtar's form shimmered, growing less ghost-like. *'I and my beloved Tammuz only wish to share power, to strengthen you both for the danger we see looming ahead. You would do well to accept our offer.'*

Dark thoughts and disastrous scenarios flew through Iltani's mind. Ishtar was a goddess of battle. If she said there was trouble coming to Sumer's shores, then it was true and Iltani would do whatever she must. *'Great Ishtar, I am a steadfast servant and am most willing to receive your gift. I would be honored to partake in the Sacred Marriage. But if I am honest, I have no interest in an unwilling male. Ditanu loves his mate.'*

'An unwilling male?' Ishtar laughed. *'Does he feel unwilling to you?'*

'No, but he loves his mate.'

A secretive smile graced Ishtar's lips. *'Yes, he does. Almost enough to resist me. I have no interest in an unwilling male either.'*

'Thank you, for understanding.'

'But that is not why he resists the Sacred Marriage.'

'No?' Iltani now knew there was some unnamed danger coming to the island and she should be focused solely upon that. Yet, Ishtar had whetted her curiosity.

'Ditanu is both stubborn and protective of you. He fears that one day his personality will completely swallow yours. He loves you too much to allow that, so he fights me to protect you.'

'That is a foolish fear.'

'Is it? You have always been in his shadow, serving his wishes, being whatever he needs. Not once have you ever challenged him for something you want.'

'But I am a Blade. Am I not to serve both you and the gryphon king?'

'Servant not slave. You must learn to stand up for what is yours.'

Iltani was mystified.

'We are out of time. You require my power. The amount you will need will be painful. Tell your king he can watch you writhe in agony or shudder in pleasure.'

'We do not have to perform the Sacred Marriage?'

'No, but that would have been the easiest, most pleasant path for both of us. You can still partake of my power, but without heated passion to act as a distraction, you will find the sharing painful.'

With that new knowledge, Iltani's decision was an easy one. *'I will not perform the Sacred Marriage, but I'm ready for your power.'*

'No, you're not,' Ishtar said as she reached out to touch Iltani.

At the Queen of the Night's touch, Iltani's own lingering desires flared up anew, burning hotter than before and she instinctively pressed back against Ditanu. Then Ishtar's power rushing into her notched up into uncomfortable levels.

"Ditanu," Iltani started slapping his arm to get his attention. He finally met her gaze. "Ishtar says there is danger coming to New Sumer and she needs to share her power to strengthen me. You need to let me go now."

"Iltani?" Ditanu's voice sounded drugged. He loosened his hold on her waist but didn't let go. "I heard our Queen's voice in my head."

"Then you heard her say the Sacred Marriage is not needed."

"Yes," Ditanu's lips were suddenly caressing the back of her neck. "That does not mean that I will sit by and allow you to feel agony when you can feel pleasure instead."

Both his hands settled on her shoulders, holding her almost delicately as he placed gentle kisses across her back, nipping gently every few caresses until he reached her spine.

His tongue flicked across her birthmark and Iltani's entire body shivered. "Ditanu..."

"Ah," he purred, "Ishtar's mark is an erogenous zone for you."

His lips started nibbling again and soon his hands dropped from her shoulders to her side where his fingers stroked up and down.

For her part, she didn't discourage him though she knew she should. Ishtar's power continued to fill her, but Ditanu's touch was so distracting, she hardly noticed.

Wanting to feel some part of him, she reached down and rested her hand against his thigh, her fingers stroking slowly up and down, feeling the slight flex of muscles as he moved.

Ditanu's hands moved from her sides to her breasts, gently palming and cupping them through the fabric of her top. He varied the pressure of the caresses. Barely felt brushes, firmer tugs and gentle squeezes—he soon had her arching into his touch.

Need grew within her, the need to touch more of him in return. Desperate, she tossed a leg over the bench and turned in his arms. She didn't care if she was breaking the rules. Her fingers ran over his chest, caressing him, learning him. It was divine, but she wanted so much more. She buried her face against his shoulder and fought not to maul her king.

"Iltani, I'll take care of you," Ditanu whispered and stroked a hand down her hair gently. "I'll help you get through this."

Iltani gasped as another wave of power rushed through her body. Ditanu whispered soothing words to her and then he dragged her closer, arranging her so her legs straddled his hips where he knelt on the bench. The new position let her feel his tremendous heat and desire. Only the flimsy layer of his loincloth and her skirt blocked them from being skin on skin.

She rocked against him and thrilled at the guttural sound he made. His passion had to be flaring as bright as her own, but he remained gentle, kissing her and caressing her oh so damn slowly. Somehow, his patience was making her own desires burn hotter. She placed open mouthed kisses upon his shoulder, the column of his neck and then his jaw line.

It was Ditanu who turned his head and captured her mouth. While his tongue was inviting hers to mate, his fingers were caressing up and down her sides. On the third trip back down, he hooked his thumbs into the scarf covering her breasts and slowly teased it down. His slow persistence won and suddenly Iltani's breasts were rubbing against his chest with each of her rapid breaths.

His right hand slid up to tease her nipples while his other dropped to brush a caress along the inside of her thigh. Even in this, he was in no hurry, and Iltani thought she'd lose her mind long before his warm fingers completed their journey to the junction between her legs. Breaking their kiss, she arched her back and spread her thighs wider, reveling in his touch as he guided her to a greater pace.

"Ditanu," she breathed out his name as she reached down to touch him through his loincloth, wanting to give him the same pleasure he was giving her.

"You must not touch me." Ditanu covered her hand with his and forced it to still.

"I'm sorry." Shame darkened her cheeks, yet she was confused too—he was caressing her and purring like he enjoyed touching her. "It's just… this is…"

He pressed kisses up the side of her neck. "There is nothing to forgive. We do this so our Queen can fill you with her power without harming you, this is not about my pleasure."

His hand released hers and returned to caressing her.

It was all well and good to say they did this for Ishtar's pleasure, but how was she supposed to survive this strange ritual and not touch him in return? She was nearly panting, on that cliff's edge where joy was but a short step off, but she wanted Ditanu to go there with her...willingly.

The king seemed to sense her confusion or just now realized that his words might be confusing, for he elaborated. "Iltani, you are allowed to take pleasure in my touch, in my body."

"But you just said..."

"I will not take you in the Sacred Marriage as Ishtar wants, but if I allow you to wrap those slender fingers around my manhood, I'll lose control and forget myself. Now, enough talk, only listen and feel. I can sense you're nearly there. Don't fight it."

"I..." Her thoughts scattered as his skillful fingers pushed her closer to that cliff.

"That's it." His voice was divine darkness, "Give yourself up into my keeping for a little while."

There was no fighting Ishtar's will or Ditanu's sinful voice in her ear as he pleasured her, destroying the last of her self-control.

"Good..." Ditanu's voice shook and she was certain he was close to his own ending.

Iltani shattered. Surely she would shake herself apart. Yet she didn't. Ditanu held her throughout the ordeal and Iltani slowly came back to herself.

That earlier strong presence of Ishtar was fading. Next came the realization of where she was, what she'd done and whose body she was clinging to. Shame burned her cheeks. Oh, goddess, how could she ever look Ditanu in the eye again?

"King Ditanu…"

"Shhh…" His warm breath fanned across her cheek as he buried his face in her hair. "We'll talk of this later. We have our home to defend."

Ishtar's presence reached within Iltani, touched her very soul, changing something and suddenly there was more than power pouring into Iltani, there was knowledge—an understanding of how to shape all that newly gifted power to her will.

It flooded outward from her, the tightly coiled power racing down her limbs giving her strength and sharpening her mind and all her senses. She felt the world around her in a different way, sensing other souls out in the ocean—an enemy army sailing into the harbor. Ships from the outside world did not belong anywhere near the ten city-states of the gryphon kingdom. Somehow those ships had breached the great defensive dome sheltering New Sumer from the outside world.

"Outliers. Many ships. They are already in the harbor." Even as Iltani shouted the words, her power continued to build within her.

Ditanu, not trapped by the same power, gently shifted her off him and onto the bench. His hand rested on the center of her back long enough to assure she was stable and then he started shouting orders.

The surprised priests and priestesses raised their heads from the ground but seemed unsure what to do until High Priestess Kammani ordered them to rise and warn the others of their order, to prepare the temple's defenses.

The king did not hesitate and shouted for his Shadows to protect his cubs. Five Shadows immediately appeared from seemingly nowhere, but Iltani knew they had been just outside the circle of light created by the torches. Iltani wanted to rise from the bench and guard the king's back, but she was still unable to move as more of Ishtar's power flooded her.

It intensified in a pool between her hands where they were still braced against the stone of the bench. A sudden surge of magic had Iltani gritting her teeth against a scream and then a brighter flash of light blinded her for several desperate seconds.

When she could see again, the power surging through her had slowed to a trickle and was no longer painful. But that was not what held her attention.

On the bench, laying lengthwise between her braced hands was a golden hilt shimmering with power, almost like it encased living fire. Her eyes travelled up the hilt to the cross pieces, and then along the entire length of the glowing blade. It was a sword the like of which she'd never laid eyes upon before but knew it was far more deadly than its mundane cousins.

Iltani reached for the hilt, her fingers closing around it as she watched the fire slowly flicker and churn deep within the blade. While she was mesmerized by the sight, the king was gathering himself and shouting orders.

"Get your priestesses and priests to a safe place, now," he ordered his aunt. He glanced in Iltani's direction, or maybe he was staring past her. It was hard to tell with spots obscuring her vision.

She forced herself to sit up straight but that didn't improve her vision in the least. Cursing under her breath, she gritted her teeth and blinked furiously.

It helped marginally.

"Take Iltani with you." Ditanu directed three of his gathering Shadows. "She is in no shape to fight. I'll rejoin you once I've found my cubs."

A figure stepped in front of the king, blocking him. "Burrukan and Consort Ahassunu will see to the cubs' safety. You must keep Iltani with you." Priestess Kammani's voice had lost some of its mellowness.

Keep Ditanu close? Fine by me, Iltani thought. She had no plans to let her king out of her sight if he was about to go into battle. She flexed her fingers around her new sword's hilt and came to her feet, lurching a bit before she found her balance. She doggedly made her way toward Ditanu.

She misjudged the distance and stumbled against the king. His arm circled her shoulders and held her snug against his side.

Kammani and the king faced off, falling into a heated debate. One Iltani couldn't follow, too distracted by the warmth and power still pouring into her from the sword.

As her strength returned, so too did her awareness of her surroundings and those new senses Ishtar had gifted her with.

"Iltani is in no condition for a fight, not yet. I don't care if she's Ishtar's Blade. She'll get herself killed if she stays with me."

That was most definitely Ditanu, sounding about as surly as she'd ever heard, too.

They didn't have time for this. Iltani's new senses thrilled a warning. "I can fight. We don't have time to argue. The cubs are in danger."

Iltani looked straight into Ditanu's conflicted eyes.

"Let's go save your cubs."

Iltani didn't wait for his response, instead following the magical guide implanted within her by a goddess.

CHAPTER
twelve

ILTANI RAN THROUGH many corridors, down flights of wide ornate stairs and out into a small courtyard filled with a crush of fighting bodies. One part of her consciousness wondered how so many of the enemy had managed to make it this far into the island, let alone this deep into the temple. Then she spotted four great grappling hooks anchored onto the north cliff wall.

As she watched, two more enemies heaved themselves up and over the wall, to drop down behind more of their kind.

They were outliers to judge by their motley dress. Pirates and mercenaries Ditanu had once called them. Never should such ones as these been able to make it this deep into gryphon territory. Even Uruk, island of the priestess, the farthest of the islands, should still have been safe under the massive dome which hid and protected the kingdom of New Sumer from the outside world.

Something had gone terribly wrong, for the impossible had happened and the outside world was here. Iltani doubted this rabble was the worst the outside world had to throw at them.

As if in answer to her silent worries, a loud sound echoed over the water. A part of the temple wall behind and to the left of her position blew apart. From her present position, she couldn't see the boats, but there certainly were boats out in the harbor, for that was cannon fire. Given the distance, that last shot was probably range finding. More luck than accuracy. She couldn't risk the king's life on a hunch. "We need to move."

Behind her, even over the noise and screams, she heard Ditanu snarl. She reached back unerringly and wrapped her fingers around his wrist. Her gifts warned her of something else. "Don't shift. There are archers on the walls and roof. You'll be too good a target."

"My people are pinned down," Ditanu growled. "We need to do something to even the odds, now."

Ditanu was correct, but it wasn't just his people pinned down. If they moved away from the sheltering bit of ledge, they were currently pressed against, they would be picked off within moments. Neither she nor Ditanu had armor—and while magic could protect the body from mundane weapons, they didn't know if this enemy possessed magic-spelled weapons. Best not to find out with an arrow through the heart. Mostly to herself, she muttered, "Next time we do the blooding ceremony, we do it in full armor."

Ditanu peered around her shoulder to survey the massacre in the courtyard. "If we're quick, we can scale the wall and be upon the archers within moments." He gestured to Etum and three of the other Shadows with him to follow his lead.

Again, Iltani felt Ishtar's presence within her, guiding her actions and body. A plan unfolded before her mind's eye. "Ishtar has a faster way."

With Ishtar's intent still clear in her mind, Iltani held out her hand and pressed it to the wall. A bright flash of magic raced up her arm and vanished into the stone. Nothing happened for three beats of her heart.

Then there was a motion on top of the temple as the enemy archers toppled over the edge, dead or unconscious, she didn't know, but they were certainly dead after they collided with the stone cobbles of the courtyard.

Ditanu arched an eyebrow at her as he rushed past. By the time Iltani matched his long-legged strides, he was already dispatching any enemies stupid enough to get between a gryphon and his cubs.

She kept pace with him, her sword's tip clearing a path before her, slashing and gutting any enemy foolish enough to come too close to her king. The crystalline blade cut like any other sword, but she felt its power, the promise of destruction far beyond what a normal sword could deliver.

Five more opponents rushed down a flight of stairs, only now realizing the king was in their midst.

Iltani dispatched the first while on Ditanu's other side, Etum felled his own opponent. Ditanu was busy with a third.

Iltani let him have the kill, but she was ready should Ditanu falter. He shoved the body off his sword while Iltani and the other Shadows made their way up to the next landing.

Here they met with more Shadows. The newcomers swiftly surrounded their king. Eluti joined his twin, Etum at the king's side. He acknowledged his brother and Iltani but made his report to the king. "Burrukan sent us to find you. He and the remaining Shadows are in the lower temple with your consort and the cubs. They are safe for now, but Burrukan wants you and your cubs off the island immediately. The lamassu have awoken and Burrukan ordered them to deal with the landing boats and the main ships."

While a lamassu guarding the king's side would have made Iltani feel more confident about his safety, even she agreed those great stone beasts were best where Burrukan had assigned them. A lamassu was best fighting out in the open. Close quarters were no place for them. After all, one didn't bring siege machines to a sword fight. The great stone behemoths were fierce fighters but could easily level the entire temple, trapping both friends and foes under half a mountain's worth of stone while trying to defend the royal line.

"How many are we up against?" Ditanu shouted over the din of battle as they continued to fight their way closer to his cubs.

"More than should have ever made it this far," Eluti growled. "Seven ships, riding low in the water. They're armed to the teeth with both cannons and men. Twenty-four cannons on the biggest three."

Ditanu cursed under his breath.

Seven ships. Not enough to seize and hold any of the city-states, but enough to bloody the rocks.

They could only have one purpose in mind: assassination.

Her heart and spirit throbbed along with the power beating in the glowing length of her sword.

One didn't have to take control of the city-states to defeat the Gryphon Kingdom. One merely had to kill the royal line, wait for all its defensive magic to die and then conquer the disarrayed islands one at a time.

Ditanu's grim expression reflected the same thoughts. He renewed his efforts to get to his cubs and Iltani and his Shadows kept pace.

As they descended to the lower levels of the temple city, they encountered more enemy troops and the vicious rounds of cannon fire. It ripped through delicate lattice walls, glass windows, and people with equal destructive abandon.

When they weren't dodging pieces of the temple raining down from above or enemy soldiers popping up in their path, they were forced to wade through throngs of panicked nobles and servants.

As if cannon fire wasn't bad enough, there were men with longbows among the enemy.

Ditanu snarled another curse. "Order the temple evacuated. It will make the task of picking off the enemy easier for both our soldiers and the lamassu."

"Burrukan is already seeing to that," Etum replied. "He ordered me to secure you."

"Secure? Really?" Ditanu said as he leaped over another fallen soldier. "What did Burrukan actually say?"

Etum chuckled, finding humor Iltani wasn't feeling. "His exact words to me were 'go find our king and drag his ass back here. The young fool has no business in the thick of the fighting.'"

"Burrukan, diplomatic as always." Ditanu gave a humorless laugh, his attention on the fighting. "I want our archers to pick off those human ones down on the beach." He made a sweeping motion with one arm "We have injured down there. I want them taken to safety and evacuated with the rest of my citizens."

"As soon as we deliver you safely to Burrukan, I will see to it myself."

"Good." Ditanu motioned the rest of his guards forward.

As promised, the way to Burrukan, the cubs, and Ahassunu was relatively clear. Still, Iltani didn't allow Ditanu more than an arm's length from her side.

They arrived at the main gate of the lower temple and guards opened the large doors and escorted the king's company inside.

Burrukan was instantly at his king's side, updating him on everything he knew. Which, Iltani frowned, wasn't much. She didn't know what else she expected. He had been on the island the whole time. As much as she doubted Burrukan, she knew in her heart he wasn't the enemy, and her newly heightened senses still did not label him a threat.

Motion to her right had her glancing away from her king, and she spotted Kuwari as he came hurtling toward her. He skidded to a halt, sliding into the side of her boot, but it didn't deter him from regaining his feet and latching onto her leg.

She reached down and gave him a reassuring rub between the ears, but turned her attention to what Burrukan was saying.

"We've mobilized against the enemy and are getting between them and our people. The south harbor is overrun with enemy ships, but many of the revelers have made it safely to the north side of the island. The lamassu have cleared that harbor. Many nobles and their families are taking to the air as we speak." Burrukan stepped to one side to make room for Ahassunu to join them. "We're ensuring that the young and most vulnerable are among the first into the air. Once they are safely out of the way, it will free up more of my men to clean out the city and capture or kill as many of the outliers as possible."

"I want some taken alive," Ahassunu said, fury edging her voice, making it deeper. "I want to know why my cubs were placed in danger and who is foolish enough to involve themselves in this action."

Once again, Iltani found herself silently agreeing.

Kill most of the invaders, but keep a few alive to discover who they were working for and what possible reward would be worth their lives.

"We'll take some alive," Ditanu agreed, "but first I want anyone with wings to help those that do not. Get everyone off this island and meet back at Nineveh. Once my people are safe, and we know this is an isolated incident, we'll return here and bleed our enemies."

The enemy, by the sound of fighting outside, was getting closer. Iltani grabbed Ditanu by the shoulder and dragged him toward the back wall of the lower temple.

"No more talk." An impending sense of doom was throbbing in Iltani's veins. "We need to get you off this island now."

"I can take care of myself," Ditanu argued. His lips thinned and parted— more a baring of teeth than a smile. His gryphon blood lust was rising. She could see it in his enlarged pupils. Now that he saw his cubs were safe, he was succumbing to the battle lust which was both a blessing and a curse to all gryphons.

He shoved his sword hilt at one of his shadows and began to strip out of this clothing. "Iltani, you will go ahead and see my cubs to safety. I and half of my Shadows will take up the rearguard."

Magic flared around him as he shifted to gryphon form.

"Ditanu, no." Iltani started toward him. "Ishtar said we must stay together. Go with your cubs."

"The enemy is too close. I will not risk them overtaking us while you and my cubs are trapped in the tunnels." Ditanu's words held the slight hissing inflection all gryphons had. "Take my cubs and their mother to the beach. Get them into the air."

Iltani wasn't happy, but she was too pragmatic to stand and fight about it while their enemies closed in on them.

Scooping up Kuwari, Iltani ordered Etum to grab a cub while Consort Ahassunu drew her sword with one hand and picked up the last cub with the other.

Iltani paused and looked over her shoulder to where King Ditanu and two dozen of his Shadows flanked him. Several were in gryphon form now. All others had swords and bows at the ready.

"Go," he ordered as he shifted in an intense flash of light.

Frowning unhappily, her crystalline sword held before her, she darted through the north doors where Priestess Kammani and several of her apprentices had already uncovered a dark tunnel. Iltani raced forward, now guided by the goddess. As the torch bearing priests led the way, the Shadows accompanying Iltani followed close on her heels.

Leaving her king felt wrong, but she had the wherewithal to know the fastest way to get him to follow was to carry his cubs from him. Instinct would keep him close, even overriding the seductive call of battle lust.

She raced through the tunnels, following the torch carrying priests, all the time wanting to shout for them to hurry. Sounds of battle came clear to her even here.

After one violent boom echoed down the corridor and rained dust down upon them all, Iltani decided the tunnels had just been breached somewhere.

"If they continue to use the black powder, they'll bring down the temple around their ears," Kammani said.

Iltani cast a worried glance at the stone ceiling above and hoped the fools didn't collapse the temple upon them until after her king was out of danger.

The stone underfoot gradually became less steep and ahead she spotted the metal brackets of two great reinforced double doors reflecting the torchlight.

They'd reached sea level. Both Iltani's sense of smell and Ishtar's new gifts confirmed as much. Ahead, two of the Shadows were lifting a heavy cross beam out of its holders while a priest unlocked the door.

The first of the shadows to emerge onto the beach were met with shouts of relief from the nobles already there. Shadows that had been ordered to help with the evacuation raced up to Iltani and the others.

Iltani ushered the rest out onto the beach and was just starting toward shore when another great boom echoed out across the ocean. Overhead, a piece of the upper temple shattered. Large chunks of stone started their destructive journey down the side of the cliff, the devastating force doubling as other boulders and debris joined the slide.

"Move," Iltani shouted as she tightened her hold on Kuwari and sprinted toward the ocean surf to get away from the avalanche of stone.

Those without wings followed her lead while those in gryphon form took to the air, grabbing their wingless neighbors and dragging them into the air with them.

With a small part of her mind not focused on tracking her king's progress, or running for her life, she noticed the sky was black with wings.

Ditanu and his men were now on the wing as well, which, she decided, was presently the safest place to be with the temple tumbling down from above.

Another explosion rocked the temple loosening more chunks of masonry. Just how much of that damnable black powder had the outcasts managed to bring with them? In her arms, Kuwari whimpered.

Then another echo rumbled across the ocean. This time, the sound came from behind her, not from within the temple.

A ship rounded the island's north cliff wall, sailing toward Iltani's position.

She shouted warnings to the others on the beach. Eluti must have heard her for he sprinted up to her.

"Why are you not with the king?"

"He sent me to get you and Kuwari."

Seeing Eluti's arrival as the blessing it was, she shoved Kuwari into his arms. "Take him, get him to his mother. I can't fight like I need to and keep him safe at the same time."

"Ditanu gave me orders," Eluti said as he fought to hold the struggling cub in his arms. "You need to come too."

"I don't have time to argue. Go."

As her magic stirred, burning along her body, setting all her nerves to tingling, a lamassu winged its way over the ravaged temple's wall and flew straight for the new threat. Somehow she'd, or more likely Ishtar had summoned the great stone beast.

Iltani, her magic now a maelstrom flowing around her body, drove her sword into the ground between her feet.

"Get going," she shouted to Eluti.

With a curse, he ran with the cub tucked safely in his arms.

Iltani turned her attention back to the ship.

A heartbeat later, both she and the lamassu knew they were too late to stop the ship from firing its next round of deadly cannon fire.

Much closer now, the ship's weapons were that much more destructive. A volley of cannon balls ripped through more of the temple's delicate stonework, reducing it to rubble while those still on the beach could only watch in horror.

Out of the corner of her eye, Iltani spotted the consort just as she took wing with one cub grasped in her front paws. Iltani sent a wave of force rushing toward the space between Ahassunu and more of the incoming projectiles. The mortal weapons struck Iltani's barrier and fell harmlessly into the ocean surf.

In the time it had taken Iltani to toss up the protection between the consort and the invaders, the massive lamassu had reached the ship. It had clasped its arms around the tallest mast. Its weight and momentum threatened to capsize the ship, exposing a large section of its wooden belly. Iltani eyed the target a moment and then launched her magic, shaping it into a spear filled with all her rage. The spear flew true and impacted the ship, gorging deep into the wooden hull.

The lamassu, sensing its prey was already experiencing its final death throws, released the mast and turned its massive body in the air—a graceful feat defying explanation. It then winged its way back toward the beach where it landed and thundered past Iltani's position, its hooves churning the sand.

Iltani lost her balance and fell to one knee.

"*Stay down.*" The lamassu's warning blazed across her mind.

She felt more than saw a massive spear fly past her shoulder and impale some other poor soul behind her.

Iltani sent her magic flying even as she tracked the new threat.

Boats.

Over a dozen of them. She'd never seen the spear launching weapons in person, but Burrukan had once told her about these harpoons. Each boat had one secured to its prow. These must have already been in the water before she and the stone lamassu had mortally wounded the main ship.

Besides the harpoons, each boat was loaded with sword and spear-carrying warriors. Again, Iltani didn't know much about the outside world—every bit of knowledge she owned was thanks to Burrukan, but her understanding was that humans from the outside world had evolved past the use of spears long ago. They now preferred weapons called pistols and muskets, which were too unstable to use near magic wielders. At close range, magic could ignite the black powder they used as fuel. But the outsiders shouldn't have possessed that information; they shouldn't have made it this deep into gryphon territory at all. A citizen of New Sumer would have had to have given these invaders that knowledge and aided them in other ways, too.

She catalogued that knowledge for later, to add to her list of crimes once she found the traitor responsible for this sacrilege.

At least, she didn't see any archers among this group, which was good. The harpoons were deadly enough.

When the first ship was close enough to make an easy target, she lashed out with power. The boat next to the one she'd intended to hit vanished in a shroud of billowing vapor. When it thinned enough to see through, she noted the ship behind it was gone too. However, her intended target kept coming. Her magic rose within her again. The second attempt took out the boat.

Ishtar's gifts were impressive, Iltani admitted, in awe of the great power riding her. Yet, as the first waves of boats made it to shore and vomited up their cargo of warriors, she feared the goddess's power given into Iltani's own unprepared hands might not be enough to defeat these enemies.

Lashing out again, another destructive wave slammed into both men and boats. Both were reduced to ash and swirling mist by Ishtar's power.

All along the beach, other boats made it to shore.

Holding her position, her crystalline sword still buried with half its blade length in the ground, Iltani continued to use magic as her primary line of defense until the very last moment. When the first wave of warriors was upon her, she gripped her sword's hilt and smiled at her enemies.

One smiled back—a giant beast of a man, a wall of solid muscle. His wide chest was covered in a black garment, similar to a robe but it open all the way down the front. Rows of tiny fastenings ran down one side. Under it, he wore yet more layers. Though none looked like armor, which stunned her. A wide three pointed covering sat atop his head, but it wasn't a helmet. The only protection it would lend its wearer would be from the sun.

She circled her enemy, and he mimicked her, studying her in turn as if she was the strangest thing he'd seen.

What strange garb. Burrukan had once told her a bit about two warring empires from the old world across the ocean. The two human empires were building colonies and warring with each other for gold, lands and other trade goods. New Sumer had always been protected and hidden by its magic, safe from the outside world, so Iltani had never paid much mind to the human's in the world beyond the ten city-states. However, she knew by the lack of uniformity in how these enemies dressed, that they were not soldiers belonging to either of the empires. No, these soldiers with their motley dress were rogues. Pirates—their services sold to the highest bidder.

It did not mean they were not dangerous.

By some unseen signal, they started toward her, only to hesitate as they were almost upon her. She wondered if they saw Ishtar looking out at them through her eyes. Whatever the cause, it gave her an opening and she gave them death with the slash of her sword.

Where sword blades met, hers melted through steel with a hiss and then buried itself into the belly of the bigger of the two. He didn't have time to scream before power crawled across his skin and he blew apart on the ocean breeze, just bits of ash and swirling smoke.

Her second opponent met the same fate. A third and a fourth fell before her. Some had more skills than others, but all succumbed to Ishtar's wrath. Iltani floated in her own body as a goddess of battle directed her.

Time passed.

Iltani didn't know how much, but ash coated her body along with sea spray and sweat. She needed to get to Ditanu's side. The blood link allowed her to sense him—he was not hurt, not yet, but the need to get to his side was increasing within her.

But no matter how many enemies she cut down, more just kept coming, preventing her from reaching her king.

Pushing aside that need for now, she focused on the battle. She wouldn't do Ditanu a speck of good if her foolish worry distracted Ishtar at the wrong time.

The newest arrivals to come ashore were more cautious, studying the lay of the land instead of just rushing forward with swords drawn. All the time, the boats still out in the water were targeting gryphons with their harpoons.

Reaching out with her senses, she felt where three gryphons already lay wounded on the beach. With a wave of one arm, she sent magic racing out to destroy another boat.

A great dark shadow appeared over her head and Iltani cursed in fear, though the cold dread in her stomach wasn't for herself.

Ditanu dropped down onto the sand next to her and slammed her to the ground, his massive wings mantling over her protectively.

A spear flew past, less than an arm's length from her head. A moment later, Ditanu moved off her and a scream jerked her back to the battle. Ditanu, in full gryphon fury, slashed out at her attacker, gutting, tearing muscle, and snapping bones with one powerful blow from his paw.

Her king had just saved her life. Shaking off a sudden bout of self-doubt, she came to her knees, spitting sand from her mouth and blinking furiously to clear her vision. She was still recovering when agonizing pain blazed along their blood link.

"Ditanu!" She screamed his name, echoing his roar of pain.

Even before she fully understood what had happened, she was summoning magic to dispatch the threat to Ditanu's life. Moments later, her eyes found and confirmed what her blood link told her.

Ditanu was grounded, a spear embedded up high near his wing joint on his left side. A human was advancing upon him with a sword poised to kill.

She lashed out with another blast of power and the human vanished, more ash into the breeze.

Iltani sprinted to Ditanu's side. Three of his guards were already with him, but she didn't have eyes for them. All her attention was riveted upon the length of a spear piercing Ditanu's wing joint. She shoved her way between the guards—there were more gathering now, thank the goddess.

A closer look at the angle of the entry wound showed the spear hadn't shattered the joint. Then whispering an apology to her king, she placed one hand on the wooden shaft and the other against his side.

The spear had pierced through muscle and cartilage but missed bone and the main blood carrying vessels. Otherwise, Ditanu's wound would have been gushing his life force out onto the sand.

"Ditanu," she shouted to be heard over the noise of the battle. "Hold as still as you can. I'm going to use magic on the shaft and then cauterize the wound."

The king flicked a tufted ear in acknowledgement and gave her a sharp nod. His beak gaped open in pain. Otherwise he showed no outward signs that he wasn't ready to continue the fight. The beloved idiot. Her hands started to shake as relieve swept through her body. He was hurt, but would heal in a few days. She just needed to get him off this beach.

Shaking off the bout of jitters, she gripped the wooden shaft and sent her magic racing down its length. Where it touched, it ate into the surface and the wood vanished in another shower of light and ash.

Ditanu snapped his beak closed with a hiss of pain as a second pulse of her magic sealed the wound. It would require proper healing later, but for now, her field dressing would do.

"That will hold for…" A thunderous roar drowned out Iltani's words. She twisted around toward the fearsome sound in time to witness the north wall and a good portion of the upper temple shear away from the rest of the cliff wall.

It crashed downed toward the beach, indifferent to the shouts and cries of fear.

Many of those shouts of alarm were cut short, silenced forever.

A cloud of dust and sand rolled out across the shore, obscuring both the dead and the survivors. Iltani's magic flared, screaming that the cubs were in pain, their lives in peril. Ditanu roared, calling for his cubs.

The fighting paused as all opponents choked in the debris-filled air.

Iltani tore a length of veil from her skirt and tied it around her face and then turned to scan the area with magic, seeking Ditanu's cubs.

Two life forces were bright spots in her mind, but the third…the third was flickering like a guttering candle.

"Stay with the king." Iltani ordered the other Shadows and began to run.

The air was thick with stone dust and visibility was terrible, but she didn't need her eyes.

Her magic guided her and she swiftly made her way through the maze of fallen rubble.

Coming around a mostly intact piece of turret, Iltani halted suddenly. After taking in the sight of Burrukan and several Shadows digging desperately at one section of rubble, her heart dropped to her stomach, knowing what it meant even if her blood link hadn't already informed her of the terrible truth.

"Move," she yelled as she joined them, a cluster of Shadows in her way. When they ignored her or likely didn't hear her over the noise of shifting rocks, she shouldered her way forward.

When the first boulder was within reach, she touched it and it popped out of existence with a snap of magic. The two soldiers nearest her turned to study her with startled looks. These two had been with Consort Ahassunu the entire night so they hadn't seen the ceremony and likely didn't know she was Ishtar's Blade.

They could figure it out on their own time.

"You!" She pointed to the one to her left. "Move the smaller bits of rock and rubble. I'll deal with the larger pieces." She glanced to the male on her right. "You, help him."

If they were surprised at standing shoulder to shoulder with Ishtar's Blade, they buried it under layers of discipline.

She touched a second, and then the third piece of rock, vanishing three pieces before Ditanu's presence was at her back again. His rage, pain, and fear flooded out across their link.

He paced back and forth, wanting to get to his cubs, but too weak to shapeshift back into human form.

Gryphon form was superior in battle, but their paws useless in this endeavor. Ditanu was rational enough to know getting in the way would not help his cubs.

Iltani closed off the emotions flowing from her king to concentrate on his cubs. With a sense of desperation, she realized she could only sense two of them.

"We're losing one," she screamed feeling helpless. There was still too much rock between her and that tiny flickering life. Rage flowed through her body. Her magic spiked, escaping her control and entire sections of rock vanished. Iltani renewed her desperate digging.

A wing. A tiny leg glimpsed between pieces of rock.

"I see one!" Iltani shouted and the two guards nearest her race forward.

"Hold," Burrukan barked as he joined them. "Careful. Or the rocks above will crush him."

Iltani froze in sick horror and closed her fist on another wave of power. It burned between her fingers but didn't leap out across the space to the boulder she'd already targeted.

Burrukan was correct.

"How many can you take out at once?" He speared her with a fierce look.

The simple answer was 'all of them' but this task would require a precision she didn't know if she'd mastered yet. "It needs to be direct touch. Ishtar's magic is too strong, too wild for me to control. I can't risk the cubs."

"Then we won't. Start with this one," Burrukan said and pointed to the one he wanted her to target.

She did as instructed, vanishing piece after piece he selected. Burrukan had a good eye for it and the pile didn't shift dangerously at any point, but she swore it was taking an eternity. Slowly the section of rubble they worked on got smaller. She could see more of the cub. It was Ilanum. His chest barely rose and fell. He was bleeding from his mouth. Iltani, heart in her throat, continued to clear the rocks Burrukan chose.

Ditanu paced forward, close enough to jam his beak into the space between two of the larger boulders and touched his cub.

He made a pitying whine, but when Iltani and Burrukan tackled the one boulder pinning the cub, Ditanu quickly snatched the cub to safety. Iltani only had a moment to see the tiny battered body before Ditanu mantled his wings around his little one.

Iltani didn't have time to see more. Burrukan dragged her to a different section of the pile.

"We are close to the consort. I can smell her." Burrukan sounded both panicked and pained. "And blood. I can smell that too."

Iltani pitied him at that moment. As much as he and Ahassunu had betrayed the king, she still couldn't hate her mentor.

"Here, this one," Iltani said, pointing to a different section than where the Shadows had been working. She could only hone in on the cubs, not Ahassunu. She hoped they were together.

They worked feverishly. The Shadows removing smaller obstacles while Burrukan's keen eye picked out the best spot for Iltani to use her power. On the beach behind them, the battle still raged on.

The lone lamassu had been joined by three of its siblings and two of the temple's smaller genies and a stone lion. The genies and the lion fought alongside the Shadows, but the great lamassu were going out into the surf.

The great winged behemoths made short work of both the landing boats and the soldiers within them. Iltani, connected to the stone guardians by Ishtar's magic, could feel their fierce joy at defending their land.

"Iltani! Here," Burrukan shouted, drawing both her attention and Ditanu's sharp, half-wild gaze. The gryphon rushed forward, so did Iltani.

She vaporized another section of rock at Burrukan's urging and then stepped back as he dragged Ahassunu from the rubble. It was amazing the weight of the rocks hadn't crushed her. Iltani glanced back at the rocks. Ah, she'd used magic. That's why the rocks hadn't crushed her.

Burrukan and Ditanu were checking Ahassunu over for injuries, but the consort shook them off and came to all fours—although unsteadily. She said something to Ditanu and he stalked forward toward Iltani and the crevice they'd just pulled Ahassunu from.

Understanding hit. Iltani dropped to her hands and knees, and crawled into the narrow space. In the far back corner, two cubs huddled together, too frightened to move.

"Kuwari!" she called. She couldn't make out which was which, but one head popped up out of the twin lumps of fur and feathers.

He squealed and tried to get up, at which point his cry turned into a series of pained yelps.

Outside Ditanu roared. It was a fresh wave of anger, not pain which washed across the link. Ditanu was just reacting to his cub's pain, not injured himself.

Crawling on her hands and knees, she made her way toward the back of the magically created cavern.

It was narrow but deeper than she'd expected. Ahassunu must have been trying to dig her way free.

Ditanu called to his cubs again, this time shoving his head and shoulders into the opening.

"Ditanu, get out of the way. You're blocking all the light." Iltani spoke to him as she did when they were children. It gave her comfort in this small tomb-like cave.

He huffed and pulled back enough to allow light in.

"I'm making my way to the cubs now. They're both alive." At least, they were both breathing. She feared to see what she'd find when she reached them, though.

There was a scuffle at the entrance.

This time, Ahassunu was there. "I wasn't able to free them without bringing down that entire back wall." Ahassunu's voice came out strained with the guilt of a parent unable to protect a child. "My magic wasn't great enough to free them."

Ahassunu hadn't asked, but Iltani heard the plea there anyway. Wiggling the last of the way, she touched Kuwari gently. Her crystalline sword gave off enough light to see he wasn't mortally wounded, but part of one wing and the tip of his tail were trapped under a solid chunk of rock.

She couldn't start randomly vaporizing pieces without bringing half a cliff's worth of rock down upon herself.

If she had no other choice, she could sever the tip of his tail and cut the trapped wing feathers. When she gently shifted Kuwari enough to examine his sister, she instantly knew the female could not be freed in such a way. Her entire hind end was trapped, likely crushed.

It was probably too late to save the tiny female, but Iltani's blood link and the steel in her own soul wouldn't let her give up either.

She glanced between Ahassunu and the cubs. "Get Ditanu and yourself out of here. Once he is at a safe distance, I'll shield the cubs and then release

Ishtar's rage upon this entire cursed beach. The power should vaporize this pile of rubble, and any enemies I can catch in the blast."

While that probably wasn't a lie, Iltani didn't know if she or the cubs would survive it, either. The thought of Ditanu losing all his cubs struck terror into Iltani's heart, but surely as long as he still had Ahassunu and the unborn cubs she carried, that would be enough to keep him safe from the clutches of grief madness even if the worse happened and Iltani failed.

Ahassunu glanced at Iltani and then the cubs, her pain clear in her eyes. "Do you really think you can save my little ones?"

"I don't know, but I will do all in my power to protect them or die trying. You have my vow." Iltani dragged in a breath, almost a sob, "That's why I need Ditanu off this beach. I need to know even if I fail, he is safe."

Ahassunu nodded her head. "I understand. You have my gratitude. I will see your will is done even if one of the great lamassu has to carry the king away from here."

The consort backed out of the passage. From outside, Iltani heard Burrukan and Ahassunu attempting to reason with Ditanu. It went on longer than it should, but at last there came the thunder of wings followed by Ditanu's startled exclamation as a lamassu scooped up the gryphon king and his cub, carrying them both away from the battle.

Through their link, she could feel the distance rapidly growing between them as the stone guardian winged away, heading for the safety of the capital, the king and the cub Ilanum, clasped in its embrace.

With her king as safe as he could be, Iltani turned her attention back to the other two cubs. Kuwari was crying and fighting to free himself. She scooted closer until she could curl protectively around him and his sister.

"Easy, little Mite," she said as she caressed his head, trying to distract him from his injuries or, at least, stop him from inflicting more damage. "I'll have you out of here in a moment and back with your parents before you know it."

She hoped that wasn't a lie, but even if it was, the cub stopped struggling to free himself. He pressed his head against her hand and turned his beak enough he could nuzzle into her side.

Iltani waited until the sounds of battle grew closer. There was another scuffle at the entrance.

A body hit the sand just outside her cave. Burrukan suddenly stuck his head inside to peer into the passageway.

"Ditanu is safe." He turned to look behind him, scanning the beach as he continued. "Consort Ahassunu and the remaining Shadows are waiting further down the beach, at the northern pier. We'll meet you there. The beach here is overrun. Give me a count of ten and then raze everything to glass and ash." He gave her a flash of white teeth. "I'm proud of you, more than I could ever say. So don't disappoint me by getting yourself killed."

With that, he disappeared back out of the passage and was gone.

"I will not fail you or my king," she whispered and pressed closer to the cubs. She closed her eyes, sending a hasty prayer to Ishtar and then summoning that full, unrestrained torrent of power which had been dancing at the edges of her consciousness since she'd first learned there were invaders within gryphon territory. The sword glowed more brightly, and Iltani formed a ring of burning power around herself and the two cubs.

Once the power was concentrated enough, she sent a small portion to eat away at the rocks pinning the cubs. Above her head, the rock shifted, making her heart pound, but the rubble didn't fall. Ishtar's magic held it back with greater force. Sweat trickled down her back and her ears felt like she was underwater as a great pressure descended upon her body.

Her magic continued to eat away at the rock trapping the cubs and suddenly Kuwari came free. He yelped in pain but shifted closer until his entire body was pressed against her breasts. She couldn't spare him the attention to sooth his fears. Dragging Humusi free, she eyed the damage.

What she saw of the cub's injuries sent a cold lance of fear straight through her heart. The cub's hind limbs and pelvis were crushed. The right hind leg was almost severed at the knee. Iltani hastily tore off a piece of her skirt and used it as a tourniquet.

She was out of time. Gathering both cubs into her arms, Iltani sat up, coming to her knees. Shifting them to a one armed hold, she grasped her sword's hilt and released the contained power. A power bright as the sun flashed through her closed lids, tinting the cavern red all around her.

Then the world exploded.

CHAPTER
thirteen

CHOKING ON AIR filled with dust and heat, Iltani struggled to her feet and found herself in the center of a crater. Blessedly, she was unharmed by the blast. Almost the opposite, she felt like she could conquer a mountain. Reining in her adrenaline-filled thoughts, she glanced down at the cubs. They were no more damaged than they'd been before, but that still wasn't saying much for Humusi's chances at survival.

More heat radiated up from the sand, some of it an odd crunching consistency under her sandals. Neither the hot air nor the molten spots slowed her as she bolted into motion, the cubs tucked against her side and a glowing sword in the other hand.

She cleared the small rise, which was actually the crater's rim, and came out on the beach and saw first-hand the destruction she had created. Burned and broken bodies. Boulders and bits of temple masonry. None of it distracted her from her destination, the small harbor just beyond the curve of the cliff wall.

Iltani sprinted across the sand, weaving around or jumping over bodies and debris in her path. This particular stretch of beach was relatively empty of enemies, which was a blessing. Encumbered with the cubs as she was, hand to hand combat wasn't something she wanted to face. Unfortunately, ahead, the sounds of battle rang out.

She stumbled more than climbed over the last rocky section and sprawled on the beach. Rolling onto her side, she shielded the cubs from the worst of the impact. Kuwari whined, but the other was ominously quiet. Iltani's focus became finding one of the Shadows trained as a healer. Etum and his twin, Eluti, both possessed healing gifts. If either of them still lived, they might be able to help.

Surveying the battle before her, she spotted three separate groups of fighting. Nearest her location, a vanguard of Shadows was dispatching the enemy stragglers that had landed on the beach during the earlier battle— the few to escape the lamassu's assault.

Further in, Ahassunu and her guards were liberating one of the enemy's boats. It was larger than a skiff, with no sail. Instead, it had oars to power it through the water. Iltani's brows drew together in confusion. A closer look showed why they were after the boat. Ahassunu's one wing was hanging limp, broken. She wasn't the only one with injuries. There weren't enough able-bodied gryphons left to fly the rest to safety.

If that were all they'd had to face, escape out to the safety of the ocean would have been relatively easy.

But fate wasn't being kind today. A large battle-damaged ship was already in the harbor. Its three masts were shattered by a lamassu's rage and there was also a large hole in its side. The ship was riding low in the water—sinking further as she watched. The ship might be dead, but its crew wasn't.

Swinging her gaze away from the wounded ship, Iltani searched out Burrukan by the sounds of battle. He was on the harbor's main dock, flanked by five of his Shadows. Together, the small group of defenders attempted to keep the ship's crew from coming ashore.

"It will be all right Kuwari, I promise," she said as she glanced down at the cubs in her arms. Decision made, she sprinted toward Ahassunu. She would deposit the two cubs in the boat with their mother, and then guard their escape.

By the time Iltani reached the nearest group of Shadows, they'd finished with the nearest batch of invaders. Seeing Iltani and her precious burden, they formed up around her and together they rejoined the consort and her guard.

Iltani spotted a large gash running along the consort's hip and she favored that leg heavily, but she did not look defeated as she walked up to Iltani and nuzzled at the two cubs. Iltani gently placed them on the sand, already knowing that even a mother's love could do nothing for the oldest cub. The cub's heart fluttered feebly along Iltani's blood-link.

Her own heart breaking, Iltani withdrew and walked toward Burrukan.

The invaders would pay for the crime of spilling innocent blood. The sword in her hand pulsed brighter, its magic flaring and dancing along the blade with renewed anger.

Ishtar, goddess of war, agreed.

CHAPTER
fourteen

ILTANI ONLY MADE it half way to Burrukan's location when one of
the tiny threads of her blood-link snapped and blinked out of existence—a
tiny life going with it. She'd only known the cub for a day, but its sudden
absence left an aching hollowness which took up twin residences in her
mind and heart.

Halting at water's edge, she focused on the first thing she saw—the boat
and its crew where they were lowering three smaller boats into the water.
Iltani narrowed her eyes and raised her sword. Her magic raced over her
body, an outward sign that didn't even begin to cover the depth of Ishtar's
rage seething within her.

Screaming, she lashed out with power, giving it no direction other than
to destroy. Ocean water boiled away as steam, the smaller boats disinte-
grated, nothing more than bits of fire and ash raining down into the waves.
Ishtar's power collided with the larger ship, racing over it, consuming it.
A convulsive ripple raced through the growing cloud of magic and with a
large crack the boat shattered, vanishing into smoke, fire and ash.

Swirling motes of magic drifted slowly down upon the waves.

A sudden fierce roar of pain jerked Iltani away from the sight of the ocean. Whipping around, she spotted Ahassunu fighting fresh enemies, but it was Kuwari's panicked cries over the sound of the surf and the shouting of men that made ice run in her veins.

Swiftly, she scanned the area. The Shadows guarding Kuwari were battling six times their number, and more of the enemy was climbing over the rocky coast to join in the fight. There must have been a second ship out of sight, just around the harbor wall.

The how or the why didn't matter now.

Iltani ran. She was halfway there when one of the Shadows guarding Kuwari was overwhelmed by sheer numbers and the enemy dragged him down, stabbing swords and axes into his body. The remaining three closed ranks around the frightened cub. Even as Iltani raced closer, another Shadow was taken down by an arrow through his throat.

Coming up behind her, Iltani heard Burrukan and the other Shadows with him gaining ground.

Iltani reached the battle first, cutting down enemies as she forced her way through to get to Kuwari's side. Every instinct told her that Kuwari was the target. Kill him and they came that much closer to ending the line of the Gryphon King's.

Ahassunu was still on her feet, fighting to reach her cub. The fierce mother dragged down enemy after enemy.

In a still moment between kills, Iltani found herself facing off against an enemy with the wildest hair and beard she'd ever seen. But it was his eyes that held the greatest wildness. A look that said he knew there was no surrender for either of them, that he wasn't going to make it off this island alive, and he might as while do as much killing and ravaging as he could before he fell.

She held her ground, looking past him to the boat just steps away where Kuwari was cowering.

The big man spat something in an ugly foreign tongue as he grinned and ogled Iltani. She returned the man's grin with a savage one of her own.

"Is this what you want?" Iltani held her arms wide, daring the fool.

Again he spoke in his language, the words unknown, but the meaning clear enough.

"Look your fill," Iltani laughed. "It's likely the last thing you'll see."

Ahassunu lunged, grabbing him from behind and shaking him like a dog.

Out of the corner of her eye, Iltani noted his head part company from his body, and then she was leaping into the boat. She scooped up Kuwari even as she summoned power, cocooning them both in shielding magic. At least, he hadn't collected any more injuries.

"Shhh, it will be all right," Iltani whispered to the cub as she rocked him. It was the only comfort she could give him as the battle continued to rage around them.

Iltani stood with her sword ready and her legs braced, matching the rock of the boat as the first soldier came at her. He made it within two body-lengths of the boat and then he burst into flames. He didn't even have time to scream. It happened all without any conscious thought on Iltani's part.

Ishtar roused, stronger than before.

Two more invaders had been approaching Iltani's location but backed away when they saw their comrade vanish in fire and ash. Iltani felt Ishtar's attention flick across them in a dismissive motion, setting them to burn while she took in the larger battle.

Burrukan and the few remaining Shadows were making their way toward the boat. Consort Ahassunu was finishing off her present opponent when a figure rose up out of the rocks to the right of the pier. He held one of those musket weapons gripped in his hand. A loud boom echoed along the shore and the consort grunted, struggling away from the human she'd been battling. After a few steps, she collapsed on her side. The new angle showed Iltani the bloody mess of a belly wound.

Burrukan screamed Ahassunu's name as he finished his own two opponents and limped toward her.

Iltani's own consciousness receded before the greater influence of her goddess. Ishtar adjusted her hold upon Kuwari, and then stepped out of the boat and walked toward the injured gryphon carrying the next generation of the gryphon kings. Iltani was still aware of her surroundings but was content to watch Ishtar. When she reached the injured gryphon's side, she dropped down on one knee in the sand. Burrukan and the other Shadows, who had been trying to slow the flow of blood backed away obediently when Ishtar motioned them to give her room.

Ahassunu was laying on her side, panting harshly. Gryphons could heal quickly. The consort might yet survive, but the four small flickering sparks of life within their mother's womb would not.

Those tiny lives were in distress. They would soon flick out of existence if Ishtar didn't intervene.

The Queen of the Night looked around, taking in the bodies, her ravaged temple, and the one ship still in the harbor, the injured consort, and lastly, the grief-stricken Burrukan. He, too, had an assortment of injuries but was still whole. He and the four remaining Shadows might be enough to get Ahassunu on the boat and away if Iltani stayed and fought off the humans still coming from the south side of the island.

"Go," Burrukan ordered her. "Take Kuwari and leave. You can't save us all."

Ah, noble self-sacrifice. Burrukan was loyal to the gryphon line and she respected that, but no one gave orders to Ishtar.

"No, not all can be saved," Ishtar agreed, "but I can save four tiny lives." Burrukan seemed to understand, but Iltani wasn't sure if she did.

Then Ishtar showed her.

Yes, the consort was already aborting the unborn cubs—her body gave her no choice. It was abort the cubs or die with them. However, Ishtar knew of another way to save the unborn cubs and honor her pact with the gryphon kings. Unfortunately, it would weaken her Blade and there would be no more glorious battle this day. This battle was lost, anyway.

But the war could be won another day.

"Save them, my goddess," the consort whispered. "If I know my remaining cubs are alive in the world, I will fight to live, fight to rejoin them. Only give them a chance at life."

What did that mean? Iltani wondered as she felt herself nod as Ishtar made a decision.

Reaching down, Ishtar curved her fingers around the consort's blood covered lower belly.

She could sense the tiny lives through her blood link to Ditanu. Then Ishtar reached into the consort with tendrils of power and scooped up each of those tiny lives and suddenly, Iltani found herself squinting to see with her eyes what her mind told her was clasped in her cupped hands. Looking down, she discerned a ball of bright light.

Four souls. Four tiny lives pulsed between her fingers and Iltani was humbled by the power of the Queen of the Night.

Iltani's sense of awe changed to surprised shock and then pain as those same hands pressed the ball of light against the bare skin of her abdomen. Iltani gasped. That was all the freedom Ishtar granted her. Had the goddess not maintained Iltani's steely posture, she'd likely have collapsed, so great was that heat and power and pain.

It faded quickly, though, her bodied growing strangely numb. A familiar lethargy settled into her bones, similar to the times her body had assimilated Ditanu's blood.

"Your body must rest or it will reject the new life I've planted there," Ishtar said in Iltani's own voice.

Iltani's vision was blurring, narrowing dangerously. She'd never fainted in her life, but this must be how it felt to do so. Ishtar, still guiding her body, tightened her hold on Kuwari and then she stumbled toward the boat. A thick fog had begun to roll in from the ocean.

To Iltani's new senses it tasted not of a natural origin, so this was a more subtle version of the Queen of the Night's power and Iltani was reminded Ishtar was also the goddess of storms.

"The cubs you now harbor will not survive the ravages of my battle magic, so we will need to find a new way to defeat our enemies. But not this day—the last enemy ship will escape for now, and we must let it. Your new duty is to survive and protect the new life you shelter." Iltani swayed as she stepped into the boat, but Ishtar kept her from falling over the edge.

As she sank down into the bottom, Kuwari hugged close to her breast, she saw Burrukan and the other Shadows holding back more humans, preventing them from rushing Iltani's boat.

It hurt to leave them behind, the sense of betrayal sharp, but Burrukan and Ishtar were both correct. Her first duty was to Ditanu and now Kuwari and the unborn cubs. She couldn't shelter or protect any of them if she were dead, she knew that. Yet, still, it hurt her heart to leave her father behind.

Iltani closed her eyes as the boat began to move, slicing through the water with unnatural speed. The boat's rocking lulled her and the presence of the goddess faded, though not completely.

CHAPTER
fifteen

ILTANI FELT TIME'S passage and the sky turning pink in the east.

Dawn came at last as the boat continued gliding through the water, drawing ever closer to Nineveh and her king.

Iltani's mind drifted for a time and then Ishtar returned, her presence strong once more.

Between one moment and the next, Iltani found herself impossibly back in the king's rooms.

And yet not, for the boat still rocked with motion and Kuwari whimpered softly. Somehow, her blood link with Ditanu, or another of Ishtar's gifts, was allowing her to see what he was seeing.

In her vision, Ditanu was sitting on his bed, stroking the still fluffy mane of his second-born cub. It took her a moment to realize the little one's sides no longer rose with life, that at some point during the battle, a second tiny thread in her blood link had snapped and she'd been unaware of its absence until now.

Grief welled up within her soul—mirroring Ditanu's pain. The blood-link, gift and curse that it was, allowed her to partake in his deeply personal pain.

Iltani wished she could offer him comfort in person, but she was still out in the ocean, in a boat guided by Ishtar's hand.

Ditanu stroked his cub's mane as he murmured a prayer to speed his little one's soul into the afterlife. Iltani sensed he was holding onto his composure by tiny little threads. Each moment that slipped by, her thoughts merged more fully with his, until there were only his thoughts. His mind was a chaotic well of emotions. Grief and rage, mixing into a lethal brew. But above all that pain and despair, was the need to know what happened to the rest of his loved ones. He refused to acknowledge the horrible possibility that they might all be…no he would not…no.

Ditanu choked back a sob and raised his eyes from the body of his cub to direct his cold stare straight at his second in command.

"Uselli, what news have you learned? Surely some of the survivors have news. Someone somewhere knows something. Where are my other cubs? Iltani? Ahassunu or Burrukan?"

Uselli shook his head. "I'm sorry my king. We don't know what has happened to them yet. More survivors arrive every hour. There is still hope. Burrukan is well trained and Iltani is your most loyal Shadow." Uselli reached out and rested his hand on Ditanu's shoulder. "Now that we know she is Ishtar's chosen…I know she will protect your remaining cubs. Iltani is too stubborn and determined. She won't let anything stop her. Besides, she has a goddess on her side."

Ditanu desperately wanted to believe that Iltani was still out there somewhere, his remaining cubs safe in her care. Nevertheless, hope was a hard thing to cling to with each hour's passing and still no word of his loved ones reached his ears.

He'd reverted to his human form, but he could feel his gryphon in his mind, pacing, always pacing, wanting to go find his true mate and cubs.

The need was nearly too much to battle, but he did. He couldn't allow his gryphon self to win. His people needed their king thinking and reasoning, not one who was raging mad.

"What else have you learned? Who are these mercenaries working for and to what extent have they compromised our defenses?"

Uselli gave his report, and Ditanu clung to each detail, hoping to fight the growing wildness within himself.

The king's mind vanished from Iltani's consciousness as Ishtar dragged her attention elsewhere.

"No, wait," Iltani pleaded with the goddess. "Ditanu is in danger. If he thinks his family is dead…"

Therein lay the true danger to the king—himself. If he thought his entire family was dead, he would succumb to a gryphon's grief madness, like his father before him.

Please, go back, Iltani begged.

Ishtar didn't listen and the world shifted and spun away.

In another moment, Iltani found her mind thrust into another body. This new body was female. There were people flocking around her. After a moment, Iltani recognized them. Priests and priestesses in service to Ishtar. Iltani was within High Priestess Kammani's body.

She stood in the throne room, on the stairs leading to the throne where King Ditanu now sat, as stone-faced as she'd ever seen him.

He was holding a war council, gathering information so he could mount some form of retaliation. Priestess Kammani was there to offer support, but Iltani could sense the deeply rooted fear Kammani had for her nephew's well-being.

Ditanu sat, listening as the reports came in, but he was so still it was as if he wasn't even breathing.

Other survivors had made it back to the king's city, but all their reports were equally unhappy. When asked, none of them had heard anything about Burrukan, Ahassunu, or Iltani. No one knew what happened to the king's other cubs.

Burrukan's second in command, Uselli, had sent out search parties to learn what happened. Now all anyone could do was wait.

Iltani, trapped within the priestess's mind could feel her despair, but was unable to talk to her, to reassure her—she couldn't give the priestess so much as a glimmer of hope to share with the king.

Time crept by. Iltani's drifting mind returned to the boat, but her connection with the priestess was still strong, and some time later, when Uselli returned with more survivors, she was thrust back into the priestess's body.

The court fell silent as Ditanu ordered Uselli forward. He came and placed a small cloak wrapped bundle in Ditanu's outstretched arms and then prostrated himself on the floor.

"I am sorry, my king," Uselli whispered.

Priestess Kammani placed a hand upon Ditanu's shoulder. "Why don't we retire to your personal quarters for this?"

Ditanu ignored her and unwrapped the bundle.

It was the oldest cub, Humusi. The one Iltani had failed to save and been forced to leave on the beach.

The king ran his fingers over her delicate head and whispered a prayer, then with such gentleness Iltani started to weep, Ditanu covered his cub back up and held her small body to his chest, as if the sound of his heart might still somehow comfort her.

If Uselli had managed to get there and back already, perhaps they had found and rescued Ahassunu and Burrukan? Maybe they were with healers even now?

Uselli's next words destroyed Iltani's naïve hope.

"By the time our troops had gathered and made the crossing to Uruk, it was too late. The surviving invaders had already abandoned the beach.

We combed through the temple and rubble. We found the bodies of Etum and Eluti as well as others." He drew a deep breath before continuing. "We are still in the process of bringing back bodies...however, there was a large pyre on the beach..."

Iltani saw a muscle twitch in the king's jaw, but he gave away nothing else. "Continue," he ordered.

"Evidence shows the enemy dragged many of the bodies there and burned them before they left."

"To dishonor the dead and inflict more pain upon the living," Ditanu's sharp retort was pain etched but he motioned Uselli to continue. "You have more to report?"

"We were unable to identify Ahassunu or Kuwari among the dead, but..."

"Burrukan?"

"No sign, my king. I'm sorry."

"Iltani?" Ditanu uttered as his voice broke. His jaw flexed again. "I would know if Iltani was dead. As long as she draws breath, there is hope my Kuwari still lives."

Uselli flinched and his eyes slid toward the Priestess as if begging for some distraction.

"You know something else." Ditanu leaned forward, his fingers gripping his throne in a white-knuckled grip. "Tell me."

It was an order clear and simple, one no Shadow could deny. Uselli didn't look happy but he continued. "We found a survivor in the ruins. One of Beletum's guards. He claims to have knowledge of Iltani and Kuwari. He would not tell me the news. If you would give me a few moments with him, to be certain this is not just some political maneuvering to gain your favor, I would like to verify this. To be certain."

"I will hear him and then decide a course of action." Ditanu gestured with his right arm, his dead cub still held in the other. Pain etched across his face, he snarled, "Bring him forward."

Priestess Kammani offered to take the lifeless cub, but Ditanu waved her off.

There was a shuffle and shifting of bodies as another person was brought forward. He wore the uniform of a guard of the house of Beletum. His appearance was as rough as the rest of the court, bloody and battle worn. The newcomer had a noticeable limp, his lower leg bandaged.

Still, he hobbled forward and then executed an almost elegant bow to the king.

"Your highness, I am sorry for your loss," he paused, his demeanor taking on a nervous quality.

Ishtar's power stirred fitfully, her hostile interest narrowing to focus upon Beletum's guardsman.

"Rise," Ditanu said in a clipped voice. "Tell me what you know."

"I was injured in the first volley of cannon fire. In the chaos, I was separated from the rest of my men, so I helped others reach what we thought would be safety on the northern beach. We were wrong. The battle was raging on the beach. I and a few other survivors made it to the harbor. We made a last stand among the rocks at the cliffs edge while the tide was low. From there I saw much of the battle." His eyes shifted to the left, scanning the faces around him.

Looking to see who all had survived? Or was that nervous evasion?

He continued on, unaware of Kammani's and Iltani's deepening scrutiny. "It was there I saw them moving the bodies of Consort Ahassunu and her Shadows. Burrukan had been killed first I believe, though, from my location, I only saw what happened afterward."

Iltani's heart constricted with new pain. So Burrukan and Ahassunu hadn't escaped. She knew they didn't stand much of a chance, but Burrukan had always been so resourceful she'd held out hope that he'd find a way.

"And what did you see?" Ditanu's cold voice pierced Iltani's thoughts. "Afterward?"

Yes, Iltani thought, what did you really see? The battle would have been over by then. Ishtar had already put her and Kuwari in the boat and escaped with them before Burrukan met his fate.

"I think Burrukan and Consort Ahassunu fell trying to protect the two cubs. Afterward, I saw Burrukan's apprentice, Iltani, running across the beach with Kuwari in her arms. One of the enemy soldiers shot her in the back with a musket. Seeing she was wounded but still alive, I and the other survivors tried to aid her. Many were slow, already injured and fell to the enemies' weapons. I took a blow to the head. I think they thought I was dead. Too stunned to move, at first, I could only watch as they toyed with her...before...before they decapitated her," he paused in his story and then nervously glanced behind him. Seeming to gather his courage, he looked up from the floor. "I am sorry, but once she fell, they made short work of your helpless cub."

"Lies!" Ditanu roared and lunged up from his throne.

Iltani agreed. For that, most certainly, was not what had happened.

Ditanu slashed out at Beletum's guard, claws extended as he shifted into gryphon form. The guard, too surprise by the sudden attack, didn't react fast enough, never seeing death coming. One moment he was standing before the king, the next, a sharp snap heralded his neck being broken by a powerful blow from Ditanu's paw.

Ditanu blasted out another roar and charged at Uselli. The Shadow was faster than Beletum's guard and he managed to escape a killing blow. Still, blood flew in a spray across the polished stone floor.

The court erupted in shouts and yelling as King Ditanu, lost to battle rage and grief madness, cut his way across the crowded hall.

He lies. Ishtar whispered.

Those two words seemed to reach Priestess Kammani's mind where Iltani's had not. The High Priestess halted in her tracks.

My Blade still lives. She guards the seeds of the future.

Kammani remained frozen a moment more, then began shouting orders. "Shadows, to me! Half of you clear the room, the rest distract your king. We must contain him."

More guards rushed in from the main doors, coming to her calls and the king's roars.

Uselli was beside her in moments and together they started to build a plan.

Iltani watched and listened, still linked to Kammani through Ishtar's magic, but she felt more ghost than alive now.

Ditanu had descended into grief madness. Iltani didn't know if even Kuwari would be enough to bring him out of it again.

Priestess Kammani rubbed a hand over her eyes, trying and failing to rub away the exhaustion blurring the edge of her vision. The King's Shadows had been successful in luring the enraged Ditanu down into the cage of magic she'd created in the sands of the practice ring.

The golden glow of the shield circling a large expanse of the sand ring didn't soften the despair emanating from the other Shadows standing guard outside the ring. By the time they'd gotten Ditanu into the cage, he'd been far beyond reason. Nothing Kammani said calmed the enraged king. At least, he was safe within the cage. Only the quick thinking of Uselli allowed them to trick Ditanu into it at all.

Uselli had sent servants running to steal pillows from the royal nursery. Using the pillows with the scent of Ditanu's cubs, they tricked him into the cage. However, once he'd learned his cubs were not within, he'd set to pacing and attacking the walls of his prison.

With many Shadows injured, their grief-maddened king far beyond help, the court in disarray, the council broken, many of its members dead,

Kammani dearly needed Ishtar's guidance, but Ishtar had been silent after that first warning. Kammani barely knew where to start.

No. That wasn't true. She knew where to start.

Find Iltani and Kuwari.

May Ishtar grant her blessings upon them all.

For only Iltani and Kuwari could save King Ditanu now, and if they were not found soon, it would be too late.

CHAPTER
sixteen

MANY HOURS LATER, the council was at an impasse. Kammani secretly wished Ishtar would come and dance upon all their heads, but of course—the goddess was busy elsewhere, keeping Iltani and Kuwari safe, she hoped. If Kammani could have simply told the other councilors Kuwari still lived—somewhere—it would calm some of this storm.

But she didn't dare risk endangering Iltani or Kuwari by repeating what Ishtar had told her.

There were traitors somewhere deep in gryphon territory.

Perhaps as high up as a council member.

Kammani glanced around at her fellow councilors.

If those traitors learned Kuwari still lived, they would do all in their power to make sure he never made it back to Nineveh.

"I refuse to believe my daughter and Kuwari both are dead. I want more proof than speculation and that questionable source of Beletum's." Councilor Shalanum stood so fast his chair scraped across the floor with a screech.

Ahassunu's father was one of the few councilors Kammani trusted. Their friendship went back a long way, but even so she feared if she told him, he would do something rash and alert their enemies that Kuwari was still alive.

"While you have us all out searching on your impossible fool's errand," Beletum sneered, "we'll be allowing the line of the gryphon kings to perish. We'll all die with it. Or is that what you want?" Beletum retorted.

"Fool's errand?" Shalanum snarled back, looking like he was going to come across the table to challenge Beletum to a physical battle, mere words not satisfying enough. "How is seeking the last hope of all gryphon kind a fool's errand, tell me that?"

Beletum waved her hand dismissively. "Your misguided theory is understandable, given your own grief at your daughter's loss."

Kammani decided she wouldn't get in Councilor Shalanum's way if he made a move to kill the other councilor, but she did wonder what Beletum was after. Clearly she had a plan. One Kammani wouldn't like, on principal alone. Beletum's father was tight-lipped as well.

A slow smile spread across Beletum's lips, confirming Kammani's earlier misgivings.

"Ishtar has blessed us with another possibility. Yes, his mate and cubs are dead, but the king still lives. The seed of the gryphon line can be renewed."

Councilor Ubarum looked up from where he'd been studying the table as if it was the most interesting thing in the room. He probably had as little stomach for the bickering of the councilors as Kammani herself. Burrukan had been his brother.

Ubarum's gaze narrowed upon Beletum. "What are you going on about?"

Beletum smoothed a hand over her hair as if in thought. "We all saw our king descend into grief madness at learning the fate of his mate and cubs. Once the rage burns itself out, it will take his will to live with it.

When that happens, he will go into an unresponsive state, and then fall into a deep sleep from which he will not wake. When he dies, most, if not all, gryphon magic will die with him. All the inhabitants of the city-states will be exposed to the outside world."

"We all know the worst case scenario."

"But have you thought about the best case? We have a little over a day to preserve the line of the gryphon kings, and by that, I mean begetting another litter in a fertile womb. With enough herbs and a fertile female willing to allow the impregnation, it might be possible to avoid doom for many more generations."

"You speak treason so easily," Kammani said in passing.

The silence in the room was absolute. Kammani could hear the other councilors breathing. No one moved. Too shocked? Or weighing the possibilities of success? When one's own life was on the line, one tended to become morally flexible. Still, no one wanted to be the first to agree to Beletum's treasonous words.

With a huff of annoyance, Beletum's father, Councilor Ziyatum stood, the sound of his chair scraping back loud in the quiet room.

He gestured at the table. "This silence is as ridiculous as Priestess Kammani's mention of treason. We are all facing our doom. The king will be dead in a day, two at most. Then it will be just us alone, trying to keep our kingdom safe as our magic dies. How are my daughter's words any more treasonous than sitting and doing nothing?"

Pirhum, the oldest gryphon on the council, squinted at Beletum and gave her father a deep frown, but he looked thoughtful, too. "What you suggest goes against everything we hold sacred. Under normal circumstances, it would be treason to take away the king's will for no reason other than to save our own hides."

He stood and went to a side table to pour himself a drink. "Yet, as you say, King Ditanu will die, and much of our magic will die with him. He loves his people, and I believe he would not wish that fate upon any of us. If he were capable of understanding our dilemma at this time, he would forgive us." The councilor shrugged. "He will likely be too far gone to realize what is happening, or that he isn't with his mate. If he can be persuaded at all." His tone suggested he doubted it.

"Doubtful," Kammani agreed, and then arched a brow, already knowing the answer to her next question. "Who do you plan to send?"

"It's no secret my mate is sterile," Beletum said with a shrug. "Yet I still cycle for him." She glanced at her mate in question. Nidnatum looked mildly uncomfortable but offered no comment.

Beletum patted her mate's hand with what must be honest affection. "I am presently in the early stages of my fertility cycle. I'm willing to risk whatever I must to ensure our culture survives. Besides, I won't ask another to do what I wouldn't do myself."

Oh, the great self-sacrificing Beletum. So noble and concerned for her people. Of course, it had nothing to do with her ambitions for the throne, to be the new consort, mother to the next generation of gryphon royalty. Kammani snorted.

Beletum was the most self-serving of the council members, and that was saying something.

"Ditanu will likely just kill you."

The momentary calm soon dissolved into the chaotic debate of earlier. Priestess Kammani could only shake her head. Ditanu was loyal to his true mate, that bond unshakable and goddess blessed. He would kill whatever female made the attempt to supplant her.

Kammani had never liked Beletum, and wouldn't be too broken up went Ditanu carved her to pieces. Better her, than some other poor innocent they might try to match with the king.

If this distraction kept the traitor on the council from guessing Iltani and Kuwari still lived, all the better. Once Ishtar's Blade and the cub were found, the Shadows would protect them from further harm.

When she knew the future of the gryphon kingdom had been safe-guarded, Kammani would turn her attention to routing out the vipers within her kingdom.

Again her eyes slid to Beletum. As much as she disliked the female, the young councilor wasn't the mastermind behind the first attack which had killed Ditanu's mother and siblings. No, she was far too young, a cub herself at the time. But Beletum's father? He warranted close watching.

Kammani was about to leave the council to their bickering, when her link to her goddess awoke, flooding her with power. Ah. Ishtar had a task for her. Kammani could only hope it was the answer to her prayers. Standing, she stepped away from the table. The vocal debate stilled. Into that temporary silence, she said, "Ishtar has need of me elsewhere. Once I have attended to that summons, I will deal with King Ditanu. In the meantime, do as you wish, but know if my nephew comes to harm from Beletum's scheme, I will personally seek you out and remove your head from your shoulders."

If Ditanu didn't do it first.

With that threat still hanging in the air, she swept from the room, heading in the direction Ishtar urged.

The tug led Kammani out of the palace, down the long twisted path of the Processional Way, and on by Shadows guarding the streets, keeping the peace and preventing panic from harming the citizens. She walked swiftly onward to Ishtar's Gate.

When she reached the gate, she motioned four of the Shadows guarding it to follow her.

"Come with me," Kammani ordered. There were many on duty, more than normal after the attack on Uruk, but instinct told her she'd need the guards.

Kammani continued on down the stairs until she stepped onto the beach. There she stood looking out into the ocean's vast expanse.

Behind her, she sensed the Shadows following. They were too well trained to question her actions, but they must be curious. She was opening her mouth to tell them she was serving Ishtar's wishes when she spotted a bright bit of magic racing toward them from far out on the ocean.

As it drew closer, it took the shape of a small boat. A clear shell of protective magic encircled the entire boat, but when it finally came to shore, propelled by Ishtar's unseen hand, the magic protecting the boat burst, vanishing in a cloud of sparks and mist.

Kammani's breath hissed out on a gasp at what was revealed and then she sent up a prayer of thanks, for the hope of all gryphon kind lay curled in the bottom of the boat.

Iltani slept, still curled protectively around the sole remaining royal cub.

CHAPTER
seventeen

ILTANI JERKED AWAKE with a gasp, not knowing where she was at first. Slowly, too slowly, she began recognizing the furniture around her. A plush quilt covered the massive bed. Brown silk drapes shrouded it from the rest of the suite. By some strange twist of fate, she was in the king's suites, his bed to be precise. She glanced around once more.

The king was nowhere near. Her blood link told her he was farther away, but still in the castle.

Alive, but terribly distressed.

Of course, he was. He'd thought everyone he loved was dead.

She needed to go to him, to let him know he still had one living cub and four tiny unborn sparks of life that would one day grow and mend the hole in his heart. The unreasoning need had her up and stumbling from the bed before she noticed there were others in the room with her.

High Priestess Kammani and several other priests and priestess were gathered around a low table, their backs to Iltani.

Kammani glanced over her shoulder at Iltani, acknowledging her with a nod, but turned back to Kuwari. After a moment, she finished with the cub. A squawk emanated from behind Kammani and Kuwari's head popped up, swiveling from side to side, searching for her.

"Good, you're awake. How do you feel?" Kammani asked.

"I need to see Ditanu." Iltani didn't want to stand around discussing useless things while she still didn't know the king's full condition. While he 'felt' wrong to her blood link, it didn't exactly tell her how far he'd already succumbed to grief madness. There were several phases, each worse than the last until finally death claimed the hapless victim. She hoped he was still in the first phase, but the sooner they reunited Kuwari and his father, the better.

Iltani walked over to the table, intending to scoop up the cub and then seek out his father until she remembered something else and her fingers rested against her own belly.

It was still unreal. So much had happened in a short time, she was still trying to process it all. No. Kuwari wasn't the only surviving member of Ditanu's family. She was the new surrogate mother to Ditanu's next litter.

Goddess Ishtar be merciful.

What a mixed up fate.

Later, she'd sort out her chaotic emotions and thoughts. For now, there was only Ditanu's need. He needed to learn he wasn't alone in this world.

Kammani made room for Iltani at the table. "We are almost finished healing Kuwari. As important as it is to reunite Ditanu with his family as quickly as possible, I decided it was best not to take an injured cub to Ditanu in his present state. He is already unbalanced. Seeing his cub in pain would only trigger even more over-protective parental instincts. Ditanu has already carved up enough of his Shadows."

"Does Ditanu have other injuries?" *Life-threatening ones?* She couldn't ask it aloud.

"A few minor wounds. The greatest threat is grief and stress to his body."

"I had dreams while I was traveling here," Iltani frowned. "Ishtar somehow linked our souls and I could see through your eyes. I saw Ditanu kill that guardsman—the one who claimed to have seen me die along with Kuwari."

"Then you know a bit of what has happened." Kammani scooped up Kuwari and then gave him to Iltani. "I would prefer to keep Kuwari here, but I don't know if Ditanu will be reasonable enough to follow you back to these chambers without the cub to lure him along."

"He might," Iltani said guardedly as she pressed a hand to the slight curve of her belly. "There's something else you likely don't know. How closely did you check me over?"

She had Kammani's attention now, the priestess looking her over with a sharp attention. Her eyes narrowed slightly and then widened when she noticed the protective hand Iltani had over her belly. "What?"

"Consort Ahassunu had taken a terrible wound to her stomach. The unborn cubs were in distress, her body already starting to abort them. Ishtar reached out and took them from the consort and put them here." Iltani touched the unmarked skin of her stomach, still in shock from the event. "That's why I was unconscious when you found me in the boat. My body needed time to adjust."

It seemed more dream than reality. Yet it was real. The blood link allowed her to sense the tiny sparks of life within her. They were strong and stable. Would those tiny unborn cubs help to ground Ditanu and convince him to surrender his rage and grief for a time?

"Ishtar be blessed," Kammani mumbled as she reached out and laid a hand over Iltani's stomach. "We could use some more good news."

A commotion at the door had the Shadows in the room jerking to attention and Iltani only then realized they had been edging closer to her. Curiosity? The need to protect? Iltani didn't know but didn't care either.

A young priestess was admitted into the room and she made straight for Kammani and then spotted Iltani. She froze, dropped into a deep bow at Iltani's feet and then glanced between the two older women nervously.

"What have you to report?" Kammani asked the young novice.

The girl's throat worked, but she found her voice. "The council moved forward with Beletum's plan as you expected they would. She slipped something in Ditanu's water before the Shadows could stop her. The council members said it was an herbal brew to increase the chances Ditanu would become fertile."

"When did this happen?" Kammani snapped.

"More than an hour ago. Councilor Ziyatum had guards outside the area. They wouldn't let me go. They kept me prisoner for an hour. Then I heard screaming. I don't know what was happening inside, but I think King Ditanu may have attacked Beletum as she entered the cage, and then I heard the councilors all shouting, and Shadows drawing weapons. When Ziyatum's guards were distracted, I escaped."

Iltani's heart started to pound, pumping adrenaline and rising magic throughout her body as it prepared for battle. She had already stayed here longer than she could stand with Ditanu in distress. She took Kuwari in her arms and she bolted out of the room at a run, leaving the others scrambling to follow. The Shadows were upon her in moments, the majority surrounding her in a wall of bodies while others moved ahead to clear the halls.

While Iltani could take care of herself, she didn't mind them clearing the way.

Kammani squeezed between the Shadows and hoisted a heavy sword harness at Iltani and then the sword itself. "You may not need it, but better to have it."

Iltani blinked at the crystal-bladed sword in her hands, a touch surprised she'd forgotten it.

"I would prefer our enemies not know you are Ishtar's Blade just yet," Kammani said as she hustled a cloak around her shoulders while Iltani fought with the harness's buckle one-handed. She wasn't used to carrying a cub and she suddenly had greater respect for mothers everywhere.

Iltani won the fight with the harness and glanced sideways at Kammani. "The element of surprise might allow us to catch our enemies off guard."

She grinned wickedly. "Besides, revealing myself might be far more opportune later."

A relatively short time later, Iltani was striding down the corridor that led to the practice ring. The main door, a massive construction of metal and oak wide enough to allow horses and chariots to pass through unhindered, was gaping open.

As she approached, there was movement at the entrance and a body came hurtling out to land in a heap on the floor. Iltani slowed her step, took one look at the fallen soldier, and noted he was still alive and mostly unharmed and that he was not a Shadow.

The Shadows surrounding her moved around the guard and on into the room. She cut around as well, but the priestess just stepped over him, her robes slapped at him as she moved.

Kammani raised an eyebrow at Iltani's look. "He's a fool fighting on the wrong side. He deserves far worse."

Iltani didn't bother with a reply. Instead, she pulled the cloak's cowl over her head and made certain Kuwari was hidden within the heavy folds. That done, she entered the practice ring to find the chaos she'd expected.

The Shadows with her spread out, quickly joining their brothers and sisters to help subdue the guards belonging to the house of Beletum. Once they made quick work of that, they shoved aside councilors and guards alike with equal disregard and cleared a path for High Priestess Kammani and Iltani.

As Iltani walked further into the sand ring, her eyes riveted upon a golden dome-like cage that took up the far end of the ring. Through the gold-tinted hazy walls, she could just make out the form of a gryphon pacing.

The closer she got, the easier it was to see inside the cage.

Ditanu was indeed in gryphon form. Iltani's eyes narrowed. Beletum was in gryphon form as well—although her formidable gryphon body had not been enough to protect her. She had collapsed on her side, panting, one shoulder and foreleg covered in blood where Ditanu had mauled her. Beletum's father stood over her protectively, a drawn sword in his hands.

He'd taken a nasty wound in his right leg, blood staining his robe and running down his leg to soak into the sand. Ditanu continued to pace and snarl at them. Iltani wished she knew whether Ditanu's drug addled mind had decided he wanted to mate the female after all, or if he simply wished to finish off his prey. It might be petty of her, but Iltani hoped his snarls meant he wished to kill, not breed.

One of the Shadows who had been with the king's contingent of body-guards, stepped forward and reported to Uselli. "King Ditanu attacked Beletum. Her father must have expected it, for as soon as it happened, his guards converged upon us and the distraction allowed her father to enter the cage before we could stop him. When we tried to pursue him, the dome locked itself down, preventing anyone else from entering. I believe Ziyatum sabotaged it to stop us from protecting Ditanu."

Iltani stepped up to the cage and reached out to trail her fingers along the golden dome. The power felt warm and familiar. Ishtar's power.

No. Ziyatum hadn't sabotaged the cage. Ishtar had. Iltani felt her goddess's presence. The Queen of the Night trusted her chosen king was capable of defeating both Beletum and her father.

Iltani frowned. Be that as it may, having Ditanu kill members of his council, even if their own stupidity was the cause, wasn't a good idea. Ditanu was wild enough, more so than she liked to see. Reasoning with him wasn't going to be easy as it was—she didn't need him descending farther into blood lust. Or any kind of lust for that matter. She eyed the big gryphon as he paced the confines of his cage.

Just what had that fool Beletum given him? And what was Iltani, herself, willing to do?

Kammani leaned closer and whispered in Iltani's ear. "He won't hurt you."

"I know."

"Good. Now go save Ditanu from killing those fools."

With a nod, Iltani paced halfway around the golden cage's perimeter and arrived at the 'door'. Two Shadows were flanking it, keeping the councilors and Beletum's guards at bay. When the Shadows acknowledged her presence with raised swords, she tilted her head back so they could see who was under the cloak.

Still, she kept Kuwari hidden from view. The cub had suffered enough traumas this day. He didn't need to see more adults waving swords at him. Kuwari made no sound, clinging to her body where she held him braced against one hip. She could feel his soft furry paws shifting against her skin from time to time, but his beak never so much as poked out of the robe to see what was going on. She doubted if the cub had any interest in anything except his father. Every few breaths, he'd draw in a deeper lungful, likely scenting for his father.

Iltani doubted he could detect anything through the shimmering of the cage's golden walls. Neither scents nor sounds filtered through that she noted. Her fingers trailed along its warm surface.

At least, she hoped that was why Ditanu still hadn't taken note of either her or the cub. If he was too far gone to recognize Kuwari, than Iltani didn't know what she'd do.

"Clear the room," Iltani whispered to Uselli.

He repeated her order with a sharp authority. The councilors started a righteous shouting and refused to leave. The Shadows started removing them bodily. Iltani touched the archway spell and the energy parted to allow her passage.

Her sudden arrival in the dome caught Ditanu's attention and he whirled towards the door, his beak gaping and his paw raised to strike. Every line in his body said he was going to charge at her, but that's not what caused her spike of fear.

Recognizing her mistake in the time between heartbeats, she reached out with a small trickle of Ishtar's magic. It wasn't enough to harm the tiny sparks of life in her womb, but it was enough to reshape one wall of the golden cage. The old councilor continued to rush at the king, his sword raised to kill, but the wall of magic got there first and Ziyatum's strike bounced off it harmlessly.

Ditanu twisted around to glare at Beletum and Ziyatum, his tail twitching angrily, but after a moment, he turned back to Iltani with a snarl.

She parted her cloak, revealing her mostly naked body with Kuwari clinging to her side.

His tufted ears rotated forward, no longer pinned to the side of his head. He dragged in a deep breath, releasing it in a huffing sound, the wordless question clear in the tone.

"Yes, it's Kuwari. He's real and alive."

After a full-bodied shake, Ditanu paced forward, stalking her.

Still holding one arm out away from her body while the other braced Kuwari in place, she wasn't prepared for the tackle Ditanu aimed at her. She didn't tumble to the floor. Instead, his weight slammed her against the cage wall. Her right shoulder made contact first, followed by that hip and then the rest of her body as two great paws planted against her shoulders pinned her against the shield. The magic at her back had some give to it, so it wasn't as painful as it could have been, but several older bruises made themselves known.

While she was still fighting for breath, Ditanu shoved her robe aside to get to Kuwari. He purred, rubbing his face against Kuwari. The cub answered, his softer calls a soothing counterpoint.

Ditanu recognized his cub. Iltani's throat tightened and tears flooded her eyes.

He made more of his coughing calls and started poking around under the robe. As quickly as the joy came, it plummeted again. Iltani's heart sank. He was looking for his other cubs. Perhaps he didn't remember they had died?

"My king, I'm sorry," she said, a hesitation in her voice. Would telling him about his unborn litter sooth some of the ache in his heart, or make it worse? She didn't know. However, the decision was taken from her when he suddenly stopped and shoved his beak against her abdomen and rubbed back and forth, pausing only long enough to press his nares against her skin, scenting a second time. His purring started up again, twice as intense as before.

The deep tone vibrated along her breastbone and unable to stop herself, she reached out with the hand not supporting Kuwari and caressed Ditanu's wild mane. She worked her fingers into the feathers on his head and then on down to where they merged into the thick rough of fur around his neck. His tufted ears twitched and he pressed his cheek against her bare shoulder, rumbling another wordless question.

"Yes, they are yours. Yours and Ahassunu's." *How I wish they were ours.* Iltani's throat closed tight, feeling dry as a sun-scorched rock, but she kept up the gentle caress of her fingers in his rough. He seemed to enjoy it and it kept him calm.

Calm was good. Calm was exactly what she wanted.

Why couldn't she feel half as mellow? Instead, she was a chaotic mix of guilt, happiness, love, and...yes...that heat curling through her body, which had been simmering ever since Ishtar had inhabited her during the blooding ceremony on the temple roof, was surely desire.

Ditanu half curled around her, his lion's tail curving along her back.

Wrapping her one arm around his head, she buried her face in his soft feathers and started crying.

"Please my king, you must come with me now. Kuwari and your unborn cubs need you to be strong. Come with me and I'll look after you." She rubbed her face against his feathers and hoped her king would return to himself.

He recognized Kuwari, but he didn't communicate and that worried her.

Still, he followed her to the edge of the cage and when she drew her cloak around herself again, hiding Kuwari from the view of those outside the cage, he paced her calmly enough.

It was all going well until they were outside the cage, and his Shadows slowly encircled him, putting themselves between him and any who might mean him harm. Ditanu snarled then, lashing out at one of his Shadows, knocking the hapless guard to the ground. Heart pounding, Iltani waited for the killing blow. It didn't come. Instead, Ditanu merely shoved Iltani farther away from the other males around them.

"Every male step back," the Priestess Kammani ordered. "He's protecting her."

The male Shadows eased back while the female ones came forward, filling in any gaps in their king's protection. When Ditanu didn't lash out at his female guards, she knew Priestess Kammani's assumption was correct.

Iltani walked from the sand-covered practice ring, Ditanu's Shadows trailing behind, clearly uncertain what to do to help their king. Iltani didn't actually know what to do to bring her king back from whatever part of his mind he was hiding in. She only hoped Priestess Kammani, who was trailing them knew enough to help.

CHAPTER
eighteen

H ER HEART IN her throat, Iltani beckoned Ditanu to follow her and then turned and started down the hall. The big gryphon paced her as she made her way back to the king's suites.

Priestess Kammani slid closer. Not so close as to gain a response from Ditanu, but near enough she could communicate to Iltani in a whisper. "Once you get back to his rooms, you need to show him he is still loved, that no matter how much pain he's in, he'll find joy again one day. Show him how to live for his cubs, if not his kingdom."

How was *she* supposed to draw Ditanu out from wherever he'd fled within his own mind? Yes, he showed recognition toward Kuwari, so she had hope that link and the tiny sparks of life in her womb would be enough to stabilize Ditanu and sway him back over to the side of the living. But beyond that, what else was she supposed to do?

Ditanu's own survival hadn't been enough for his father.

When the old king had lost his mate and most of his cubs, he'd snapped, attacking everyone and everything until his own body turned on itself.

Never having witnessed it, she didn't know if the old king had shown recognition of Ditanu after he'd descended into grief madness or not.

Her nagging doubts kept pace with her the entire length of the walk back to the king's chambers.

Turning to look over at Kammani, she asked, "Do you think he's past the worst of it?"

"I do," she answered calmly. "As long as you stay and shower him with love and keep Kuwari near, I think our king will recover. He'll need careful watching, but I have hope."

The heavy weight which had been threatening to crush her heart lifted. She would do anything Ditanu needed her to do, anything Ishtar asked, anything at all—raze mountain ranges, wage war until every beach turned red with blood, call storms the like the world had never seen to sink their enemies' ships—she'd do anything to see Ditanu safe and well once more.

Please let Kammani be correct.

So far, he'd been docile with her even though he showed a more aggressive side toward others.

Ditanu paced in front of her again, forcing her to stop. He pressed closer to Iltani, trying to nuzzle under her cloak to touch his cub. Kuwari huffed softly at his father and Ditanu relaxed marginally.

Although distracted by his cub, his vigilance never lessened, not even once they were safe in his rooms.

Continuing on to his bedchamber, Iltani crawled onto his bed and then gestured for him to join her. He paced the room's perimeter, seeking signs of enemies in the shadows and corners of the room. When he found nothing, he paced back toward her, huffing softly to catch her scent.

"Come, my king, join your cub." Iltani patted the bed and deposited the cub in the center while she moved closer to the head board to give him more room. Kammani's words still echoed in her head. Iltani just hoped rest, Kuwari's love and her own was enough to heal his grievous emotional wounds.

She doubted she could accomplish that on her own and prayed for Ishtar's guidance and aid.

When she patted the bed a second time, he bound up onto it and nuzzled his cub for some minutes. After Kuwari had fallen asleep, Ditanu rose to all fours. He came straight for her, not halting until he was standing over her, his massive bulk dwarfing her and making her feel tiny and vulnerable.

Ditanu's large front paw batted at her and she was suddenly on her back, pinned down by his paw as he pressed his face into her stomach. First, his smooth hard, beak and then the soft feathers of his cheeks rubbed over her belly. Iltani made herself go limp, giving Ditanu no reason to strike out at her, although in her heart, she refused to believe that he could or would hurt her.

He purred and then began scent marking her. The soft rasp of his feathers against her skin tickled and she fought the urge to laugh. After long moments of scent marking her, he finally stopped and allowed her to sit up. While she was gaining her composure, Ditanu had picked Kuwari up by the scruff of his neck and was carrying him back over to Iltani. After a moment, he gently lowered the cub into Iltani's lap.

Kuwari wiggled and circled, making a nest out of the tattered fabric of her skirt. It was blood-stained and sand coated, but the cub didn't seem to care. She petted Kuwari for long moments until the exhausted cub fell asleep again.

Turning her attention to Ditanu, she raised her right hand and carefully caressed his face and neck, her touch light and rhythmic. "That's it. Relax. Stop fighting and rest for a while."

"He must not fall asleep while still in gryphon form, not weakened as he is." Priestess Kammani pulled aside one of the hanging drapes to peer in at Iltani, Kuwari and Ditanu. "The greatest danger now is that his human side will slip away, leaving behind only predatory instincts to rule him."

Frowning with renewed worry, Iltani's gaze darted between her king and the high priestess. Then Kammani held out a bowl filled with some kind of liquid.

"Get him to drink this. It's an herbal stimulant. After he drinks it, you need to convince him to shift back into human form."

"How am I supposed to do that? He's exhausted. Even if the stimulant works enough to bring him around again, I don't think he's rational enough to understand we want him to shift back to human form."

Kammani didn't look up from her satchel as she sorted through the contents. After she had dumped another dusting of ground herbs into the 'drink', she looked up at last. "He doesn't have to be particularly rational—we just need him human. Once he's human, you can work on healing him, both mind, body and spirit."

She held the drink out to Iltani.

"Fine. Rational, not required." Iltani came to her knees and laid Kuwari on the pillows beside her. A large paw swiped out and knocked Iltani flat. Again.

Body tense, she waited for the sharp claws to tear flesh, shredding her fragile skin. The wide paw flexed gently. Lethal claws dimpled the skin of her lower back but they did not draw blood. A moment later a wing mantled over her prone body while a paw dragged her back to his side.

Now that Iltani was back where he wanted her apparently, he drifted off to sleep within moments.

"Hmmm," the priestess's voice rose to be heard over Ditanu's purring. "Getting that great lazy lion to shift back may require some rethinking on our part."

The crackle of paper wrapped herbs and Ditanu's purring were the only sounds that reached her under the shelter of his wing. While being pinned belly down on Ditanu's bed might have, upon rare occasions, snuck into a few of her dreams, this was not how she imagined it.

Fool of a woman, she scolded herself, get your mind on more important things.

"Kammani, what if I summon my magic? Use that to see if he'll rouse?"

"No, we can't risk it. Your body and the unborn cubs need to adjust. To use any great working of magic—not just battle magic—in the coming days might cause your body to abort them."

Cold dread lanced through her middle.

No, she would not lose Ditanu's cubs. They were hers now, hers to protect. She'd failed the other two. She wouldn't fail these little ones.

"Get him up. I don't care what you have to do." Kammani pushed the drink closer to Iltani. "He needs to drink this. Now."

Pushing up onto her elbows, she shoved his wing back and rolled to her feet. She walked toward the dish of herb-laced water and picked it up. Ditanu rumbled in warning and came to his feet, too.

Well good, that was easier than she thought.

Iltani navigated the bed, keeping her feet under her even when Ditanu pounced across the distance to block her escape.

"I'm not trying to escape." She ran her fingers through his mane. "I only wanted this." She held out the drink for him to sniff.

"Once he drinks that," Kammani's voice intruded again. "I have something you should drink too. It will give you much needed energy."

Iltani glanced over her shoulder, her eyes narrowing. There was something in the priestess's tone. "You make it sound like the battle has yet to begin."

"Hmmm," Kammani huffed humorlessly, "I don't doubt for a moment we have many more battles before we put an end to our enemies, but that is not what I was referring to."

Tapping a finger against her thigh, Iltani watched and waited for the rest, but the priestess didn't elaborate. Well, fine. Jerking her attention back to

Ditanu, she held out the bowl of water toward him again. To her complete surprise, he dipped his beak down and drank it dry.

Well, that was easy.

"Good," Kammani commented.

More Shadows arrived. Uselli eased into the bedchamber, while others waited in the outer rooms and the hallway beyond. Still, she could sense them all. It didn't matter how far away they were. They were linked to the king, and her blood link to Ditanu allowed her to sense all his Shadows.

Ditanu rose from where he was resting on the bed and glared at Uselli. His tail flicked with agitation, but he didn't attack. That had to be a sign of improvement. He was far more wakeful than earlier, his eyes clear and focused as he watched everything going on in his domain. Still, for all there was the look of returning vigor, there was no sign of Ditanu the king. Presently, the watchful male on the bed was all gryphon parent.

Kammani had stopped what she was doing when Uselli arrived and they talked in soft voices. Ditanu growled softly, clearly not liking a male in his territory. Iltani sidestepped, blocking Ditanu's line of sight of Uselli.

Ditanu's pinned ears relaxed, and his growls switched to purrs.

"Yes, that's it. Focus on your unborn cubs and me. Ignore poor Uselli." Iltani allowed her hands to rest lightly upon his head, giving his ears another soft scratch.

The big gryphon continued his purring, but he now ran his beak along her bare belly and pressed his ear against her skin. His eyes drifted closed and she felt the tension leak out of him.

Priestess Kammani and Uselli communicated in hushed voices, unaware they'd been moments away from being attacked. Iltani's heart was slowing back to its normal rhythm and she started to pay attention to their whispered conversation. The words 'Sacred Marriage' sent her heart back to pounding. Her stomach turned leaden as a cold sweat broke out on her skin.

"Sacred Marriage? You can't possibly expect us to. . . .there's no way. He barely made it this far before he collapsed."

"The herbs will give him stamina." Kammani half turned and raised one elegant eyebrow at Iltani. "This is Ishtar's wish. How she plans to heal our gryphon king."

"He has a mate."

Kammani gave her an amused look. "Yes. He does."

"It's not possible, not physically. He's still in gryphon form."

"Yes, yes he is," Kammani said and rolled her eyes. "But Ditanu will shift to human form if you give him a compelling reason. Ishtar already gave her blessing, earlier. We all witnessed it. I am certain if you both please the goddess, she will grant Ditanu a long life."

Iltani would do anything to see Ditanu restored, but this? This wasn't anything like what her heart craved. She'd always wanted Ditanu to choose her, not be forced into it by Ishtar.

When Iltani didn't answer, Kammani sighed. "Well, you know Ishtar is the goddess of fertility, love and war. Today you've seen her aspect as a war goddess," Kammani paused and pointed to where Iltani had set down her crystalline sword and then next pointed at Iltani's slightly rounded belly, "and you've seen her as a granter of life. Soon you will see her as a goddess of love."

"I understand." Oh, dear goddess. Those two words made it sound so easy.

"Good," Kammani said with a gentle smile. "You'll need to convince him to return to human form. I don't think you'll find that too difficult."

"Of course." Iltani felt a flush creep up her face.

"Now, see if you can get Ditanu to part with Kuwari for a while. I'll see to his care for tonight. You'll have enough on your hands. I'll stay in Ditanu's study with Kuwari. That is about as far away as Ditanu will allow, and even then, you'll have some trouble convincing him I imagine. "When you're ready, bring the cub to me."

Iltani glanced at the drowsing Ditanu where he'd laid back down, curled around his cub.

Yes. Iltani would have a lot on her hands tonight. Come the morning, would she even be able to look herself in a mirror after she'd stripped all Ditanu's choices away in the night?

To save her king, she would have to betray her king.

CHAPTER
nineteen

ER EMOTIONS AND self-doubt shoved aside until tomorrow, Iltani approached Ditanu. Seeing her, he sat up and greeted her with a purr. She didn't even know if he still had the resources needed to shift forms.

"I know you're tired, but I need you to shift back into a man soon." She scratched around his ears. The big gryphon stretched and purred, pressing into her touch, but still he didn't communicate verbally.

"I'm going to give Kuwari into Kammani's keeping for a little while—he needs undisturbed sleep and milk to recover fully." Something the cub wasn't likely to get here if Ishtar had her way. This was the dicey part. Iltani slowly scooped the sleeping cub up into her arms. "Kammani has some milk for him. He won't be far, just over here in the other room."

Iltani eased off the bed. Ditanu didn't attack, but he jumped down and followed her as if in a trance. When Iltani crossed the threshold, she quickly spotted where Kammani had settled among the pile of pillows by the fire. A bowl of milk and a rag sat next to her.

Ditanu oversaw the cub changing hands, only watching silently as Kammani settled down among the pillows and took the sleeping cub.

"I think it's best if Kuwari remains asleep until later," Kammani was saying as she held out the milk dampened rag for Ditanu's inspection. "If I thought Ditanu would let him out of these suites, I'd take Kuwari to the nursery to give you a touch more privacy."

There would still be an audience of Shadows.

There were always Shadows.

Besides, it wasn't like they hadn't heard or glimpsed their king and his consort together before.

At least this Sacred Marriage would only be witnessed by a few Shadows unlike the highly ritualized ones of the past where ruler and Blade performed high up in the open air temple with all the citizens of the ten city-states looking on from below.

The knowledge that it could be so much worse helped ground her enough, her pounding heart and the nervous flutter in her stomach calmed.

While she'd been woolgathering, Ditanu had begun pacing back and forth between his bed chamber and his study, clearly wanting Iltani and the cub in the same room, and confused by the separation and becoming unhappy about it. He turned to start back to his cub for the fourth time when Iltani called him. He paused at the threshold, looking over his shoulder.

Not seeing a better time, Iltani shrugged off the cloak that Kammani had given her and then untied the scarf covering her breasts. After a small fight with the ornate belt, she got it loose and the remnants of her tattered skirt fell to the floor. She glanced down at her scarred, blood smeared, and bruised body.

Iltani only hoped Ishtar was with her and that Ditanu would find her somewhat appealing.

A soft, heated magic swirled through her blood, expanding out with each beat of her heart. Ah, Ishtar hadn't abandoned her to deal with this alone.

Naked, she dropped to her knees and moved closer, hoping to appear as non-threatening as possible because Ditanu was getting more worked up about his aunt having his cub.

Iltani's throat tightened with fear and nerves. It took two tries before she managed to spit out the words that wanted to stay trapped in her throat. "I know I am no substitute for your mate, but I'm still here and won't leave you ever again."

Crawling the last of the distance, she wrapped her arms around his neck in a fierce embrace. He didn't strike out. Encouraged, she ran her fingers through his thick lion's rough—the mix of fur and downy feathers incredibly soft against her skin.

Ishtar's blessing came in a wave of mellow power flooding outward from a knot under her heart and racing down her arms and fingers, and on into Ditanu. The big gryphon purred and rubbed his face against her torso, nearly knocking Iltani over backwards.

After slowly rising to her feet, she stepped backward, heading for the bed directly behind her. Ditanu followed though the occasional glance behind told her he still hadn't forgotten his cub. Iltani yelped in surprised when her legs came in contact with the bed, and she sat down heavily. Ditanu barely gave her time to recover her balance before he jumped up beside her.

He examined her, his sharp gaze roving over her from the top of her head to the tips of her toes and then back again. There was something else in his look now, a new heat that hadn't been there before.

Interest. Male interest.

That was good, that was what she'd hoped for. Still, it made her feel deeply uncomfortable.

Iltani crawled backward, shuffling toward the head of the bed.

"Ditanu, I need you to shapeshift into a man so we may better honor the Queen of the Night."

If her words penetrated far enough into his mind to touch his human side, nothing in his expression showed it.

Iltani very much wanted his human side, not his gryphon nature, to be in command for the next few hours.

Come on, shapeshift. How much more obvious can I be? Shift, damn it.

Iltani ran into one of the pillows that marked the head of the bed. Wanting something else to keep her fingers busy for a few heartbeats more, she reached out to the sash holding the drape aside. With a couple tugs, the ties came undone and the gauzy drapes fell into place. At least, it gave some semblance of privacy. She couldn't reach the opposite one without crawling across the entire width of the bed, so she left it, allowing her eyes to track back to Ditanu.

Gasping in surprise, her hand twisted in the bedding as she took in the form of a very human and very naked Ditanu crouched at the end of the bed, poised less than two body lengths distant.

She wanted to feel relief that he was human and no longer gryphon, and she did. However, she'd have felt much more relieved if the old human Ditanu was present, but it was the intense gryphon soul that looked out of Ditanu's eyes, not the gentle king she'd grown up with.

Perhaps it was better this way.

It would feel less like she was betraying the man she loved.

Yes, she told herself, this was just about serving Ishtar.

Ditanu crawled across the bed toward her. It was more stalk than crawl she admitted, and damned sensual, too. Only he could make scrambling across a bed in slow motion look anything but awkward.

Iltani issued a startled sound when Ditanu reached out and wrapped strong fingers around her ankle and pulled her down the bed toward him.

It wasn't painful or violent, but the show of strength still convinced that small pit of fear in her stomach to double in size. He lowered himself onto his elbows so he could plant a kiss on the bottom of her foot.

The new position hid some of his nudity from her, but she'd still seen that he'd become aroused. His body had filled out over the last four years. Even as an adolescent, he'd been breathtaking to behold. Now he was easily the most beautifully masculine thing she'd ever laid eyes upon.

She licked her lips nervously. The banked desire which had been simmering it her blood, uncoiled, making her ache deep inside. Self-consciousness had her pressing her thighs together.

Ditanu drew in a deep breath, his nostrils flaring to catch her scent, and then he studied her long moments, his expression unfathomable.

"Yes, I'm nervous," she said, still unable to read anything in his expression of the Ditanu she knew. "You would be too if our positions were reversed."

"There is no need," Ditanu said. "Ishtar and I have been lovers for an eternity. We will take care of you and your king."

"Who?" Even as Iltani asked, Ishtar's presence grew within her mind.

Tammuz, god of the harvest. My beloved husband. He will heal your gryphon king and make him whole again for you.

"All we ask is that you allow us to enjoy your bodies this night," Tammuz continued, "and in exchange, all our power is yours to call upon in times of need. Come morning, your beloved Ditanu will be healed." He crawled farther up her body to caress her cheek. "We will not force you, but I have missed my beloved Ishtar and hope you agree. I dwell in the underworld, Ishtar in the mortal. This is the only way her sister, Ereshkigal, will allow me to leave her underworld." Tammuz laughed. "I promise, Ishtar and I will leave you and your king with very good memories."

His tone, so similar to Ditanu's, made her body flush and ache, her breasts suddenly overly sensitive and heavy. One powerful hand stroked up her side, his thumb caressing the underside of her left breast, and her mind ceased all function.

Tammuz leaned down and pressed Ditanu's mouth against her navel. Iltani nearly jumped out of her skin.

"Shhh, Little Blade. No harm will come to you. This is the power of Ishtar's pact with the line of the gryphon kings. Even Ereshkigal cannot prevent us from coming together for the Sacred Marriage."

Ishtar's power swirled stronger, but still it didn't take over Iltani's body. A slow realization dawned—the gods were waiting for her permission.

"Did Ditanu agree?"

"He did," Tammuz answered. There was no deception in his look and his lips curved with a familiar slow humor. "And he instructed me to call you his beautiful Little Shadow."

His words and warm breath slid across her body, causing a case of fresh nerves to tighten her stomach. Ditanu needed this. The gods promised to return him to himself, healed and whole. As for Iltani herself, she wanted to know what it felt like to make love to her king.

"I agree." Iltani slid her hands up Ditanu's arms, caressing her way up to his shoulders. Tammuz or Ditanu leaned down for a kiss, and she welcomed him. As a fire built in her blood, she arched her back, pressing her breasts against his chest as she parted her thighs to better cradle his.

Ishtar rose within her then. Iltani surrendered her body to the Queen of the Night, sure in the knowledge Ishtar would have her Tammuz for a few hours and come the morning, Iltani would get her king back.

"Welcome, my beloved," she heard Tammuz greet Ishtar, his love for her clear in his voice.

The thought of the Sacred Marriage ceased to frighten Iltani and she drifted, a passenger in her own body, but no longer afraid.

CHAPTER *twenty*

ILTANI'S SLEEPING MIND told her it was close to dawn and yet she dreamed as if still deeply asleep. Although, now that she thought about it, this didn't feel like a normal dream. This was sharper, edged with Ishtar's familiar power. It nudged her spirit, demanding she follow. With a sigh, for she truly was tired, Iltani's spirit followed where Ishtar led.

Once again, Iltani's viewpoint of the world changed as the Queen of the Night dragged her consciousness into another body. Taking in her surrounding with a glance, she recognized she was in a seldom used part of the island. There were catacombs below the palace where she and Ditanu had used to explore as children.

The catacombs had once been used as cold cellars for storage until one of the mountain streams had changed its course over time and the storm season runoff had started to find its way into these tunnels.

Now they were abandoned even though they only flooded part of the time.

Or they should have been abandoned. Except they weren't. Whoever Ishtar had merged her with was slowly making her way through the corridors. The slowness of her walk had nothing to do with her unfamiliarity with the tunnels. Some injury slowed her and she limped.

A slim hand held the torch before her as she walked, carefully picking her way around debris from past floods.

Female. Cloaked and hooded. Walking with a limp down never used tunnels. She certainly wasn't here for a pleasant walk.

A stranger the Queen of the Night, wanted Iltani to see.

One of the traitors?

Most probably.

As much as Iltani would have preferred a few moments rest after the events of the last day—this too was important. It might be the only lead she'd get about the traitors.

Thank you, for this, great Ishtar.

The woman continued to walk until she came to a door. It opened smoothly under her hand. No noise, only the smooth glide of recently oiled hinges. The stranger preceded through another door, entering a dimly lit room. Three other strangers turned at her arrival.

Cloaks of dark gray, good quality wool hid their identities. With the cowls pulled up, the dark recesses didn't offer Iltani as much as a glimpse of the faces inside.

"You're late," said the tallest of the cloaked strangers, his voice deep with a slight gruff edge to it. Older? Or perhaps a voice damaged by smoke from the fires which had very recently burned on the island of Uruk? Neither possibility told her much about his identity, unfortunately.

"I couldn't get away without causing suspicion. Would you have preferred I led a bunch of Shadows to our meeting?"

"Your sarcasm is not welcome," the man snapped. "None of us will be safe if we fail Ereshkigal again, she is not as forgiving of failure as her sister."

"And Ishtar is not forgiving of traitors," the woman said. "So we won't fail Ereshkigal."

Ereshkigal? Back in the bed where her body still slept, Iltani's heart started to pound with adrenaline. These traitors were serving Ishtar's sister, the queen of the underworld? That would explain how they had sabotaged the city-states defenses. But why? What did they have to gain by destroying their own kingdom?

More important at present: whose body was Iltani inhabiting? Iltani's first suspicion was Beletum, but the king had given her terrible wounds. It was doubtful Beletum would be back on her feet so soon. Not even gryphons healed that fast.

"How can we fix this disaster?" Another male growled. He was slightly shorter than the first man and broader across the chest, too. "One of Ditanu's cubs was supposed to survive the battle so we could convert it to worship Ereshkigal, assuring her rise from the underworld. Ditanu's cubs are dead and he is mad with grief. Ereshkigal will be livid."

How had these strangers lived to plot so long? There must be more to their network of traitors than just these four. How much power did they wield? How high up did the corruption run?

Back in the king's bed, Iltani's hands curled into fists as rage rushed over her body. She would hunt down all the traitors and cut out this infection before she let any of them near Kuwari or her king.

Iltani's host body nodded in agreement to the shorter cloaked male. "I agree this has not gone as we planned. Yes, we need a cub, but I think Kuwari still lives. That cloaked figure Kammani brought to the king—he was very interested in getting under her cloak, and I do not mean in a mating way. I am certain that was Iltani with Kuwari."

The fourth stranger spoke for the first time. "Ereshkigal be merciful. Let it be true."

"I am certain it was Iltani. No one else would have been foolish enough to go in that dome at that time." The woman shivered. "She was lucky Ditanu didn't try to tear her apart, too."

"Do you think the king will survive?" The fourth cloaked figure spoke for the first time. A male, but a mild sounding one. Young perhaps?

"You saw him. He was worse than his father. No, Ditanu is already dead or will be by nightfall, and then Kuwari will be vulnerable. The council will name a regent."

"Your hunch better be correct for we have no other plan. If we fail, we will be found out. Ishtar will kill us and send us to Ereshkigal. Ereshkigal will torture us for an eternity for ruining her plans."

"There is that." Iltani's host body agreed. "It will not be an enjoyable wait, but we must. Once Ditanu dies, his Shadows will protect the cub most viciously. We will have to slowly earn their trust while at the same time gaining control over the council."

"Kammani will be a problem," The broad-shouldered man reasoned, and reached up to scratch at his jaw. "She will likely try to assert herself as regent."

"She'll have to be taken out," the woman agreed.

"I'll worry about that," the older man said.

The room with the four traitors faded and Iltani's spirit was cast adrift once more.

A moment's dislocation and she was housed inside her own body once more, her dreams became normal nightmares.

CHAPTER
twenty-one

THE DREGS OF sleep threatened to pull Iltani back down into sleep's arms, but there was something important in the waking world she should face. Doubt nudged her closer to wakefulness. Something was wrong. Normally she awoke easily.

Either Burrukan had been particularly vicious in his training session yesterday or she'd been celebrating and drank far too much wine. Still, this didn't feel anything like an over indulgence of wine.

Safety, warmth, and comfort cocooned her in a way she'd rarely experienced—and not for many, many years at that. This was different than that long ago time when she and the cub Ditanu had shared a nest in their old nursery room.

Then memory returned and so too did all the horrors of yesterday's attack: the battle, the death of two of Ditanu's cubs, and Ahassunu and Burrukan's sacrifice to give Ishtar time to spirit her away.

So much horror, death, and betrayal.

Last night came back to her. It was impossible not to remember with Ditanu's arm around her waist, his warm breath caressing the back of her neck. He was still asleep, curled around her. Her blood link to him allowed her to feel his sleeping mind. There was a calmness that had been lacking the night before.

Dare she hope Ditanu was himself again?

It would make what she'd done last night more acceptable if New Sumer had had its king restored to them. If she'd been looking for a scapegoat, she could blame it all on Ishtar's ways, but Iltani would still know the truth. She'd most certainly enjoyed making love to Ditanu and waking in his arms easily made the list of her most pleasant experiences.

The arm around her waist tightened suddenly and Ditanu muttered in his sleep. If he were anything like he'd been as a boy, he'd still be a heavy sleeper, hard to wake even on the best of mornings. She hoped that was true because she needed to empty her bladder, and there was no way she still wanted to be in Ditanu's bed when he awoke.

She didn't know how much he would remember from the night before. Even if there were blank spots, he'd realize what had occurred quickly enough. Gryphons had a superior sense of smell even in human form. He wouldn't miss the evidence of their lovemaking.

However, she could and would give him a few moments to wake up and make peace with what had occurred between them. If their roles had been reversed, she'd want a few minutes to come to terms with the knowledge she'd betrayed the memory of a mate before their body was even cold.

Sitting up, Iltani gently moved his arm and then looked down at him. Even though he was in desperate need of a bath, he was still the image of male beauty, just breathtaking.

The guilt Iltani expected to feel this morning was strangely absent.

"I don't regret anything I did to save you," Iltani whispered and she shifted away from him and eased out of the bed. "But if you have to hate me a little for accepting the Sacred Marriage, I'll understand."

A quick search of the bed revealed two robes had been placed at its foot. Another quick scan of the room showed several Shadows stationed at various points throughout the room. Mostly by doors and windows.

None tried to talk to her.

Thank Ishtar.

Not paying them any more mind, she made for the bath chamber.

She didn't want to so much as look anyone in the eye. Ishtar and Tammuz had been anything but quiet.

Once she'd attended to her needs, she eyed the bath, wondering if she had time to get a quick one before Ditanu awoke. She settled for a quick wash and then exited. After a look to confirm Ditanu still slept, she padded to the other room where Kuwari and Priestess Kammani were sleeping.

Iltani crouched down next to them both and gently shook the priestess awake. Kammani blinked her eyes open and glanced around with far more composure than Iltani thought possible.

All business, the older woman first looked over Kuwari and then Iltani. "Ishtar awoke me in the night so I could check on you and the king to know you were both well." The priestess stood, smoothing out her wrinkled robes. "You both pleased the gods."

A wave of heat climbed Iltani's cheeks. She wasn't sure what was worse. That Ditanu's aunt had checked on them in the night or that Ishtar had been sharing intimate secrets with her high priestess.

"Ditanu will be himself when he wakes?" There had been times near the end when she thought Ditanu recognized her, but he'd fallen asleep moments after Tammuz had retreated. Iltani hadn't had a chance to ascertain how aware Ditanu was of his…surroundings.

"Yes," Kammani gave her a pat on the shoulder, "You saved our king, the unborn cubs, and Kuwari. That should gain any mere mortal a few days' rest, but not you. We have much still to do. Here," she handed Kuwari into Iltani's arms, "I need to see about getting this one some fresh milk. He wasn't interested in drinking last night, but I imagine he'll wake up hungry."

Two Shadows burst in from the bedchamber at the same moment Iltani heard an anguished cry from that direction.

"The king has awakened," they said in unison.

"Go, go." Kammani shoved Iltani toward the sound. "Ditanu needs to see both you and his cub alive. There's no telling how much he'll remember from last night."

Oh, great goddess. Panic flooded Iltani's mind even as she broke into a run, Kuwari held tight in her arms. The motion jostled the cub awake and he gave a plaintive grumble. Iltani ignored him as she burst into the bedchamber.

The gauzy drapes around his bed obscured Ditanu from her sight.

"Ditanu!" She brushed away one curtain, the gauzy fabric tearing in her haste. Her feet tangled in the bits hanging down and she miscalculated the height of the bed. Her jump fell short, her foot catching on the side of the bed, tripping her. With her arms full of cub, she couldn't get her balance in time and had to roll in mid-air so as not to crush the cub. She landed with a grunt and had the wind knocked from her. Before she even had her breath back, she was on her knees, holding Kuwari out to Ditanu.

"Iltani? Kuwari?" His voice came out hoarse, strained, his great emotional pain evident, but so to was a hint of incredulous hope.

He sat up so quickly he sent pillows toppling sideways off the bed. Kuwari decided it was time to play and pounced on his father. His big hands scooped Kuwari against his bare chest and then he buried his face in the cub's fluffy down.

Tears came to her eyes as she watched Ditanu. His shoulders shook as he cried silently and curled forward around his cub.

Needing to do something to offer comfort, she reached out and stroked her hand along his shoulder and partway down his back.

After a time, her touch must have penetrated for he quieted and then glanced up at her. "Iltani? It's really you?"

"My king," she acknowledged and bowed to him. "You are not alone."

"You're not a spirit here to guide me to the afterlife?"

Iltani glanced up through her lashes, debating what to say. At last, she huffed, "A ghost would have made a much more elegant entrance, I imagine."

"When I woke….I thought last night was…that you were dead and Tammuz took you to the underworld with him…and last night was your goodbye to me." His words came out halting. "I couldn't face a future without you in it."

Iltani didn't know what to say so she hugged him fiercely. The arm not holding Kuwari circled her back and he shook with silent tears.

"I know I wasn't able to save everyone you love, and I did things that you might see as a betrayal, but Kuwari needed his father." Her free hand went to her stomach and curved along the slight belly she now sported. "And your unborn cubs will need you in the coming days."

Which was a truth Iltani was only coming to realize now. The blooding ceremony would need to be performed several more times over the coming months to allow her body to complete its change to gryphon. She would die without further exchanges of Ditanu's blood, and the unborn cubs were only exasperating the stresses on her body, but now wasn't a good time to bring that up. He needed to come to terms with the fact she was his litter's new surrogate.

Again, shock marked his expression, but his eyes narrowed after a moment, turning thoughtful. He reached out, unceremoniously parting her robe and then pressed his hand against her belly. His gryphon magic raced over her skin, studying her. His glance sought out hers again.

She answered his unasked question. "Ishtar took them from Consort Ahassunu after she'd been injured."

Ditanu still watched her, silent and unmoving, his unreadable king's mask back in place. Nothing in his expression gave his thoughts away.

Swallowing hard, she debated telling him the rest, but he deserved to at least know what she'd seen. "I was protecting Kuwari, and after Ishtar had placed the unborn cubs with me, I saw Burrukan and Consort Ahassunu and the few remaining shadows make a desperate last stand. Ishtar had already put Kuwari and me in a boat and then called fog in from the ocean to hide us. I'm sorry. I didn't see what happened to them in the end." Iltani looked down at her hands, not able to meet Ditanu's eyes. "My body was still accepting the unborn litter and Ishtar put me to sleep."

Still he said nothing, and she didn't look up. The rustle of blankets told her he moved and then he was placing Kuwari back in her arms. While she was still securing the cub, Ditanu reached out, his one arm going around her shoulder and the other under her knees. Yelping in surprise, she found herself lifted up and deposited back down in Ditanu's lap. Once he had her settled, his arms wrapped around her shoulders and dragged her against his chest.

"Iltani, thank you for saving Kuwari and my unborn cubs. Thank you for not leaving me." A sob shook his frame a moment before his lips brushed her hair. After a second silent sob shook his body, he rested a cheek against the top of her head.

Her earlier insecurities melted away. This was Ditanu. They had spent most of their lives together. As desperately as she wanted to know just how much he remembered from last night, in another way, it didn't matter at all. She was both his Shadow and his Blade and would forever serve him in whatever capacity he needed.

He rubbed his cheek against her hair again. "I know there is much I must do to assure my kingdom and its people are safeguarded, but the part of me who is simply a man wants to grieve. I will need your strength in the coming days."

"I will be whatever you need." If that was a friend's shoulder to shed his grief upon, she would be that shoulder, even if her own body's cravings threatened to steal her sanity.

"I know." Ditanu's one hand slid down her arm and then ventured back up, he repeated his gentle caress twice more before he stopped. Iltani would be surprised if he were even aware of the action. "And you have always been whatever I needed, haven't you?"

Iltani could pretend ignorance, but she knew what he spoke of. How could she not, it was the only thing she could think of. "Yes, Ishtar and Tammuz healed you by having us perform the Sacred Marriage."

"Ah," He grunted softly.

"Ah?" she asked, needing to hear something more.

He pulled back enough he could look down at her. A long finger hooked under her chin and tilted her head back so she met his gaze. "Were you willing? Or did Ishtar overwhelm you with her desires?"

His question caught her off guard. Was it asked out of curiosity? Or fear and guilt that she was a victim? Iltani was already feeling vulnerable with all that had gone on, but she wouldn't allow Ditanu to feel even the slightest guilt, even if by answering truthfully she was revealing more about her own desires than she might want.

"I was willing. You know Ishtar's Blade would do anything for her gryphon king." It sounded far too intimate even saying it that way, but it was true. Ditanu needed to hear many truths if their kingdom was to survive.

Kuwari had been silent and mostly still, but he kept raising his head and looking up at her expectantly. Finally with a disgusted sound of annoyance, he squealed.

"He's hungry," Ditanu said, and not bothering to get up, he called for a servant to bring him milk for the cub.

Kammani soon returned with the milk and a converted water skin. Iltani had wanted to move, to give Ditanu a few moments with his cub, but he wouldn't let her out of his lap.

"You are Kuwari's mother now," Ditanu said simply, a peaceful expression in his eyes as he watched his cub nuzzle at Iltani's breasts. "He'll expect you to be the one to feed him, even if it is just from the milk skin."

Ditanu reached around from behind and cupped her breasts, protecting them from Kuwari's more vigorous attempts to nurse as he explained the way of it to his cub. "Kuwari, I know you are hungry, but you will have to settle for the milk skin."

The strong fingers at her breast had her thoughts scattering in all directions. Ditanu might not even be aware of what he was doing to her body. It wasn't until he shifted his hands to Kuwari and stuck the water skin's 'teat' into the cub's mouth that she was able to master speech.

"That isn't. I wasn't. I have no intention of trying to replace your mate. I know gryphons form strong, unbreakable mating bonds. As for Kuwari and the unborn cubs, I am not as presumptuous as to usurp Consort Ahassunu's role. I care only that the next generation of gryphon kings prospers. If you would prefer someone else nurture Kuwari, I understand."

His grief, she could do nothing for, but Iltani hoped her words would give Ditanu some peace and free him from any guilt he might feel about what had occurred.

Again a finger hooked under her jaw and tilted her head until she was looking into Ditanu's eyes. His hand shifted to cup the side of her face. "Why would they need another mother when they have Ishtar's Blade to protect and provide for them? I am happier than I can say to know you survived and are here with me in this dark time."

Iltani didn't know what to make of the look in his eyes, but it breathed new life into an impossible hope, one which was probably better left buried.

He tucked her against his chest, her face buried against his neck. After another moment, he rested his head upon her hair. "I am thankful Ishtar chose you for the Sacred Marriage and not one of her other priestesses. I couldn't have abided anyone else. You are a part of me. My Shadow."

His statement didn't require an answer, for which she was grateful. In her present state, she'd spill her heart to her king in one embarrassing long speech. She closed her eyes and relaxed against him, content to stay exactly where she was. Besides, Kuwari was still nursing from his milk skin. Iltani arranged it so the 'teat' was suspended in the valley between her breasts at a somewhat natural angle for the cub to nurse from.

"You do that well." Ditanu reached out to stroke his cub's head.

Iltani grunted in acknowledgement. It was good Ditanu was already a father and knew something about the care and feeding of cubs. Iltani didn't know the first thing about being a mother, but it probably required a strong inner strength, something she had in abundance.

She'd make Ditanu proud, and maybe one day, she could give him comfort outside of the Sacred Marriage. The traitorous thought refused to go away no matter how many times she tried to shove it back into the part of her mind that housed her deepest, most foolish desires.

His mate was barely cold for Ishtar's sake, and Ditanu had no idea his consort was unfaithful.

Slowly her whirling thoughts calmed, soothed by the sounds of Kuwari nursing and of Ditanu's heart under her ear. She drifted to sleep feeling the rhythmic stroking of his hand down her hair. Firm lips pressed against her cheek and grazed the side of her mouth, but that might have been nothing more than the beginnings of a dream.

CHAPTER
twenty-two

ILTANI AWOKE SLOWLY to the sounds of conversation. Shifting out from underneath a heavy cover, she sat up and scanned what she could see of the room from behind the partly closed drapes. Someone was pacing.

First Ditanu's and then his aunt's voice drifted to her. She tossed back the covers and realized her robe was gone. She was naked again—it was becoming an alarming habit. She found a clean robe laid across the end of the bed for her. She shoved her arms into it and was still tying the belt when she emerged from the shadowy sanctuary of the bed.

Ditanu was standing next to the hearth, Kuwari snuggled in his arms while he had a heated debate with Kammani. It looked to have been going on for some time.

"I need to go before the council now. My kingdom is in shambles!"

Priestess Kammani planted a fist on her hip. "Send Iltani. You are not ready to face the council yet. Wait another day. Grieve. Bury your cubs."

Ditanu's jaw flexed and his skin paled. "I will grieve later, once I know everyone else who depends on me is safe."

"I repeat, send Iltani in your place. Let her ferret out the traitors before you give them another chance to end the line of the gryphon kings. If you die, Iltani dies, your unborn cubs with her—she still needs your blood until her metamorphosis is complete and she can take on gryphon form. And if you and Iltani both die, how long do you think little Kuwari will last? Send Iltani! Let her do her job."

Iltani joined them in front of the fire. "I've only heard the tail end of this conversation, but Kammani speaks wisdom. The council might not fear lowly Iltani, but once they learn I am Ishtar's Blade, they will. Fear breeds desperation and desperation breeds stupidity. I can use that to expose the traitors. Only after they are outed, will we be safe."

Ditanu frowned, but his expression was thoughtful. Before her stood Ditanu the king. There was no sign of the man. Good. Because Kammani was wrong. Ditanu the man would be a grieving mess. They needed the iron-willed king if they were to survive.

Ditanu and Kammani needed to learn what Ishtar had shown Iltani in the night. "You're both correct. The ten city-states need to see their king strong and recovering, but they need us to find the traitors even more."

Iltani explained the dream Ishtar had shown her and told them about Ereshkigal's plan.

"Ereshkigal?" Ditanu said at last, thoughtful, and quiet—many plans flicking behind his eyes.

"Send me to the council. I will bluff—tell them half a truth, that Kuwari survived but I will let them think you died. They will know I won't long outlive you, a week at most without your blood. It will make them bold, and they will think Kuwari an easy target or a pawn they can use." Iltani stepped up until she was nearly nose to nose with Ditanu. "Let me separate our enemies from our allies. I don't even need a week. Just give me this day to find our true allies among those who will simply grab for power. And then tomorrow," her voice softened, "when it is time to bury your little ones, we will show all the gatherers that the king of the gryphons and Ishtar's Blade are very willing to hunt down all who mean New Sumer harm."

"Iltani is correct," Kammani crossed the room and paced a circle around him. "Her plan is sound. This way neither you nor Kuwari will have to expose yourselves to the council for another day. And stronger is stronger. The council respects strength."

"I don't want to send Iltani into danger when I don't have her back."

"Allow Iltani to fulfill her role as Ishtar's Avenging Blade. Let her deal with them for Ishtar will have her back. Which gives me another idea. Order Iltani to tell the council of Kuwari's survival and to also say she is now the cub's regent, by Ishtar's decree and your last command."

His expression darkening, he paced away from Kammani and then turned and paced back. "Your words are wise, and I will agree to this since it is best for all ten city-states if we find the traitors quickly, but I still don't like sending Iltani to face those sharks on her own." He turned to Iltani. "You may do this, but you will have an escort of twenty Shadows. I will not have the mother of my unborn cubs put at risk." There was a simmering anger underlying his words.

"As you wish. I will take the Shadows and I will learn all I can and then return with what I've learned."

"Good. It's settled then," Kammani said. "I'll help Iltani bath and prepare. Time is of the essence. We don't want the council naming a new regent or something else equally silly."

Iltani bobbed her head. "Kammani's correct. We need to hurry." She looked down at herself and winced. She was still covered in dried sweat and patches of flaking blood that she'd missed during her swift scrub in the bathing chamber.

Ditanu's free hand landed on her shoulder and he squeezed gently. "You may do this for the good of our kingdom, but afterward, you will return to me and I will decide what is to be done with anyone you deem a traitor. You will not go after them yourself. It is too dangerous. If you're not concerned for yourself, think of my cubs."

"I will never forget and I will never put them directly in harm's way."

"Good. We understand each other. Return to me quickly. That's an order too."

CHAPTER
twenty-three

ILTANI HAD BATHED quickly. Afterward, the priestess had helped with the mess that was her hair, toweling it dry and then working out the mass of tangles. There wasn't time to braid it, but Kammani had commented Iltani possessed a natural beauty that needed no outward enhancement. Iltani had never wasted much time wondering if she was beautiful. But with the way Ditanu just stood gazing at her with Kuwari in his arms, as Kammani dressed her, Iltani couldn't help but wonder if the king thought her pretty. She soon pushed aside her frivolous thoughts and focused on what she must do next.

That was how she came to be striding toward the council chambers, a new many-veiled skirt fluttering around her legs. Flowing along behind her, making less noise than the soft rustling of her skirt, twenty Shadows marched in her wake.

A harness held her scabbard and crystalline sword across her back where she could draw it swiftly if there was need. She didn't think she would be slaying any of the councilors in this first meeting. Still, she believed in being prepared and looking like she was ready to rain down Ishtar's rage upon them all.

Kammani had tried to convince Iltani to go bare-chested as the goddess herself often did. Iltani had declined the offer. At which point, a dower faced Ditanu had handed her a long veil to help secure her breasts and she'd mumbled that perhaps goddesses didn't have such issues as inconveniently large breasts.

Ditanu had laughed, a smugly male chuckle. After she'd gotten over her girly reaction to his voice, she'd wanted to tell him he could wear the flimsy finery. Instead, she'd strapped on the arm blades he'd gifted her with. Another long dagger she strapped to her thigh. The skirt of veils didn't really hide it, but she wasn't trying to hide her weapons.

A simple leather tie held her hair bunched at the nape of her neck. Kammani had artfully pulled it over her right shoulder where the weight of her hair held it in place. It wasn't done for beauty. No, Kammani had wanted Iltani's indigo and golden swirling birthmark to show.

In the end, Iltani now stalked toward the council chambers wearing less than she'd have wished, but more than she might have been, so she'd held her tongue against further debate. Besides, there would be enough debating with the council members.

Two Shadows moved ahead of her and reached the council chamber doors a few strides ahead of Iltani.

She was now their new leader, as was her right as Ishtar's Blade. That would still take some time for her to accept. The Shadows shoved open the door hard enough to cause them to swing back and clatter against the wall. Once through the threshold, she stormed into the council, seeing what she expected to see.

Chaos.

She approached the central table, took one quick look around and then shouted over the noise of the council. "I order you to stop fighting amongst yourselves like a pack of hyenas. The next one to speak about claiming the throne will find themselves in the underworld."

All around the table mouths dropped open in shock.

Beletum's father forced himself to his feet—he'd been one of the few actually sitting down at the council table. Most of the others were on their feet already, as if taking a stronger stance against their opponent would win them whatever argument said councilor was waging.

Once Ziyatum made it to his feet, he wobbled a touch, then grabbed up a walking stick and used it to steady himself. His grimace of pain did not elicit even a glimmer of sympathy. It didn't matter that he'd earned the wound while trying to save his daughter from Ditanu's wrath. If they hadn't concocted the foolish plan to have Beletum attempt to seduce the king during his grief madness, neither one of them would have been injured. She'd never forgive Ziyatum for raising his sword to Ditanu.

Iltani would have just executed them both—she didn't trust either in the least, but she had no real proof of their guilt either and without it the other councilors would start fearing for their lives. Killing large numbers of New Sumer's ruling body wouldn't be beneficial to its people. Besides, Ditanu wasn't likely to be impressed if he suddenly had minor nobles from all over the ten city-states badgering him every moment.

Ziyatum put on a fierce face. "What is the meaning of this? The council chambers are no place for a girl barely into her womanhood."

"Old man, your sight is going," Iltani bit back, and she started walking toward the head of the table. "And your mind, too, if you think I'm still a child. I have lived twenty-one summers upon these islands and have already seen a lifetime's worth of betrayal and power mongering."

"Blah!" Ziyatum sneered. "Simply because you chased the king like a bitch in heat since before you were ever a woman, and he permitted it until even he tired of it, sending you away to choose a real mate, doesn't mean you have any authority here."

Killing any of the councilors might be out of the question, but offending them or putting a little healthy fear in them wasn't out of the question, so Iltani started to laugh. "You shoved so many insults in there, it doesn't even make sense."

She unclasped her cloak and pulled it off, folding it over one arm as she walked the length of the table. There were a few sharply drawn breaths. She ignored them and continued forward, past the table and to the king's chair. There she took a moment to fold the cloak neatly, to give the councilors a good look at the birthmark running down her spine.

Turning toward the speechless councilors, she drew her sword and stepped up to the table where she gently placed the sword upon the polished stone surface. The fire within the crystalline blade flared with renewed life, casting a light across the table and reflected off any smooth surfaces.

"I shall clarify something here and now. The throne belongs to none of you. Ditanu's youngest cub has survived. Kuwari is the next in line for the crown."

Leaving the sword where it lay, because she wanted to see if any of the councilors were brave enough to touch it, she continued her walk around the table. By this time, the twenty Shadows had taken up places along the walls and at either end of the table, which effectively cowed anyone else who might feel the need to start a debate.

"There shall be no more bickering." She nodded to some of the councilors as she passed. Grabbing a shoulder here or a belt there, she shoved their owners down into their respective seats. "I am Kuwari's protector. Ishtar herself has tasked me with protecting him and providing for him. If any of you have a problem with that, you may take it up with Ishtar. I am more than capable of seeing your soul freed of its flesh so that you may better commune with the goddess."

There was shock and confusion on many a face, but several were also clearly relieved that the line of the gryphon kings had not failed. Consort Ahassunu's father, Shalanum, was clearly still filled with grief, but immediately nodded his head at Iltani.

"How may we serve you, Regent?"

His alliance didn't come as a surprise. She had saved his remaining grandchild.

And yes, that was honest grief she saw in his eyes. While she didn't know if he was aware that his daughter was betraying her king with Burrukan, Iltani decided he would still be a potential ally.

Hmmm, perhaps later she will tell him that one of Ahassunu's last acts was to ensure her unborn litter still had a chance at life and she gave them into Iltani's keeping.

"It's past time we got down to business. Our kingdom has need of us now."

The war council turned out to be an exercise in frustration. Instead of narrowing down the list of enemies as she'd planned, her list of suspects had only grown in size. While most seem to accept her rule, for now, there were a few who clearly would try to take command from her.

One shrewd councilor, a woman by the name of Nakurtum, who was the newly appointed governor of Nippur since her mentor had been killed in the battle, noted that Iltani would need to name a regent to guard the cubs after her death. She'd been quick to realize Iltani would not live more than a week without the king's living blood to sustain her metamorphosis.

She did make a note never to let her guard down around any of them. After several frustrating hours of bickering and political maneuvering, she'd ended the session with the command to strengthen all defenses across all the islands, because she didn't believe for a moment that the traitors and the outlander humans were no longer a threat to their kingdom. Iltani's last order was for all to return to Nineveh by dawn, for they would hold the funeral rites then. The council thought she was talking about a funeral for both Ditanu and his two cubs.

She didn't correct them.

CHAPTER
twenty-four

Weariness a deep ache in her muscles and bones, Iltani returned to Ditanu's suites, feeling much like the last few hours were the most pointless of her life. How her king managed to persuade his councilors to do anything promptly was beyond her.

Hah. At least after tomorrow, Ditanu would take up the mantle of kingship once again, leaving her to simply guard his back and listen. She'd be most pleased to never have to talk to a councilor again.

At her approach, the Shadows outside the king's suite came to attention and two of them held open the door for her. She gave them a sharp nod in passing. Inside, she didn't see the king, but knew he was here, her blood link guiding her on through to his bedchamber.

Uselli, Burrukan's second in command—and now hers, she supposed, was standing, overlooking some maps and other messages piled high upon the king's writing desk.

"Good, you're back."

"Where's the king?" But she already knew. He was in the bathing chamber beyond.

"He's bathing Kuwari."

"Iltani?" Ditanu's voice carried to them easily, as did Kuwari's squawk of greeting. "Report."

After a short pause outside the threshold, where she listened and heard the sounds of water splashing, she raised her voice. "I learned nothing we didn't already expect to learn. The report can wait until you're finished with Kuwari."

"You are not interrupting," his voice was muffled as if he had turned away.

She steeled her spine and pulled aside the curtain. Hesitating a fraction too long, Uselli gave her a firm shove and followed her in. The last place she wanted to give her report was here while the king was bathing, and now the fiery blush crawling up her cheeks would only make her discomfort all the more obvious.

Turning, she scowled at Uselli, but continued on in and walked around the ornate screens that blocked her view of the bathing pool.

"It was as we suspected. The council was in chaos—a power struggle to determine who would take the crown." She kept her eyes planted firmly on the decorative tiles marking the pool's edge, but her peripheral vision still picked up movement as Ditanu waded back toward the steps. "Though they seemed more interested in talking each other to death—or shouting—than solving it by swifter means. When it became clear their dissidence wouldn't be tolerated by Ishtar's Blade, things proceeded in a more beneficial manner."

Ditanu mounted the steps, Kuwari tucked in his arms. "You threatened to part heads from necks I presume?"

"There may have been mention of that, yes." Iltani forced her eyes back to the designated spot on the floor, that one tile with a slight crack in its corner. Ditanu walked in front of her and against her will, her gaze followed him. He was just so damn easy to look at. She sighed and then wanted to kick herself when he glanced back at her.

"Did you learn anything, anything suspicious about a particular council member?" Ditanu grabbed a couple towels. One he tossed over the cub, giving him a brisk rub down and then he slung the other around his own waist. Ditanu had never been modest—for that matter, Iltani hadn't been particularly body shy around him either as younglings. But that was then, and *now* was very different indeed.

"Over half of them triggered Ishtar's warning within me. They were all scared for their lives and uncertain who to align with if there was a power struggle—so that isn't really a surprise. When they learned Kuwari was still alive, they switched tactics. Debating who would make the best regent. Political ambition at its most bloodthirsty. As planned, they think you're dead. I didn't enlighten them." Iltani shrugged. "Three-quarters of the council seemed willing to follow my orders and acknowledged me as Kuwari's regent. Though that might be because they think I won't long outlive you, knowing without your blood to complete my metamorphosis, I will die."

"You did well. My Shadows will follow and observe everything the councilors do. We'll see if you have ruined the plans of the traitors. Their desperation will betray them. If not today, then tomorrow, when I reveal myself at the funeral rites. Or in the days following, but I will have my revenge."

His shoulders tensed and she imagined his hands had just closed into fists even though she couldn't confirm from this angle.

Iltani hoped his words were true, but she doubted it would be resolved so quickly. Whoever had the gumption to plan an assault of this magnitude might just see her as a small inconvenience and not be flustered in the least. Those gray cloaked strangers in her dream didn't look the type to roll over and piss themselves at the first sign of trouble. That didn't affect Iltani's own plans for them. She didn't care if they were secure in their evil plotting or not, she'd kill them all the same. It wouldn't be revenge, it would be duty.

Kuwari tossed off the corner of the towel covering his head and craned his neck to see around his father. She was coming to recognize his 'hungry' expression.

"Kuwari's hungry," Ditanu commented as if reading her thoughts.

Well, if anyone could read her thoughts, it would be him.

"Here," Iltani offered. "I can take him while you get dressed."

Ditanu had refused to allow even his body servants to know he was alive.

"Actually, let me send a Shadow to go get some milk first, then we can help each other prepare." He did as he said and then returned, "Because there is no way I'm putting all those tiny braids back in by myself. I'll do yours while Kuwari feeds and then you can help me with mine."

Iltani would appreciate the help, but wasn't really comfortable with the whole domestic intimacy the thought conjured up. No graceful excuse presented itself, so she said, "I'd be grateful for the help."

The need for sleep blurred her eyes as she finished the last of the tiny, neat braids. Blinking, she surveyed her work. "Not half bad," she said, "I even managed to get an even amount of beads in each one."

"You sound surprised."

"It's been a long day—you're lucky I didn't fall asleep halfway through."

Ditanu had done her hair first even though she'd said he didn't need to, but he'd insisted, saying he didn't want to sleep yet and he didn't want to think. So she'd allowed him to fashion her hair into artful little braids

Kuwari had fallen asleep half way through, and Iltani had wrapped him in blankets and sat him on the bench she and Ditanu were also occupying.

"I should have realized," Ditanu mumbled as he turned to look at her. "I've been selfish—you need your rest for your body to continue its change." His hand dropped, his fingers brushing along her belly, a look of wonder still on his face. "The pregnancy has likely sped up your need for my blood. How are you feeling besides tired?"

"You've been through so much yourself, I don't want to be demanding, but I think I'll need blood soon. I'm sure it wouldn't normally be so frequent. It's just with the battle and the unborn litter..."

"Nonsense. You are now the mother of my cubs. I will shed blood as often as you require."

His words caused another of those cursed blushes to bloom, but the tone also warmed her heart. He might never love her as a mate, but he did love her, it was there in his voice, his looks, and his actions.

After another blooding ceremony, Iltani felt revived but still sleepy. It was a good tired, not a dead on her feet exhausted. Ditanu was just wiping away the residue of blood from his chest. Iltani took the damp cloth from him and finished the job. The magic unleashed during the ceremony had healed the wounds until only thin white lines on his pectorals showed where the cuts had been.

This time, Ishtar had left them alone during the blooding ceremony. Iltani was secretly pleased not to have the goddess of fertility fanning unneeded flames. Ditanu was more relaxed, too. The awkwardness of the earlier times was not in evidence. Perhaps they were both too exhausted. Or maybe it was just that they were falling into their old routine. Iltani grinned and touched the pale scars on his chest like she would have before their separation.

"What does that little smile mean?" Ditanu brushed an errant braid back over her shoulder as he spoke. "I would know what thoughts whirl through your mind behind those beautiful eyes."

Iltani laughed at his words. He wasn't complimenting her to be flirtatious. It was simply their old way, to speak whatever was on their mind without worry. She was glad he wasn't the stone-faced king with her.

At last, she sighed and removed her hand from his scars. "I was thinking I'm glad we are still friends like old times. I did not like our separation. Nor did I like that earlier awkwardness."

"I never felt awkward around you, not for one moment." He laughed and stroked her shoulder so she would look up. "And I'll prove it to you."

"There is no need." A bittersweet smile touched her lips and then vanished. "We each should go find our beds. Tomorrow...will not be pleasant."

"I know." Pain flashed across his expression, and then he glanced away and said softly, "but it is tonight I fear. The nightmares already hunt at the edge of my consciousness."

Another habit from before their separation had Iltani clapping a hand on his shoulder. "Then I will stay with you until you sleep and should those nightmares come hunting, I will slay them first."

Ditanu had always had nightmares—his gift allowed him to see bits and pieces of dark possible futures, mostly they were all jumbled up, too chaotic for his sleeping mind to make sense of. Iltani, always the protector, had stayed and soothed him after particularly nasty ones, staying until he slipped into a more peaceful sleep.

"Thank you, Iltani." Ditanu picked up Kuwari and then reached out and clasped her hand in his. "I would like to hold all my living cubs this night."

Iltani's free hand trailed down to her belly for a moment, and then together they left the bathing room and entered his bedchamber.

Iltani stayed with Ditanu until his grip on her relaxed in sleep. She still held Kuwari in her arms for a few moments more, but reluctantly let the cub go. After carefully extracting herself from between Kuwari and his father, she glanced back at Ditanu's sleep softened expression. On impulse, she leaned down and brushed her lips against his.

He murmured something in his sleep but didn't wake.

"I love you," she whispered and then brushed her fingers against his lips. "Although you read me so well I think you must already know that, I still had to say it. Rest well, my love."

She eased off the bed. Looking around, she spotted a heavy blanket draped across the foot of the bed. She grabbed it, eyed the two chairs in front of the fire, and then decided against them in favor of the floor. It would be better for her back.

She laid down and rested her hands against her belly. Sleep eluded her for a long time.

CHAPTER
twenty-five

"THE MOTHER OF my cubs does not sleep on floors!"

Iltani jerked awake and found herself almost slamming foreheads with Ditanu. The king was crouched down, leaning over her.

"My king?"

"You're in my suites. I'm Ditanu here. Remember? And stop trying to change the subject."

"I wasn't. I'm not," she stammered as she tossed back the coverlet and rolled to her side.

Ditanu held out his hand to help her up.

She took it and he lifted her easily.

"The mother of my cubs does not sleep on floors. Repeat it after me."

"I…"

"Ishtar's Blade shouldn't be found on the floor either. One doesn't just carelessly toss aside one's favorite weapon." Humor was slowly working its way into his voice, and she could see he was having a hard time keeping a straight face.

"I will remember that in the future."

"Good." His expression lost some of its animation. "We have much to do today."

His cubs. Their funeral. Oh, by Ishtar—poor Ditanu. "I will not leave your side for a moment this day."

He looked her in the eyes. "I am glad."

Iltani fingered the heavy, elaborate torque that circled her neck and draped down to cover her bare breasts. Her hair had been pulled forward over her shoulder so the tiny braids didn't hide Ishtar's mark emblazoned down her spine. Ditanu told her it now covered half her back. It would be impossible for anyone to miss it. Gold glinted in her hair and circled her wrists and ankles. Another skirt of a hundred wispy layers hugged her waist, its many streamers fluttering in the slight breeze coming in from the garden. Around the waist, several of Ditanu's gryphon feathers plucked during the blooding ceremony two days ago, had been worked in among the fluttering streamers.

She caught a glimpse of herself in the polished silver mirror secured to the east wall. The voluptuous woman reflected there was an opulent creature of golds, tans, and indigos to match the tattoo running down her back. She was unrecognizable. The only things that soothed her at all was that the king was equally as decked out. No one was likely to notice her.

Well, until they noticed their matching torques and learned the meaning. High Priestess Kammani had dug them out of storage, saying these had been worn by previous monarchs and their Blades who had performed the Sacred Marriage.

Iltani fingered her torque and flushed a deeper shade of crimson. Somehow it seemed a touch obscene to her to wear a heavy chunk of gold and jewels that screamed for the entire world to see, that she and the king had had sex. It cheapened what her heart said should have been something just between the two of them. Not that Ishtar or a hundred centuries of tradition cared what Iltani might think.

Her eyes slid sideways toward Ditanu and caught him echoing her motion and touching his own torque with an unfathomable expression.

Voices from out in the hall had announced company before Priestess Kammani came through the door. "Good, you're both ready. All is prepared. The councilors and most of the high-ranking nobility are arriving in the temple as I speak. The Processional Way is already lined with your people. I know this will be hard for you, but you must show your strength so your people will know they are still protected by the line of the gryphon kings and greatly blessed by the Queen of the Night." His aunt touched his shoulder then. "Later, you will finally have time to grieve for your lost cubs. Until then, be strong for all our sakes."

Kammani gave him a motherly kiss.

"Go, put those councilors in their place and show the traitors their plan has failed."

Ditanu, his king's mask back in place, scooped Kuwari up in his arms, bracing the cub against one shoulder and then reached behind him for Iltani's hand. His strong fingers closed firmly around hers and she matched his strides, his Shadows falling in around them. They would show their enemies a unified front.

The Processional Way was as Kammani said it would be. Many of the watchers whispered silent prayers or said nothing at all as the first horse-drawn chariot rolled past, carrying the body of Humusi, next came the second chariot with Ilanum's equally tiny body. Several of the King's Shadows were on horseback and rode ahead of the chariots and beside them. An honor guard as was traditional.

Iltani drove the third chariot herself though she would have much preferred to have her hands free to draw her sword, but Ditanu had said he wanted Iltani in the chariot with him. As for himself, the king stood stoic, his living cub held firmly in his arms—on display for all to see.

As the chariot passed the first of the onlookers, and the prayer changed into a wave of whispering and pointed fingers, growing in volume until it caught the attention of others farther down the Processional Way. The city guards had to fight to keep the crowd from pressing further in, but the people started chanting the words 'Ishtar is merciful' over and over until it took on a multi-voiced roar.

A funeral should have been a somber thing, but Iltani couldn't begrudge the citizens of New Sumer their joy and newfound hope for the future.

King Ditanu simply nodded to his people in acknowledgement.

It wasn't until they were almost to the temple complex that the crowd must have noticed the golden torque around hers and Ditanu's necks, for the chant changed then to 'Sacred Marriage.'

At last, they arrived at the main temple, where the dead of the gryphon kings had been buried since they first came to these islands almost eight thousand years ago.

After the last chariot had rolled into the temple courtyard, Iltani studied each of the councilors where they waited upon the stairs leading up to the temple. Each one was equally shocked to see their king very much alive.

If Priestess Kammani and a wall of her brethren hadn't come forward at that exact moment to tend to the tiny bodies in the first two chariots, Iltani sensed the councilors would have flocked around King Ditanu, demanding to know why they were only learning now that he lived.

Kammani's interference gave Ditanu a few more hours' peace.

CHAPTER
twenty-six

AFTER THE DAY long royal funeral rites, Ditanu ordered his Shadows to clear a path for him to return to the palace. Iltani followed silently in his wake. She didn't voice useless platitudes, merely holding her silence and being a solid presence at his side. Once they returned to his palace, Iltani ordered food brought for Ditanu and herself and milk for Kuwari. Normally, she'd trust the errand to a passing servant or one of the palace guards, but knowing traitors could be anywhere, she only trusted other Shadows.

The first of the Shadows started away, but something else occurred to Iltani. "Wait," she called softly. A female Shadow turned back to her. It was the twins' cousin, Takurtum. Iltani was glad to see the young woman had survived the massacre on Uruk. There had been too much death and Iltani knew, later, she would find time to grieve for Etum and Eluti properly. "I'll need a pallet brought to Ditanu's suite and made up for me there."

Because he'd have another fit if she slept on the floor again, but there was no way she was sleeping in his bed. She didn't trust herself. What if he'd woken while she'd kissed him last night?

She didn't want to complicate things as they were just starting to fall back into that routine she loved so much.

When they reached Ditanu's chambers, he ordered his steward Warassuni to report to him, saying he needed to see how his city-states had fared without him. Iltani had hoped Ditanu would give himself time to heal before throwing himself back into his work, but it wasn't entirely unexpected, either. Ditanu cared for his people. It was part of why she loved him.

While he was busy discussing matters of the kingdom with his steward, Iltani took the opportunity to stake out a place to call her own. After poking around in Ditanu's vast suites, going room to room with Kuwari and a compliment of Shadows trailing her everywhere, she eventually found her spot.

Ditanu wouldn't be happy, but perhaps the king needed to hear the word 'no' a little more often. With a grin at the cub, she waved her arm encompassing the small room which was actually the king's wardrobe. "My territory. What do you think?"

Of course, Kuwari didn't answer in words. Instead, he scampered over to the lowest shelf where the servants stored the king's sandals.

"I think you're a little too young to wear those just yet," Iltani told the cub.

After picking through them for the one he liked best, Kuwari started to chew.

The servants soon brought the things Iltani asked for. However, the food came at the same time, and that won out over the pallet and blankets on her priority list, so she instructed the servants to arrange her 'room' whatever way they liked. By the tittering of the servant girls, they were discussing how to turn a closet into something befitting Ishtar's Blade.

Iltani couldn't care less. It was a place to lay her head. She'd slept on bare ground a time or three while back on New Assur as part of her training.

Food in one hand, Kuwari tucked against her side with the other, she made her way into Ditanu's receiving room where he, Warassuni, Uselli, and a few others in charge of running a city were already gathered around a table discussing reports.

She offered her plate of food to Ditanu, who took it with a smile in greeting before returning to his impromptu meeting. Servants brought in more food and laid it out for the others.

Her king's needs dealt with, for now, she carried Kuwari back to Ditanu's bedchamber and sat in one of the chairs by the fire so Kuwari could nurse from his converted water skin in relative quiet. An hour later, Kuwari had emptied his milk skin and fallen asleep. She heard the approach of feet on carpet long before the servant reached her position.

"Lady Iltani, your room is prepared," the servant said. Iltani recognized the girl from the time she'd helped Iltani do her hair the first night she'd returned to the island. It seemed like weeks ago now, not less than a handful of days.

"Thank you." Iltani couldn't remember her name. She'd ask one of the Shadows later.

The girl bobbed a curtsy. "We had your belongings brought over from your other room in the consort's...old suites."

The poor servant flushed and verbally tripped over the word consort. Iltani couldn't blame her. She was probably trying to figure out if Iltani was now her new mistress.

"I am a servant the same as you."

The girl looked absolutely doubtful, but only mumbled, "If you say so, my lady."

She dismissed the girl and took Kuwari to her new room.

It was tiny, but the floor space was long enough to fit a travel pallet in as she'd expected. Some of the pillows and ornate tapestries had made the move from her new room in the consort's chambers to her newer room in Ditanu's closet. Ah, the bag she'd brought with her from the training island was there as well.

She made a thick nest for Kuwari alongside her own sleeping platform, intentionally not putting him directly upon it because she wasn't sure if he was fully trained to go all night without accidents. He'd been good the last two nights and he seemed to know where the sand pit was in the bathroom, but there was no point making the servant's task more difficult than needed.

Once Kuwari was snuggled down in his blanket nest, and he'd purred himself to sleep, she went over to her bag and pulled out an old shirt to sleep in. A bundle of letters fell out in her lap.

Her breath caught in surprise. These ones weren't the well-read ones she'd always had; these were the ones Burrukan had given her just before she set foot on Nineveh. In all that had happened since, she'd completely forgotten about them.

She was just picking them up when the curtain comprising her 'bedroom door' was drawn back and Ditanu braced a hip against the frame.

"The closet isn't a proper place for Ishtar's Blade to rest her head, either."

"Hmmm. It's not the floor. I figured that was your only stipulation. It's just temporary," Iltani said, and then added in her mind, 'until I have a chance to hunt down every last traitor and make them pay for hurting you.'

His expression brightened and she sensed a playful argument on the horizon, at least until his gaze dropped to the letters in her hand.

Suddenly his king's mask was back in place—though she'd thought she'd seen a flash of pain before it was firmly in place.

"You did not read my letters?"

Iltani glanced down and swiftly pulled out the other well-read tattered ones.

"More times than I can count," she admitted with a blush. "These ones are new to me."

"New?" That one word was asked by Ditanu the King, definitely not Ditanu the man.

She hesitated, sighed, and then gave him the truth. Insofar as she knew it. "Burrukan only gave these to me the day I returned, before I stepped foot upon the island. He said if he didn't, he would be committing treason."

"That cantankerous old goat," Ditanu said with a chuckle, his king's mask falling away as quickly as it had come.

Now that he had an explanation as to why she hadn't read them, he seemed unsurprised by the news.

"Did you know or suspect some of your letters weren't making it to me?" she asked.

"Looking back, yes, I admit I suspected a few of my earliest ones may have gone astray until he deemed you ready to read them. You were in training and didn't need the...distraction." Ditanu rubbed at his clean-shaven face. "Your return letters to me never made comment as to some of the more delicate topics I wrote to you about. At first, I didn't understand, and then it occurred to me that Burrukan might be censoring my letters or your replies. I decided it was best not to question him about it, for fear of putting my mentor in a difficult position. I didn't always like what Burrukan did, but he always did everything in his power to protect us and our kingdom." He gestured at the stack of letters. "However, I did not expect this amount to have gone astray." Ditanu sighed. "He saved me from my own foolishness more times than I can count." He fell silent for several moments and then with his voice thick with emotion, he said, "I will miss him."

"I, too," Iltani whispered, and then hesitantly, "Do you still wish me to read them, or would you...prefer if I not?"

Ditanu cleared his throat and then nudged the pile of letters closer to her. "Keep them hidden. Our enemies would very much enjoy what I reveal in those."

"I should destroy them now, then, if they are that dangerous."

Ditanu shook his head. "I would have you read them first. Our friendship has a four-year gap in it I'd like to see filled one day. These may help fill that gap for you." He rubbed a hand over his face again and then looked chagrined, "Is there, by chance, another stack of your letters that might not ever have made it to me?"

Iltani swallowed and then felt around inside her pack for the last stack of letters. These were the ones she'd written to Ditanu that Burrukan had withheld. The pile wasn't as thick as Ditanu's letters.

"Ah, Burrukan always saw things right in the end." He reached out and took them from Iltani. "He was probably correct in this too. He was a military tactician until the end. Guard my letters well against our enemies, read them, and then burn them afterward."

Iltani started to reach for one of the letters, but he was quicker and wrapped his long fingers around his wrist. "But not today, nor tomorrow and not in any of the days until the end of this lunar cycle. I want to give us a chance to become reacquainted. If we haven't managed to share our every secret by then, we'll open our letters and read them aloud over a jug of wine." He glanced at the stack of letters. "Though this mountain might take two or three nights and several pitchers of wine."

It almost sounded like courtship. What, by Ishtar, did he mean? She had to know. Iltani parted her lips. It took two tries to convince her clumsy tongue to form words. "Are you asking? I mean, do you intend for us to...?

He pressed a finger to her lips to silence her.

"My grief over Ahassunu is too new. I simply need my most faithful Shadow, to be my rock and place of solitude for the next turning of the moon. Ishtar chose well when she picked you to be her Blade. I will need a blade that will not break and will not betray me."

His words were plausible and should have been the truth, but Iltani's new gift of knowing a truth told her the very first words were a lie. His grief was too new? That was the lie, but then that could only mean his grief over his consort was old. Did he know about his consort and Burrukan after all? Her poor king, to have lived with the knowledge that the woman he loved didn't love him, was in fact in love with the man who had raised him. What a terrible knowledge to have had to carry around with him. Obviously, he'd never betrayed that knowledge. Why not? She'd figure that out later.

Iltani laced her fingers with his. "I will never betray you."

He leaned down and placed a kiss on top of her head. "I know."

CHAPTER
twenty-seven

ILTANI STOOD TO the right and just a step behind Ditanu's throne where she'd been stationed since noon meal. It was time for final meal. How much longer could these councilors and high ranking nobles talk? Actually, some of the nobles were worse than the councilors. At least, the councilors' talk had a purpose.

She shifted positions to relieve a cramp in one calf. The move was slight, but enough to catch Ditanu's attention. How he was even aware was a mystery. He sat his throne while he listened to his council and nobles drone on about every trivial problem they had encountered in the three days since Ditanu had last held court.

The king held up a hand and the noble at the foot of the stair halted mid-word. Ditanu motioned her closer. She shifted until her hip was butted up against the arm of his throne. Still he gestured her closer, making it clear he wanted her ear.

Keeping her face blank, she leaned down while Ditanu picked up his goblet of wine.

He took a sip, holding the drinking vessel in front of his mouth as he whispered in her ear. "Are you growing tired? Your body is still undergoing changes. Plus, with my cubs, you are burning through resources more quickly. I can end the session early. There is precious little to learn here anyway. Our enemies have been planning this for more than twenty-five years. They won't give themselves away just now."

"I'm good for another hour or more. Do not end the session early on my account."

Ditanu grunted and his look said he didn't quite believe her.

She was two steps behind his shoulder. Really, how had he even seen her move? Damn heightened gryphon senses. Hmmm. Although, she was growing tired, more so than simply standing for five hours should have made her. She could run entire circuits of the small training island without breaking into a sweat. Perhaps he was correct and she should allow him to make excuses. He likely could use the rest too.

"We have done what we can to renew the protections around the islands. The repairs have already started on Uruk, and new safeguards are being woven into the structure to prevent such an attack from being so deadly ever again." Ditanu waved to one of his scribes. "I've assigned more guards to patrol the waters between the islands."

Steward Warassuni stood to Ditanu's left, swiftly making notes.

Iltani rather admired him for it. He had several scribes already present and he didn't need to write anything himself, but he did anyway. It showed his dedication to his work.

"There is only one other thing I can think to increase our defenses." Ditanu's eyes narrowed and his jaw flexed. "I should have seen to it more faithfully. Our city-states are dotted with hundreds of the lamassu, only a few of them have been maintained by my aunt and myself. At first light tomorrow, myself, High Priestess Kammani, and Ishtar's Blade shall start going from city-state to city-state, anointing ever last lamassu we have within my borders."

There were mumbles of agreement for Ditanu's plan. Iltani was secretly pleased. It might take a fair bit of blood to complete the task, but had there been more lamassu, it might have prevented some of the tragedy that happened on Uruk.

"That is indeed wise council, my king." Councilor Ziyatum approached the throne.

The Shadows closed rank, only allowing the councilor to come as close as the foot of the stairs. It wasn't something against Beletum's father in particular; they treated everyone as a possible threat to their king's life.

Ziyatum stopped a couple steps away from the first stair. "However, I think you forget one important detail. If you wish to ensure the safety and prosperity of our beautiful islands, you need to give the people some kind of reassurance that should something happen to you, they are still looked after, made safe by well-laid plans."

"Why don't you just say what you truly mean…never mind, I'll do it myself. You want me to confirm my choice of regent. Strange, I thought Iltani had explained the way of things to you."

"Ah, wasn't that just deception to confuse our enemies?" Ziyatum asked as he tilted his head in question. "It would only be wise to name your true regent for Kuwari now, thus preventing possible future civil disturbances to the ruling body of these great city-states. The cub could likely also benefit from the loving guidance of a new mother figure. So perhaps the new Regent should be female."

Iltani winced at the councilor's callous words.

"And I imagine you have someone in mind already." Ditanu smiled coldly. "Strange, Beletum doesn't seem the motherly type. I suppose I'm lucky that Kuwari has taken to Iltani so readily. Besides, since she is also carrying Consort Ahassunu's unborn litter, Iltani will fill the role of mother for all my cubs rather nicely. I have already named her regent with Ishtar's blessing. I assume that solves your worry?"

Ziyatum made a noise which Ditanu must have taken as assent, for he stood and then held his hand out for Iltani.

She hesitated for a moment longer than Ditanu's patience lasted. He glanced over his shoulder at her as if to ask why his hand was still empty. She slipped her fingers in his.

Ditanu descended the stairs and crossed the length of the hall, his Shadows flowing around him. Iltani scrambled to match his longer strides. His blessedly quick departure saved her from having to fend off the councilors' questions.

In the end, only one of the councilors chased her down, or more likely, was allowed to follow by the Shadows. Consort Ahassunu's father.

"Is it true?" Shalanum asked, doubt mixing with pain, hope and joy in his expression.

She supposed if anyone had a right to know, it was the cubs' grandfather. Shalanum had always doted upon Ahassunu and her younger sister. His mate and other children had been killed in the same attack which had killed Ditanu's parents and siblings.

"Yes," she answered truthfully. "High Priestess Kammani has examined me and says the little ones are healthy, unharmed by their ordeal."

He drew in a deep hitching breath, and said simply, "I'm glad something of her lives on."

King Ditanu remained silent for the entire trip back to his quarters, leaving Iltani to handle the other grieving father. She didn't blame him. Ahassunu's father must have brought up memories of Ditanu's own loss.

"Would I be permitted to visit with Kuwari for a few hours over dinner?

The king turned to Shalanum. "Of course. You, too, have suffered great losses. I imagine Kuwari misses his grandfather."

"Thank you, King Ditanu. You have always been just."

CHAPTER
twenty-eight

OVER DINNER, KUWARI and his grandfather played while Iltani and Ditanu looked on and ate their meal. After a long hour of play, Iltani wondered which one would wear the other out first. In the end, Kuwari fell asleep in his grandfather's arms.

"Kuwari needs his rest," Ditanu said and then surprised Iltani by continuing, "However, I think he and his grandfather are good for each other." At which point, Ditanu ordered Shalanum to take Kuwari and a large unit of Shadows and go stay in the nursery.

After Kuwari and his grandsire left in the company of an appropriate number of Shadows, Uselli came and stood at his king's shoulder, looking unhappy.

Ditanu sighed. "You have something you wish to say? Out with it then."

"I don't like having you and Kuwari separated."

The king wandered over to his desk and sorted through reports, ledgers, and some other unknown letters. "I trust Shalanum."

"That's not what I'm worried about. Anyone can see he dotes on Kuwari." Uselli followed Ditanu over to his desk, but Iltani stayed where she was. She could hear the conversation well enough from by the fire. If the way Uselli just squared his shoulders was any indication, he planned to dig in and stand his ground on this subject. Iltani was exhausted. There was no way she was getting involved.

Besides, her link with Kuwari had grown and was equally as strong as the one she shared with his father, and the cub was close enough she could sense any danger that came near. If Ditanu wanted some time alone with his grief, she'd give him this evening. Tomorrow, it was back to being a king and a father. He could be just a man for a few hours. The hall outside would be close enough. She could guard her two wards from there.

While she'd been making her decision, Ditanu had poured himself a goblet of wine and continued the conversation with Uselli. "Does it really matter? The suites are housed on the same hallway."

"Still, if something were to happen, it would be safer if you were both together."

"Our guard is up, our enemies won't attack now. They'll lay in wait until they think our guard is relaxed again. Sadly, Kuwari is probably safer now than he has been in the months leading up to the attack." Ditanu's expression darkened. Iltani could see him going down dark corridors in his mind. "I wish to be alone with my thoughts tonight. At least, as much as I'm ever alone."

"Fine," Uselli said with a huff. "But you're going to take years off my life with worry."

Ditanu turned to spear Iltani with a look. "To sooth some of your worries, I'll keep Ishtar's Blade no more than an arm's length away."

"I'll reduce the number of guards in your chambers, but double them outside in the gardens and the hall."

In the end, Uselli agreed to his king's demand and he left to go guard the cub.

After a time, the servants came and prepared a bath for the king. Ditanu waited at his desk, drinking wine and reading through a few of his reports. The three servants exited the bathing chamber.

Ditanu ignored them.

"My king, your bath is ready for you," Warassuni prompted. He'd served Ditanu's father as well. Iltani had always liked his quiet confidence, his ability to keep the simple day to day routines of the city running and the king's surprisingly few needs attended too without issue.

Iltani knew Ditanu liked the old human steward, and they normally shared a few pleasant words of conversation until it was time for the king to see to other things.

"Thank you," Ditanu said without inflection of any kind. "I will not need your services further this night."

Dismissed, each servant bowed as they departed in haste. Apparently, Iltani wasn't the only one to notice her king's darkening mood. Ditanu downed his wine, poured another cup and then unrolled another scroll, squinting at the handwriting.

The guards rearranged their positions as Uselli instructed, leaving only two Shadows standing at the door leading out to the hall. Iltani moved away from Ditanu's desk and took up a position another guard had vacated by the wall. At least here she was out of Ditanu's direct line of sight, and maybe he would find the solitude he so clearly craved.

An hour later, Ditanu still sat at his desk. He tossed the scroll down he had been reading and picked up his wine goblet. Finding it empty, he refilled it and drank that one down almost as fast as the one before it. When it was empty again, he reached for the pitcher only to find it empty. He huffed something under his breath and set it back down on the table with an overly cautious movement.

Her king was thoroughly drunk.

Pushing up from the table, he started toward his bathing chamber.

"I doubt wine can actually drown your sorrows. However, it might manage to drown you in that big bath of yours," Iltani called as she stepped away from the wall and started toward him.

Ditanu paused, turned with an overstated slowness and then looked her up and down.

"I have faith my Blade would prevent me from drowning." His words weren't slurred and his motions were still smooth and coordinated, so perhaps he wasn't as far gone into his cups as she'd thought. Gryphons had a naturally higher tolerance for the stuff than humans did, and they sobered up quicker, too. She'd yet to meet a gryphon who had ever suffered from a hangover, either. Lucky bastards.

The last time Iltani had drunk to excess had been four years ago at the king's coronation. Burrukan had shown no mercy the next morning when she was still suffering a raging hangover. He'd bundled her onto his skiff with no regard for her pounding head or heaving stomach. Iltani didn't touch drink after that. It clearly turned her into a raging fool—she was grateful she didn't remember anything from that night.

Ditanu's gaze travelled up and down her body once, and a secretive smile softened his firm lips.

What the hell was that look about?

When he met her gaze, his eyes had that glassy look which came with too much drink. "Letting my Blade save me from drowning might be enjoyable."

"You're drunk, my king."

"Yes, I am. And it's Ditanu here. Not king, sire, or majesty—I hate majesty. It's just Ditanu. Remember?"

Damn him. Even drunk he remembered that stupid rule.

"As you say."

"Yes," he gestured back toward the bathing chamber, "And I say I shall have a bath. I'm a king and can do as I wish."

He turned from her and made a relatively straight line toward the chamber.

Rolling her eyes, Iltani followed. Ditanu rarely drank to excess, but when he did, he was never dull or mean. He was playful and downright.... adorable.

Oh, this was going to be interesting.

Ditanu's head started to nod for the third time. Unlike the first two times, he didn't jerk awake. Cursing, Iltani pushed off from the wall where she stood guard and darted forward. Her powerful strides quickly covered the distance and powered her halfway across the pool before gravity won out and she plunged into the water.

Fragrant, but cooling, water was displaced by her sudden arrival and a great wave washed up and over the sides. Her skirt's streamers floated in the water all around her. Cursing under her breath, she pushed them out of her way and waded over to the king where he was slumping forward, still asleep and unaware he was actually in danger of drowning. She reached his side just before he slumped face first into the water. With a grumbled curse, she braced his shoulders against the back wall of the bath.

Even her sudden arrival hadn't been enough to wake him. Maybe he actually might have drowned. She'd only been joking with him earlier. Delayed fear set her heart to pounding and she just stood in the bath, her skirt swirling around her, her harness, scabbard, and sword half under the water. Worst of all was the heavy golden torque around her neck. The cooling water stole her body heat from it. Now it was heavy, cold, wet and chafed her breasts every time she moved.

What a stupid, foolish token. Why couldn't monarchs and their Blades have exchanged something more sensible like a hair ornament or bracelet?

"Wake up, damn it!"

He didn't respond.

Annoyed, she slapped the water directly in front of his face.

He jerked awake with a surprised grunt, and she gave his shoulders a good shake while he was still trying to orientate himself.

"Get out of this water right now, or I swear..." her words were cut off mid-sentence.

Ditanu grabbed her and lifted her halfway out of the water to sit her across his lap. "I would have gotten out sooner if I'd known you wanted to take a turn," Ditanu reached behind him and his groping hand eventually closed over a cloth and a cake of soap. "But we can make this work. Besides, we used to bath together as cubs, this isn't that much different."

Not much different? Hah. Iltani disagreed. She wiggled out of his arms before he could start to bathe her as he clearly planned.

"You," she scolded and pointed at him to reinforce her statement. "Almost drown. Out of the pool now!"

In case he resisted, she hooked one of his arms over her shoulder and wrapped her own around his waist. With a grunt and a mighty heave, she got Ditanu to his feet.

With some trouble and a considerable amount of laughter on Ditanu's part, she managed to extract him from the pool and navigated him back to his bedchamber. She grabbed a couple towels from a bench on the way by before she continued on to his bed. One she wrapped around his head and shoulders, the other she just tossed at his lower extremities without letting her eyes focus on anything.

She helped him dry off while having to avoid his grabbing hands. He kept trying to drag her into bed with him. By the time she was done, a blush was burning merrily upon her cheeks but Ditanu was dressed in a robe and more or less tucked into bed.

"Iltani, stay?" There was great loneliness in those two words. "I need you."

"Shhh, my king. You're still drunk. That's the wine talking. You don't mean it. You won't remember it come the morning anyway. So just go to sleep and everything will be better when you wake."

"Hmmm, yes, I'm drunk." His voice had mellowed to a deeper tone which did things to her she was better off not thinking about.

He was silent for a time, but then he turned to her and reached out to cup her cheek. "But I do mean it. I have always needed you, always loved you. I'll still remember that come morning." He traced a finger along her lips.

His words held her frozen. She should pull away. She really should. She didn't.

"Gryphons never forget. Though some memories are better than others." He made a rolling sound in his throat which sounded a lot like a gryphon's purr. She hadn't known he could make that sound in a human body.

It was surprisingly appealing.

Her curiosity peaked, she asked, "What are you remembering?"

"My coronation. Afterward, when you seduced me."

"What? Oh, by Ishtar, I was drunk out of my mind that night. I was such an idiot, wasn't I? I should have known better—you were always complaining about females continuously coming after you. I would have apologized once I sobered up but Burrukan had me bundled up and away...I didn't even get to say goodbye."

"You were sweet. I welcomed your attentions." Ditanu took advantage of her distraction, and suddenly his hands were roving along her sides. "You're wet."

"I jumped in a bathing pool to keep your drunk ass from drowning." One of his hands tried to go up under her gold torque to fondle a breast. Too surprised to think, she smacked it away. "What are you doing?"

LISA BLACKWOOD

"I want my mate."

"But…we're not…I mean."

"Ishtar has made us mates. You are now mother to Kuwari. You shelter my unborn cubs. How much more of a mate could you be?"

Iltani honestly didn't know, and she wanted to be his mate in a most desperate way. She couldn't tell him that, though, not drunk and grieving as he was at the moment. Perhaps in a few months?

Instead, she frowned at him and said, "You are drunk. I will not take advantage of you." He might think he craved her now, but come the morning and a clear head, he might have regrets.

"I won't have regrets," he said as if reading her mind, and sounding a lot less drunk than he had earlier. "Ahassunu wasn't a true mate to me."

Even as her heart lurched in surprised shock at his words, hope bloomed in her heart. Cautiously, barely daring to believe her ears, she asked, "What do you mean?"

"Ahassunu and I begot children, and she was a good friend and a wise consort, but we were never mates."

Ishtar's magic whispered that Ditanu's words were impossibly true.

"How? Female gryphons will only come into heat for their mates." Even as she asked, she knew.

"Ahassunu and Burrukan were mates. They had been in love secretly for years."

While she was mulling that over, Ditanu captured her wrist and gently dragged her under the covers with him. Iltani tensed but relaxed when he did nothing more than wrap an arm around her waist and draw her closer.

His voice continued to rumble above her head. "At the time I learned about Burrukan and Ahassunu, you were almost a year into your training. The council had been leaning on me hard to take a mate or, at least, spend some time with a creature of the opposite sex. Beletum's father was the most determined. Ziyatum almost succeeded in convincing the rest of the council that Beletum and I should be betrothed for a trial year." Ditanu shuddered.

"Nobles have been throwing their daughters at you since you turned fifteen."

"Earlier, actually, you were just too innocent to see it."

"That's disgusting." Her fists clasped and unclasped, wanting to throttle the ones responsible for making a boy grow up too fast.

"Tradition mixed with desperation, actually. I was the last of my line."

"Still," Iltani countered. "Doesn't make it right."

"No, but I used you to keep all but the most determined at bay."

"Hmmm, is that why I always happened upon harlots lying in wait for you?"

"Probably. I figured chasing away unwanted females was an honorable way for Ishtar's Blade to serve her king."

"Duty. Ha! Not sure if I was feeling the 'honor of serving my king' at those times." She huffed and then clarified. "I saw way more bare asses and breasts then I should have had to endure."

"It was always entertaining to watch you convince them to give up the hunt."

Iltani heard the smile in his voice. "I guess we were quite the pair when we were younger."

"I think the councilors might think we are still quite the pair."

"You're right." Iltani started to laugh. "You were starting to tell me about how Ahassunu came to be your consort but is not your mate."

"The council wanted me betrothed and to complete a year of courtship to increase the chances a female might go into heat for me."

Iltani hated the idea of Ditanu having his hand forced. A year's betrothal wouldn't guarantee a female would become fertile for him, but it would force a kind of intimacy between the two betrothed. Even as a young woman, it had not sat well with Iltani. It also influenced why she'd been an idiot the night of his coronation. That hadn't been a snap decision, but something she'd been working up the nerve for days in advance. As her younger self had judged it, if Ditanu were going to have to take a mate, it should be someone who at least loved him.

Ditanu nuzzled her wet hair. "The thought of getting betrothed was bad enough, but when Burrukan pointed out something very disturbing, I listened to him."

"Was there some danger I wasn't aware of?" The thought disturbed Iltani.

"Burrukan had noted that three other females around my age and of suitable bloodlines had died over the years, leaving only a few candidates for potential mates." Ditanu sighed. "That was when Burrukan broached the topic of making Ahassunu my consort."

Relief washed over Iltani's mind. "I knew Burrukan was loyal, but that must have been hard for both of you."

"Yes, but he said it was better to beget heirs with a trusted female, even if she wasn't in actual fact, my mate, than finding a viper in my marriage bed that might desire my throne more than me. As he pointed out, I would also have Ahassunu's powerful family at my back in the crucial first few years of my reign."

Iltani felt her throat thicken with unshed tears. Poor Ditanu. "The last four years haven't been easy for you either."

"I would have endured nobles tossing their daughters at me for an eternity, and I would still not have taken any of them as my mate willingly." Again, Ditanu shuddered. "But Burrukan told me there are drugs that could be given to both a male and female that would make a male ache and ensure the female went into heat even if she didn't have a deep emotional bond with the male."

"That's what Beletum gave you…" Iltani cleared her voice and tried again, having to shove aside the terrible imagery and jealousy the thought conjured. "Is that how you and Ahassunu…?"

Ditanu started to cough, when he had himself under control, he said, "Even Burrukan isn't that loyal, and I had no interest in another man's mate."

"Then how?"

Ditanu swallowed another laugh. "My hand and a cup to catch it in, if you must know. I never asked how Ahassunu and Burrukan worked out what to do with my donated seed." His hand slid from her hip to cover her belly. "I imagine it was done with magic, much like how Ishtar planted my little ones within you."

"I knew Burrukan couldn't have been betraying you as it seemed."

"Ah, you caught them. The first night?"

"Yes. It was a shock."

"Burrukan must have thought I'd keep you up all night reminiscing."

"I didn't tell you that first night because I didn't know how to go about it, and my power didn't judge them as a direct danger to you."

"That must have been stressful for you," Ditanu said distractedly. The hand against her stomach had started to wander again.

"Not as much as this," she mumbled under her breath.

"Your clothes are cold and wet, and you're still wearing your sword and harness. That can't be very comfortable."

"Whose fault is that?" In a louder voice, she added, "You're still drunk, my king. Let me go before I get your bed any damper."

"It's big. We can move over."

His hand rose up and she felt him working loose the buckle of her harness. A few strong tugs got it loose. After a moment, he eased it off her shoulders. The combined weight of the sword and sodden scabbard made a hefty thump as it landed on the carpeted floor beside the bed. Next his fingers felt around at the back of her neck for the clasp to the heavy golden torque.

"Ha!" He sounded rather delighted to have conquered the collar's clasp.

He reached across her, and part of his chest and arm brushed against her breasts as he tossed the torque over the edge of the bed. Her breath quickened at the contact but she didn't say anything or try to draw away. If she was truthful with herself, she didn't want to be anywhere but where she was. She remained silent as Ditanu's fingers glided between the valley of her breasts and then continued their slow, caressing journey to her navel before venturing the last of the way to the ornate belt of her skirt. The muscles of her abdomen quivered at his touch.

He hesitated a moment and then as if he couldn't stop himself, skated his fingers along the sensitive skin just above her belt. "This is developing faster than an honorable man would allow—we were supposed to read our letters to each other, become reacquainted over several evenings. I was going to court you properly if a little belatedly. My noble intentions seem to have departed."

"It's all right." And it was, Iltani decided at that moment. She'd never wanted a fancy courtship or any of the other elaborate trappings that went with the crown. She'd only ever wanted Ditanu, and he was offering himself to her.

Warm lips caressed her shoulder, following the curve of her neck to a sensitive spot just below her ear. Iltani's breath hitched.

Again Ditanu's voice washed over her senses, more intoxicating than wine. "Your scent calls to me, your voice soothes me, your smile sets my heart pounding, and your lush body makes me ache for you." His tone turned raw and desperate. "Do you grow aroused when I'm near, as I do for you? Do you dream of me when you're alone at night? Touch yourself even though it's never enough to fill the emotional need?"

Her throat tightened with sudden emotion at the loneliness she heard in his voice and she couldn't get words out to answer his heated questions. The silence stretched longer and she felt foolish tears pooling at the corners of her eyes.

He pulled away, bracing himself above her with an arm planted to either side of her head. He watched her, his king's mask suddenly in place. "If you don't want this, tell me now and I'll stop and never accost you in such a way again."

"You overwhelm me. A feast offered to a starving woman. Can you blame me for not knowing which delectable dish to start with?" Iltani touched him then, running her hands slowly up his chest, savoring warm skin and hard muscle. "Be assured I want this. I've wanted you since I first became a woman."

Ditanu released a strangled breath and lowered his head down to her lips, sealing them together. She slid her hands along his sides and kissed him fiercely in return.

They kissed for a long time, neither in a hurry, but eventually Ditanu freed her of her sodden skirt and then rolled with her so she was resting atop him in a dryer part of the bed. Between kisses, she helped him out of the robe she'd just gotten him into.

"Told you not to bother with the robe, but do you ever listen to me? No." His throaty chuckle hitched and changed to a deep purr as she brushed her fingers across his right nipple and then sealed her mouth over it. She moved to the other one, giving it equal attention before planting a kiss over his sternum. As she worked her way downward, his purring increased in volume. Taking her time at his navel, she nuzzled him and then kissed her way down to one hip bone, ignoring the one part of him that was standing proud for her attention. When she ran the tip of her tongue closer to his groin, his hips jerked.

The desperate sound he made had her own body clenching with need.

She sat back on her haunches then, just studying Ditanu's masculine beauty.

"Iltani?" he sighed out her name and then raised his head to look at her, humor and desire mixing together in his gaze. "Would you like me to get you pen and parchment to draw on?"

243

"Maybe later." Never one to pass up a challenge, she reached out and wrapped her fingers around his thick length and he jerked under her.

"Then perhaps there is something else you would like to...say?" he asked lazily as his hips rocked into her caress.

After trailing her nails along his length, she wrapped her fist around him again. "You are breathtaking, my king."

"It's Ditanu, remember?"

He sounded rather hoarse. She grinned wickedly and squeezed him, flicking her thumb over his crown, collecting the tiny beads of liquid gathering in a groove there.

Ditanu bucked, thrusting up into her fist and hissed out unintelligible words.

"I'm sorry. I didn't catch that."

He growled at her words but answered her. "That feels so much better than my hand. Keep that up and you'll end me before we get to the good part."

Iltani didn't want to stop and debated keeping up the playful caresses to see how long he would actually last, but her curiosity could wait. She simply wanted to join with him. In the end, he pulled her back up to capture her lips again.

Ditanu grew less passive, his kisses and caresses more demanding before he suddenly flipped her over onto her back. Iltani was still gasping in surprise when he took one of her nipples into his mouth. He soon had her gasping for an entirely different reason. He seemed to particularly like her breasts, kissing and toying with them until Iltani wanted to cry out in frustration.

His hands stroked up her sides, feather light caresses that made her shiver. He touched her everywhere but where she most needed him to. Thinking he needed some encouragement, she wrapped her legs around his hips and arched up, rubbing against him. He hissed appreciatively, but only continued to kiss her.

She broke their kiss and glared at him. "Ditanu, you do *actually* know what you're supposed to do with a woman, right?"

He grinned. She could see the flash of his white teeth in the darkness. "And if I don't? Are you going to teach me?" His words were accompanied by gentle little thrusts that promised relief from the desire tormenting her if he would just get on with it. She spread her thighs further and wrapped her legs around his hips, trying to force him deeper.

He chuckled in that purely masculine way. "Not so fast. I think you're forgetting something."

Iltani shifted under him until they were better aligned, and then she reared up, impaling herself on him. She and Ditanu groaned in unison and finally he started to move.

"Damn it, tell me you love me," Ditanu growled as he thrust into her.

Lost to sensation, she nearly didn't understand his words. Then she did and understood he had desires greater than just the physical that needed sating. "Ditanu, I have always loved you." To punctuate her words, she kissed him with a fiercer passion, until his purrs vibrated against her chest. He made a hissing sound of pleasure and increased his rhythm. His passion drove her that much closer to her own end. His one hand found its way between her legs and the added stimulus was almost enough to send her over the edge. "My king, I have loved you for years."

"Iltani," he gasped out and froze suddenly, his body tensing as he came. "My beautiful warrior. Forever and always the Queen of my Heart."

His words, his voice, his powerful body still grinding against her, it was enough and she shattered moments after he had.

"My beloved king," she sighed out. "That was better than wonderful."

"Not bad for being half drunk?"

Iltani started to laugh.

CHAPTER
twenty-nine

THE SOUND OF drapes being drawn back registered on her ears. A moment later, light from an east facing window found its way unerringly into Iltani's eyes. Squinting, she grunted something unintelligible. Dawn came. Mmmm. So too did servants. Damn it.

She'd been having the nicest dreams, too.

An arm around her waist tightened, dragging her naked body back against another equally naked body.

Ditanu, never easy to wake, growled something under his breath.

"Tell them to go away," he said again, slightly clearer.

Iltani was still coming to terms with a few new realizations as the servants continued laying out a table with two settings. The sound of a throat being cleared behind her had her blushing harder. She rolled over and peered over Ditanu's broad shoulder to see Uselli standing there with Kuwari.

The cub was wiggling and fighting. Only an occasional soft growl could be heard—that was when he wasn't chomping on Uselli's fingers, trying to chew his way free.

Kuwari's head snaked around, narrowing in on Iltani at which point he loosed a cry fit to rattle teeth. Ditanu bolted into a sitting position, taking the blanket and Iltani's cover with him.

Uselli released the cub and Kuwari bound across the bed, leaped over his father, and landed in Iltani's lap.

"My king," Uselli mumbled, "I'm sorry to disturb you, but Kuwari was fussing and wouldn't be calmed. His grandfather said he'd been fine all night, it was just this morning. We thought he must be hungry, but he wouldn't drink from the milk skin."

Ditanu took the milk skin from Uselli and held it out to Iltani. She took it but the cub had already settled down, purring contentedly while he waited. When she offered the milk, he took it willingly.

Kuwari was still nursing happily when a servant came over carrying robes. Iltani put hers on without a word.

Ditanu was standing on the opposite side of the bed belting his in place when he looked up at her and grinned. "Welcome to my world. No privacy at all. And no, you won't really get used to it as much as learn to tune everything out."

"If you say so."

Really, it was a small price to pay for finally being with the man she loved.

Ditanu, as expected, didn't have the slightest hint of a hangover. While Iltani would have been happy to stay in his chambers and make love again, repeatedly, he had kept his plans to go island to island to rejuvenate all the dormant lamassu. Her logical mind agreed it was important to have a better warning in the future if another fleet of ships ever managed to breach the dome protecting the city-states.

Their first stop earlier in the day had been Nippur, the island of Ahassunu and her line. Shalanum was trusted enough to keep a secret so they went openly to wake the lamassu there first. Between herself, Ditanu, and his aunt, the work of waking the dormant lamassu went faster than Iltani thought it would, although it still took a few hours at each stop, and it was draining work. Ditanu decided they would do two a day, with a day of rest between.

Ditanu had wanted to finish one island in particular. Kalhu, the city-state ruled by Beletum and her father. It was a little-known fact that the lamassu could also be used to spy. Even if they were asleep, they could still hear and see everything within their domain.

Iltani agreed Kalhu should be one of their first stops—but done in secret so their enemies would not be aware. Ditanu hadn't wanted her to come, saying she should stay behind and guard Kuwari. She'd only laughed at her king's naivety and told him he was welcome to explain that to Ishtar, then. Iltani had sensed her goddess near from the moment Ditanu had mentioned going island to island and waking all the dormant lamassu.

That was how Iltani found herself beside one of many boats being dragged silently up a beach in the middle of the night with only the moon to light their way. Well, they did have unlit torches with them should they have a need. The rocky shore at the base of the cliffs was a good place to hide their boats from casual observation. If anyone happened to be patrolling an empty beach they might happen upon them, but that was why several of the Shadows would stay behind with the boats and subdue any soldiers belonging to Beletum. They could make an apology and sooth ruffled feathers later should Beletum prove innocent.

If the lamassu did report something treasonous in nature, Iltani wouldn't be concerned with ruffling feathers. She'd be taking heads instead.

Once the boats were secured, she, Ditanu, and Kammani surrounded by a group of sixty Shadows led by Uselli made their way off the beach and followed the stairs cut into the cliff a century past. The stairs were still in good repair if a little weather-stained and salt-eaten. At the top, a large door made of solid planks and reinforced with metal was in much rougher shape. Its hinges were rusted. A cloak shoved against one and a blow delivered from a sword hilt was all it took to shatter the lock. Inside it was dark, silent, and dank.

"No one patrols this area," Uselli muttered in angry disbelief. "Who allows their defenses to be so compromised?"

Ditanu cleared his throat. "Someone who has too many other things to accomplish, perhaps?"

"Or," Iltani added and Ishtar's magic flared a stronger warning. "Someone who doesn't fear being attacked, because the mercenaries who attacked us are in their hire. Ishtar's warning magic awoke as soon as I stepped foot on this island."

"We should go back, gather more men before we return," Uselli urged.

Ditanu shook his head. "No, we need to investigate this now. We'll wake the Lamassu as planned and then go to the council with evidence. I can't wipe out one of the ruling houses just because I do not trust them. We need evidence first or risk having the other city-states respond in fear."

"But Ishtar is warning there is danger here."

"How many of the councilors did your power label a threat to me?"

Iltani scowled but grudgingly replied. "Most of them."

"You see?"

"That doesn't mean Beletum and her father are not a true threat."

"Then think of it this way. If we only take the head, the body might still survive and grow a new one someday."

"I'd like to see someone grow their head back after I've cut it off."

Ditanu reached out and caressed her cheek. "It is not that I don't trust you, but we must be certain first."

"Noted." Iltani drew her sword. "I still don't like it."

"Dislike noted," Ditanu said with a cocky grin. He shielded his eyes when the first torch was lit and when he lowered his hand, his expression had changed. The flash of humor was gone, replaced by something far more predatory.

So he did believe her when she'd warned of the danger. Now he wanted to hunt down that danger and kill it. She drew breath to say even killing every last traitor wouldn't fill the hollow in his heart where the love of two of his cubs used to live. Closing her mouth, she remembered again the pain and hollowness in her heart when the first tiny thread in her blood link had snapped. She'd only known those tiny lives for a day. Ditanu had known them since birth. Iltani's hand tightened on her sword's hilt. Perhaps Ditanu had the right of it after all.

Maybe healing couldn't start until after his need for revenge was satisfied and laid to rest next to his two dead cubs. Whether it would heal him or not, she would help him slay his enemies even if it hadn't been her duty. Child killers didn't deserve to keep breathing.

A guard stayed behind at the broken door where he could pass messages between the two groups of Shadows.

Ditanu forged on, and Iltani stayed at his side while his Shadows paced ahead.

They met no one in the tunnel or in the root cellar where it emerged. From there, they exited the cellar and made their way higher up into the palace. Ditanu had scoured ancient maps detailing Kalhu's layout before he'd chosen the place they came ashore. That was how he knew of the hidden entrance and that it led up into the palace and not elsewhere in the surrounding city.

They found a few guards on duty, but easily avoided detection.

The Shadows' dark cloaks were woven with magic to hide them from enemy eyes. What their cloaks couldn't hide, their training did, assuring they moved with silent feet and smooth grace, barely stirring the air as they passed.

She and Ditanu moved almost as swiftly and silently. They'd been trained by Burrukan, after all. Still, she had to nod at the other Shadows' training, skills which took years to perfect.

At last, they came upon the first of the dormant lamassu—one of four statues guarding the great hall of Kalhu. These ones were lacking the beauty and luster of the ones back in Nineveh. She ran a finger along one stone feather, dislodging flakes of paint from centuries past.

"These ones are old," she whispered so only Ditanu would hear.

"But they are loyal and they will still serve." He patted one of the lamassu's great bull's legs. "I and those of my blood will take better care of you in the future, too. I promise."

Ditanu drew a blade and then brought it to his forearm and made a nick. The sharp blade sliced cleanly and a few beads of blood welled up and then a few more. He muttered under his breath and made a second deeper slice.

Anointing the lamassu might be one of New Sumer's best defenses, but it still hurt.

Iltani gave Ditanu a nod in acknowledgement and then went to the far corner of the hall to her own lamassu. Priestess Kammani was already marking the one before her with blood.

"Well, old fellow, it's time to wake to the world once more." Iltani sliced her own arm with a soft grunt. "I imagine it has changed a bit since last time your hooves made the ground shake."

Priestess Kammani prayed solemnly while she anointed her lamassu. Ditanu remained silent. While Iltani chatted nonsense at hers. It had been exactly the same for the other eleven she'd already awakened this day. Each city had a varying number of the lamassu depending on how large the islands were and how much beach they had to guard. Between thirty and forty seemed the normal number.

Iltani anointed her statue more by route now than careful skill, and so she was startled when this one started to shift under her hands. Iltani whipped around to see the others already waking.

The lamassu of Nippur hadn't moved at all upon waking. They had only acknowledged Ditanu as their king and Iltani as Ishtar's Blade, accepting each as their commander. As for Kammani, they had drawn upon her power and acknowledged her as one of the line of the gryphon kings, but did not ask her how they should serve.

However, all that had been done in the silence of their minds, the statue never moving. Lamassu only moved when they sensed danger.

These ones were moving.

'King and Blade, beware,' the one before her spoke. 'Treachery breeds upon this island. They mean to slay every last one of your line.'

The lamassu nearest Kammani started across the room, shaking the floor under Iltani's feet. Priestess Kammani lost her balance and stumbled. One of the Shadows helped her back to her feet.

Kammani's lamassu spoke four words. 'Ereshkigal seeks to rise.'

'The Queen of the Underworld has grown jealous of her sister,' Ditanu's lamassu added its weighty voice. 'She sees a way to rule this world too.'

Iltani knew if Ereshkigal gained a foothold in this world, it would change beyond all recognition.

The lamassu confirmed what Ishtar had sent her in a dream, but its words were clearer. If Ereshkigal set her own puppet upon the throne, she would merely have to wait. With more worshippers praying to her, she would grow stronger while Ishtar grew weaker. There wouldn't even need to be a battle.

"We need to get out of here now." Iltani rushed over to Ditanu's side.

He was nodding his head when the second lamassu spoke again. 'Your false consort and her mate are here, below in the dungeons. I can feel them through the stone. They are weakened from battle wounds and torture. While *they might survive a few days more on their own, it is unlikely Beletum will leave them alive once they learn of our awakening and your nocturne visit.'*

Iltani's heart plummeted to her stomach. If what the lamassu said was true and of course it was, Burrukan and Ahassunu were alive, and in need of rescuing, but if they waited, likely all they'd find would be their corpses.

"I won't leave them," Ditanu said with a steely note of finality. It silenced Iltani's and Uselli's voices before they even raised them.

"I agree, or else they are dead," Iltani said, "but we don't have much time. Dawn is fast approaching and servants will be waking soon. The more people we have to hide from, the more likely we'll be caught. I don't care how skilled the Shadows are. Even they can't hide in broad daylight."

"We will hurry then. The dungeons are below us from what I remember of the map." Ditanu closed his eyes and frowned as if retrieving the mental image of the map he spoke of. "If we hurry we should be able to reach the dungeons, free our friends, and escape back to the beach before our enemies know we were ever here."

Priestess Kammani just shook her head at them. Iltani knew she wasn't afraid for her own life. "If either of you gets killed, Ereshkigal is that much closer to winning."

"We won't die," Ditanu said with surety rising in his voice. "This is why Ishtar sent her Blade. Together Iltani and I are stronger than any force Ereshkigal has drawn together, slave to her will."

Iltani hoped he was correct.

CHAPTER *thirty*

THE DUNGEONS WERE dark as she expected and the air was less than fresh but it could have been worse. There was no scent of violent death or old decay. Iltani breathed a sigh of relief. Now they just had to get Burrukan and Ahassunu free.

There had been five guards stationed at the dungeon. They were all now dead by her blade. She didn't feel guilty. They were holding Consort Ahassunu prisoner. While they might not have been willing subjects of Ereshkigal, they had remained complacent. Had even one of them been willing to get word to Ditanu or his Shadows, the lot of them would have been freed and rewarded.

Well, Iltani had given them the reward they deserved.

One at a time the Shadows broke open the doors. Inside they found other victims and survivors of the island attack. Ditanu had taken one look at his citizens and ordered his Shadows to start delivering them safely back through the palace and on into the root cellar and freedom.

More cell doors were forced open. Iltani started down another corridor lined with yet more doors. Closing her eyes, she rested her hand on her belly and whispered a prayer. "Ishtar guide me to these ones' mother so they can grow up knowing us both."

Ishtar's answer was a slight tug upon her soul. She followed her goddess. Ditanu and his personal guard followed in her wake.

She came to a door and raised her hand. Her fingers uncurled to show the glow of Ishtar's power. It was the barest trickle, just enough for the task at hand, not enough to harm the unborn cubs in Iltani's womb.

Reaching forward, she touch the lock and it vanished in a puff of smoke and a hot metal smell. Inside it was dark, but Iltani summoned a touch more power, not the vast draws of battle magic, but a gentler, healing light which illuminated the room

Burrukan was in human form, a heavy metal collar fastened around his neck. A chain attached to it secured him to the wall. The chain would only allow him to move a few feet in any direction. Presently, he lay on his side, drugged or unconscious. There was no way Burrukan would have slept through someone coming into his cell otherwise. Consort Ahassunu was resting beside him in gryphon form. She didn't look good. The belly wound she'd taken just days before was infected and oozing. Iltani could smell the corruption.

"We need to get her out of here," Iltani whispered.

Ditanu and the shadows were already moving. They had backed out of the cell to find something to carry Ahassunu upon. Iltani knelt by Burrukan's side and gently shook his shoulder, hoping she wasn't causing him too much pain.

He blinked up at her, and slowly his owlish look changed, sharpening.

He spotted the open door and the other Shadows outside. "You must go." His voice sounded as broken as he looked.

"Not without you and Ahassunu." Iltani touched his collar and then changed her mind, vaporizing a link in the chain instead. She did the same for Ahassunu, who didn't stir at all.

"She is dying," Burrukan said, his voice so full of pain.

"But is not yet dead. I won't let these traitors kill another one of my people."

Ditanu and six guards came back in carrying one of the other cell doors.

Well, that would work, she supposed. Priestess Kammani came forward and examined Ahassunu. When Kammani declared her stable enough to move, Ditanu and several of the Shadows gently lifted the consort and placed her on the door to carry her out. Iltani helped Burrukan to his feet. Another of the Shadows handed him a spare sword. He closed his fist around it and nodded sharply.

The shadows had their rightful leader back and hope flared in more than one gaze for the first time after the dire news the lamassu had whispered about Ereshkigal's rising.

The trip back up to the lamassu's chamber took twice as long. It couldn't be helped with carrying Ahassunu and several of the other prisoners weakened from Beletum and Ziyatum's hospitality. Each moment stretched by longer than the last. Iltani's fingers tightened upon her sword hilt until she noticed and forced them to relax.

They had just reached the hall leading to the lamassu when there was a cry of warning. The cry was cut short a moment later, but the damage had been done. Holding her breath, she listened and waited. Then she heard the thump of boots.

Two guards belonging to Beletum's house burst through a set of doors at the end of the hall. Seeing the prisoners, they froze. The taller one on the right shouted over his shoulder and then started forward.

Iltani and the other Shadows still had the advantage of their concealing cloaks. All the enemy soldier would see on first glance was unarmed prisoners, attempting escape. Three of the nearly invisible Shadows were easing closer to the two enemy soldiers. They were nearly upon them. If they silenced these soldiers and the ones coming up behind, Ditanu and his people still had a chance of escaping without a fight.

The front most Shadow was within three body lengths of his target, his long dagger already in his hand. Two other shadows were converging upon the scene when the other guard, the silent one who was studying the scene in more detail, suddenly turned and ran back through the door.

"Intruders!" he bellowed as he ran. Reaching the door, he turned back and hesitated, looking back in time to see his partner grunt softly and fall to the ground, already dead from a dagger shoved up under his chin and up into the brain.

The door slammed closed and Iltani heard a latch being slid in place. Then muffled somewhat by the door, other shouts of 'King's Shadows' and other answering shouts in the distance.

"So much for secrecy," Ditanu muttered under his breath and then gestured to his men, "This way."

Iltani followed the king's direction while keeping an eye on the passageways behind and to either side. Her senses stretched outward, Ishtar's defensive gifts flowing outward with them. Minds that had been sleeping but moments before were now waking. Other guards were rushing toward the cries of warning.

When her group reached the room where the lamassu waited, Ditanu gathered half his men around him and then ordered the prisoners, Consort Ahassunu, and their Shadow guides on ahead. To Burrukan, he said, "The rest of us will slow the enemy while you go on ahead. The escape tunnel and the stairs leading down the cliff are narrow. Some of the injured will have to be carried."

"My king…"

"This is not open for debate. Go. Get to the boats. The lamassu will aid us in holding back our enemies and then cover our escape." Ditanu took Burrukan by the shoulder and forcibly shoved him toward the other prisoners. "Once the boats are loaded, take them out to sea. The rest of us can shift and follow on the wing."

With a grumbled oath, Burrukan limped after the others.

Once he and the other prisoners made their way through the opposite door and on down the passage leading to the root cellar, Ditanu gestured for his men to spread out.

The Queen of the Night's power uncurled within Iltani and the goddess's presence flared to life in her mind. She knew her goddess was watching, and Ishtar wanted her to stay here, to end the threat tonight.

Iltani knew she couldn't use the full force of Ishtar's destructive power without risking the unborn cubs, but that didn't mean she couldn't use her brain. She smiled.

"My king, wait. I have an idea."

Brushing her still bleeding thumb across the forehead of the last painted lion in line, Iltani stepped away from the wall and eyed her work. Much of the mural now glistened with smears of blood. Ditanu and Kammani were hastily finishing their walls when she looked up. Already, the first painted stone tiles to be anointed had begun absorbing the drops of blood.

"That's all we have time for," Ditanu called. "Outside in the hall, they have worked up the nerve or gathered great enough numbers to feel safe in confronting us."

Iltani sucked on her bleeding thumb as she rejoined Ditanu in the back corner of the hall, where the rest of the Shadows held their position. Their new plan required their enemies to cross the width of the hall. Ditanu said he knew what to use for bait and then tossed his hood back and stood ready, a sword in his hand.

Iltani mimicked him. "You'll be Beletum's favorite dungeon fixture if you get captured. She's been sniffing after you for years."

"Thanks for that cheery thought." Ditanu grimaced and raised his sword.

Something slammed into the hall's main doors. The two heavy stone tables the Shadows had dragged in front to act as a barricade didn't budge. Sharp hammering came again. Harder this time, and in quicker succession. The tables held, but the wooden door did not and slowly plank by plank, the soldiers of Kalhu started to break through.

"Here they come," Ditanu shouted.

"You sound too pleased by that," Iltani said and frowned. "Don't do anything stupid...your majesty."

He didn't have a chance to respond to her barb. Across the room, the wooden door gave way. The first of the guards rushed through the hole, scrambling over the tables and taking up positions to protect the others coming in behind. When there were enough of them, the first ones through the breach pushed aside the tables and kicked the door wide. More guards rushed in.

The front runners lined up across the room, coming only about half way. They wouldn't risk attacking the Shadows until they deemed the odds more in their favor. Iltani doubted they could fit enough guards in this hall to make it an even fight. One only became a Shadow by being the best.

Beletum's house soldiers organized themselves quickly. Iltani would give them that bit of credit.

Thus, they held their ground, not attacking even when no more flowed in behind the last. There was a hesitation, and then they parted making an opening for their leaders to walk. The power within Iltani notched up again, but this was not deadly battle magic. This was warm, mellow and pleasant—Ishtar in her aspect as a giver of life. She hoped this power wouldn't harm the cubs, but if Ereshkigal gained a foothold in the mortal world, it would threaten more than just the tiny sparks of life sheltering inside Iltani.

Footsteps approached and then she laid eyes on Beletum. Her father, Ziyatum, was right beside her. A few steps behind, Beletum's weak-willed husband, Nidnatum, brought up the rear.

Beletum made for the center of the room, showing no fear. Her stride carried her toward King Ditanu, her cloak flowing around her. Iltani noticed two things. One, her cloak was like what the traitors in Iltani's dream had worn. Secondly, Beletum wasn't wearing much else underneath.

Ishtar's power flared through Iltani as the goddess focused on a mark directly between Beletum's breasts. It shimmered dully, its power not of the mortal world, but of the underworld. Ereshkigal had somehow found a way to anchor herself in the mortal world and that magic was tied to Beletum's brand-like mark.

If ever there was a perfect target for the tip of Iltani's sword, she imagined she was looking at it.

"King Ditanu," Beletum smiled in welcome but stopped out of sword range. "We had not expected you, but here you are."

Ditanu arched a brow. "Yes, here I am. What interesting things I have learned while here. Traitors and misguided goddesses, both of which should be content with what they have, and yet are not."

"Ah. You know of Ereshkigal's plan." Beletum fingered the brand. "She has so much to offer New Sumer, all the city-states would prosper under her rule. She plans to expand out beyond these islands. United, we would never need to worry about dangers from the outside world. If we aid her in gathering worshippers, she has promised us we may rule them in her name."

"Worship should be freely given, not forced," Iltani said. Or perhaps that sentiment came from Ishtar herself for her essence was growing stronger.

"Ishtar, my dear sister, that is why you will be defeated this night," Beletum glanced down at Iltani's belly, "Well that, and your obsession with the line of the gryphon kings. You doomed yourself by trying to save the cubs. Now your Blade can't use the full force of your battle magic without killing them. That oath you swore eight thousand years ago to the gryphon kings will be your doom. You cannot win, but I can be merciful and let them live if they will serve me instead."

Ereshkigal narrowed her eyes upon Ditanu. "I like your strength, your fierceness, your loyalty." She gave him an assessing look. "I imagine there are many other things to like about you as well. Together we would have strength enough to conquer the entire world."

Ah, so that was the way of it.

A slight shifting of Ereshkigal's expression told Iltani that she wasn't lying about that. She really did covet the king of the gryphons. "King Ditanu, perform the sacred marriage with me and form a new pact—I assure you, my offer is much more interesting than what Ishtar first offered your ancestors."

Ditanu's stone-faced expression gave nothing away, but Ishtar's attention shifted from Ereshkigal and rested upon the king of the gryphons as if she was about to witness something interesting. Iltani's blood link to Ditanu blazed to life as his emotions swamped her—pain, hatred, a smoldering volcanic rage, a desire for vengeance—it all merged into one burning thought.

"Never! You killed my cubs! I would rather perform the Sacred Marriage with a lamassu! This world will never be yours." Ditanu's hand snapped out, the blade which had been balanced between his fingers for a second, flew true to its mark. Only Ereshkigal slapped it out of the air at the last moment.

She licked a few drops of blood from a slice on her palm. "I will wait for the cub to grow up then. Kill them all."

With that, Ereshkigal stepped back as her guards came rushing forward.

That was the sign Ishtar had been waiting for. Iltani began to dance.

She needed no music, for Ishtar needed no music, just the clear ringing tones of her crystalline blade cutting through the air. The sword glowed, its power shimmering bright, rising up from the depths of the blade. Its glow ignited the air around them, glorious bits of light and fire. All around her, the Shadows engaged the guards loyal to Ereshkigal. Ishtar in her aspect of a goddess of fertility and love danced a rare counterpoint to battle.

"You lack passion," Iltani sang to her sister. "That is why none of the line of gryphon kings will ever take you in the Sacred Marriage. You are the death of the afterlife. You are needed. Yet you belong in the mortal world no more than I belonged in the underworld. Do not make the same mistake I did, or you, too, might lose something dear to you if you cross into a realm not your own."

"If you wish to talk," Ereshkigal said. "I will send your Blade to the underworld and we can continue this conversation there."

Fear did not exist in Iltani's new understanding of the world, thus, Ereshkigal's threats could not touch her. Iltani continued to dance, power shivering in the air—a gentle power, love and fertility, not war. This power could not harm the tiny sparks of life. Instead, it strengthened them as well as those linked to the line of the gryphon kings and all Shadows were linked to Ditanu, making them stronger.

Ereshkigal laughed. "Are you seeking to sway me with love? It will not work. The only power in your arsenal that can kill me is your battle rage. You are wasting my time."

Iltani raised her blade high above her head and brought it down with all the strength in her arms and came to rest on one knee with her head bowed. The blade's tip burned its way into the floor, through tile and stone as if it was water. Magic flowed out from the sword, racing across the floor and up walls anointed with royal blood.

When she looked up, she sought out Ereshkigal's gaze. "Dear sister, who said it had to be me to kill you?"

Stone lions and dog sized dragons freed themselves from the walls all around the hall even as the four great lamassu reared, storming forward, crushing enemies beneath their hooves. The lions and dragons darted in, taking down the surprised guards, but most converged upon Ereshkigal's host body.

The Queen of the Underworld fought back, destroying many of the lions and dragons, but she was no match for the lamassu, for they were deities in their own right. Two of them herded Ereshkigal toward Iltani's location.

"A gift for you and your king," Ishtar said as she withdrew from Iltani's mind.

Again Iltani was alone in her own body, but she felt Ishtar near, watching.

Well, it was always good to please one's goddess.

Dragging her sword free of the floor, she rose from her crouch and darted forward, her sword's blade singing in the air moments before it bit into Beletum's side. The councilor squealed in pain and staggered sideways. Iltani toyed with the other woman for a moment as she looked around for her king.

Ah, she didn't have to look hard. He was facing off against Ziyatum, but the battle was over almost before it had started and the governor of Kalhu collapsed on the floor dead. Ditanu continued cutting his way through enemy soldiers. When he was nearly at her side, she reached down and dragged Beletum up by the hair.

"Mercy," Beletum cried. "Ereshkigal forced me to be her host."

'Lies,' Ishtar whispered. 'My sister can only venture into my realm invited. Beletum summoned that power here. She is a willing victim. As was her father before her.'

At Ditanu's arrival, Beletum repeated her plea for mercy.

"By New Sumer law," Ditanu ground out, "you should be brought before your peers and they would decide how death would come for you."

Iltani loosened her hold on Beletum's hair and was about to render her unconscious when Ditanu leaned forward suddenly and got in the councilwoman's face. "But you killed my cubs," he stabbed a dagger into Beletum's heart. "So there is no need to drag this out."

Bracing the body, Iltani sliced the traitor's head from her shoulders. When Ditanu arched a brow, she said, "I'm just thorough."

"We'll burn the body just to be certain."

By the time they looked up the rest of the battle was over, but Iltani knew setting their world right again would take days and days of work.

"My king, I know we will have to root out others that were loyal to Ereshkigal, but we can't do anything else here tonight." Iltani sighed and took his hand, their fingers entwining. "I want to go home and see to Ahassunu and Burrukan and the others."

"As do I." Ditanu took her into his arms and placed a kiss on her forehead. "And then later, I simply want to sit with you and Kuwari, enjoying your company. Perhaps even reading some of those letters like we agreed."

"That sounds lovely," Iltani agreed and then kissed him as a promise of other things they might do as well.

CHAPTER
thirty-one

AFTER THEY HAD landed back on Nineveh, Ditanu was greeted by his council to learn they'd already been briefed by Uselli. Iltani wanted to thank Uselli for his swift efficiency in rounding up the council, seeing to Burrukan and Ahassunu's needs, and then chasing away the council again afterward.

While Iltani was visiting with Burrukan, he'd started barking orders from his sickbed about troop placements, rotations, and sending the most skilled of the Shadows to hunt down any traitors who might still be faithful to Ereshkigal. All this bluster was really about his fear for Ahassunu, but after a long night with the healers Priestess Kammani had come in and said that Consort Ahassunu would have a long road to recovery, but she would heal.

After another hour, they were told they could go see Ahassunu. When he first laid eyes on her, Burrukan started to shed silent tears, but no one would dare call it crying. She grinned and promised to have Kuwari brought to them. In the end, it was Ditanu himself who brought the cub.

"I thought this one might like to see his mother."

Ahassunu, now in human form, held out shaking arms for her cub. While mother and cub got reacquainted, Ditanu sat down with Burrukan and clapped a hand on his shoulder.

"My old friend," Ditanu said with a smile. "I was starting to think I wasn't ever going to see you again. Glad to see you're too cantankerous to die."

"I'm glad I can say the same about my king. Iltani told me she nearly lost you to grief madness."

"Yes," Ditanu said. "We have long stories to exchange. But first, I think you have some explaining to do about some very tardily delivered letters."

After a long talk and exchanging stories, Ditanu told them he planned to tell the council the truth about Ahassunu being Burrukan's mate. Since Ahassunu was the mother of the next generation of gryphon king's she would retain the title of Consort and Ditanu's co-ruler, but she was free to publicly claim Burrukan as her mate.

Burrukan had only laughed, saying their relationship was likely going to be written up as the most complicated and unusual in gryphon history. Ditanu countered by saying it would make a wonderful ballad.

With that, Iltani and Ditanu left with a promise to have servants check on them to see to Kuwari's needs so the healing couple could rest.

They'd left the healer's quarters together, Ditanu looking as tired as Iltani felt. All she wanted was food, strong wine, and a bed. Preferably Ditanu's. When she cast him a speculative looked, he smiled and nodded.

"As I recall, we have a courtship ritual planned, one involving food, wine and letters."

"Yes," Iltani agreed. "I do believe we might have mentioned something about that."

When they reached his suites, Iltani had to wait for the servants to finish bringing food, but finally, over dinner, Ditanu pulled out his stack of letters and a large pitcher of wine.

They read each other's letters over a number of hours that involved laughter, tears, and a few lingering caresses which led to other longer interruptions.

"Were you really going tie Burrukan up somewhere and kidnap me?"

"I had had a touch too much to drink one night after Burrukan had returned to Nineveh to report on your progress. I sobered up by morning, but I had still wanted to return my mate to my side. Alas, I realized Burrukan was doing his best to protect us."

"Mates? What? Wait, but that was before the Sacred Marriage."

"Yes."

Iltani felt her mouth form an 'o' of surprise, but then her brain kicked in. "But how?"

"After the Sacred Marriage, I would think you'd know enough about how a male fits together with a female…."

Iltani smacked him on his shoulder, holding nothing back.

"Ouch!" Ditanu said on a laugh, and then, once he got himself under control, "It happened on the night of my coronation. Honestly, I'm not sure which of us passed out first, but the act proceeded far enough to form our mating bonds. You were my mate from that moment on, and I haven't regretted it for a moment."

Iltani was still speechless. Why hadn't he told her this from the beginning? Finally, she managed, "Why all the deception if I have been your mate all along?"

"Because, Burrukan was correct in one thing. We were both too young to deal with the dangers of court. You were still years away from coming into your power as Ishtar's Blade. It would have been easy for our enemies to end the line of the gryphon kings. I was the last. All they had to do was learn we were mates and kill one of us. I would not have survived your death."

Iltani swallowed hard. "I...I knew I was supposed to start my training the day after your coronation, and I convinced myself that I was trying to protect you from getting betrothed to some harpy who liked your throne better than the man who sat upon it. Now I realize it was also because I couldn't face leaving you without making my feelings for you known." Iltani felt another of those horrible blushes burn up her cheeks and halfway down her chest. "I'd had too much wine at your coronation, and came up with the foolish plan that I would show you I was a woman, no longer a child. That I could fulfill your every need. But, deep down, I think I feared losing you to another while I was away training and wanted to stake my claim."

"Oh, I had noticed you had grown into a woman. I was a very head-strong young male entering his prime. Trust me, my beautiful Iltani, I had stopped thinking of you as a child a few years earlier. Even then, I think I knew it would be wrong to act on it. As Burrukan has said on more than one occasion, I have a very powerful personality and tend to bend others to my will."

"But that's not what happened that night at all," Iltani said, as the need to finally confess became overwhelming. "I'd planned it all out days before. After the coronation, I led you back to your room, saying I couldn't sleep, that I was having nightmares at the thought of leaving you, and that I just wanted to spend a few more hours with you. When you agreed, I put on the flimsiest nightdress I could find and intentionally placed the wine in front of the fire to warm so I could stand in front of that damned fire every chance I got. I hoped if I flaunted my body and plied you with wine, you'd get drunk enough to finally take me to your bed."

Ditanu coughed into his hand. He was laughing at her. "You were keeping pace with me in regards to the wine, only I had greater body mass. You got drunk faster. I think even then I would have done the noble thing and tucked you in bed, alone, had you not then shimmied out of that flimsy bit of cloth you called a nightdress. Once you came to me and started removing my robe, my noble intentions vanished. We became mates that night. I truly don't actually like the taste of wine or any alcoholic drink, but I must say I hold a fondness for it in my heart all the same. It's why I drink it—to remember wonderful memories of you. Besides, you seemed to come to my bed when I'm half drunk. You even called me adorable once."

Iltani started to laugh. "Oh, by the great Queen of the Night, I seduced the king of the gryphons! Isn't that a treasonous act?"

"It's only treason if it goes against my will." He reached across the table and cupped her cheek. "I imagine Ishtar was proud when her Blade claimed her king. Nothing you did that night, or any night since has ever been something I did not want."

"I understand why you would hide this knowledge from others, but why keep this from me?"

"When Burrukan found us in the night, he was livid and tossed a bucket of cold water in my face to sober me up. He then told me I had just put you at risk if my enemies ever figured out that my Little Shadow was, in fact, my consort. By the pre-dawn light, when the fires in my blood had cooled somewhat, I realized there was truth in Burrukan's words, but that's not why I allowed him to separate us."

Ditanu pulled Iltani to him. She went willingly and rested her ear against his chest. When he continued, his voice was a deep rumble.

"Burrukan asked if I knew why you gave yourself to me. I told him we were in love, had been for years." Ditanu sighed. "At which point, he said how could I know if you did it out of love for me, or perceived it as some kind of duty—even if you weren't aware of it on a conscious level, for you would do anything for me, be anything for me, even if it might not align with your personal wishes or desires naturally. You would still fill whatever needs I might have. I think he was correct, too." Ditanu started to chuckle. "When Burrukan said I dominated and overshadowed you all your life, I realized you might love your king out of some sense of duty, but I did not know if you loved Ditanu the man."

He reached out and ran his thumb across her lips. "That's why I did not tell you we were mates, even after we performed the Sacred Marriage. I needed to know—I still need to know. Do you love Ditanu the man?"

"Is that all?" Iltani laughed. "I loved Ditanu the boy long before he was either man or king. And, yes, I've grown to love both the man and king equally now."

Ditanu kissed the top of her head. "I had to ask, to be certain."

Iltani poked him in the side. "Well?"

She waited and pretended to take offense.

"Well, what?" he asked with humor.

Huffing, Iltani smacked him on the shoulder again. "Say it back to me. Or I'm going to have to beat it out of you. In the last days of my training, my skills were enough to defeat Burrukan in battle—I'm sure I could take you."

Again he laughed, a sound so full of delight it brought tears to her eyes.

"I think I'll withhold the words just to make you try," he purred. "I think I might enjoy being 'taken' by you."

She huffed with greater indignity, but her eyes drank in his form and desire flared to life within her at the thought of attempting to 'take' him as he implied.

He tilted her chin up to look her in the eyes. "You have had my heart forever. I've loved you before I even knew there was a way to physically express that love. You are my greatest love, the Queen of my Heart."

Her heart did that little lurch and her stomach answered with its familiar little flip. She leaned closer and took command of his lips. After a time, she broke away to breathe. "That's better. I've only been waiting all my life to hear it."

Ditanu grinned and claimed a kiss and then opened the next letter in their stack and started reading it out loud. Iltani decided this would be a lifelong tradition, this writing and reading of love letters.

the

END

other books by

LISA BLACKWOOD

The Avatars

Beginnings
Stone's Kiss
Stone's Song
Stone's Divide
Stone's War (Forthcoming Spring 2016)

In Deception's Shadow

Betrayal's Price
Herd Mistress
Death's Queen (Forthcoming)
City of Burning Water (Forthcoming Fall 2016)

Warships of the Spire

Vengeance (Forthcoming March 2016)

AFTERWORD

THANKS FOR GIVING *Ishtar's Blade* a try.

I also have a monthly newsletter for fans, highlighting future projects, sample chapters, freebies, review copy giveaways, contests and a chance to grab 99c new releases! To gain access to those kinds of fun tidbits and bargains, just click here to visit my website and sign up for my newsletter.

about the

AUTHOR

LISA BLACKWOOD GRUDGINGLY lives in a small town in Southern Ontario, though she would much rather live deep in a dark forest, surrounded by majestic old-growth trees. Since she cannot live her fantasy, she decided to write fantasy instead. An abundance of pets, named after various Viking gods, helps to keep the creativity flowing. Freya, her ever faithful and beloved hellhound, ensures Lisa takes a break from the computer so they can rid the garden of cats with delusions of conquest.

To find out more about me and what I'm up to, come visit my website.

LISABLACKWOOD.COM

and my blog:

BLACKWOODSFOREST.WORDPRESS.COM

Printed in Great Britain
by Amazon